One Man's Island

One Man's Island

*Reflections on Maine Life
from Slightly Offshore*

By Caskie Stinnett

Down East Books, Camden, Maine

All of the pieces in this book were published in Down East *under the title of "Room With A View." The Foreword and the Postscript, however, originally appeared in somewhat different form in* The Atlantic Monthly.

Copyright 1977, 1978, 1979, 1980, 1981, 1982. 1983. 1984
by Down East Enterprise, Inc.

ISBN 0-89272-248-7
Library of Congress Catalog Card Number 84-51561
Design by F. Stephen Ward
Composition by Roxmont Graphics
Photographs by Davis Thomas and Jon Francis
Printed in the United States of America

5 4 3

Down East Books
Camden, Maine

For Joan B. Werblin

Books by Caskie Stinnett

Will Not Run Feb. 22nd
Out of the Red
Back to Abnormal
Grand and Private Pleasures
This Great Land (Co-author)

Contents

Foreword . . . 1
Author's Note . . . 7

Chapter 1 — *Progress Here and There* . . . 9

Demolition . . . 10
Stake Out . . . 12
New Room . . . 14
A Little Electricity Never Hurt Anybody . . . 16
Plution . . . 18
Chic . . . 20
Withholding Consent . . . 21
Over My Head . . . 23
In the Name of Progress . . . 25
New Hope . . . 27
Goodbye, Central . . . 29
Enter the Utah Lobster . . . 31
Passage . . . 33
The Great Breakdown . . . 35

Chapter 2 — *Unexpected Treasures*. . .39

Gifts from the Sea . . . 40
Refuse du Jour . . . 42

Chapter 3 — *The Boxer* . . . 45

The Myth of Protection . . . 46
The Case for the Dog . . . 48
Upper Hand . . . 50

Chapter 4 — *Minor Grievances* . . . 53

My War with the Outboard Motor . . . 54
Cloying . . . 56
There's Been Enough Talk . . . 58
Who Says It's Vacationland? . . . 60
Where There's Wood Smoke . . . 61
Backsliders . . . 63
Tilt . . . 65
This Isn't Massachusetts . . . 67
Stay Tuned . . . 69
Burglary . . . 71
Frustration . . . 73
Lament . . . 75

Chapter 5 — *Memories* . . . 79

First Trap . . . 80
Bahnhofangst . . . 82
Morality . . . 84

Chapter 6 — *The Seasons and the Elements* . . . 87

First Day . . . 88
Fickle Mistress . . . 90
New Wharf . . . 92
Summer . . . 94
Fog . . . 96
Autumn . . . 98
First Snowfall . . . 100
Christmas in Maine . . . 102
Wind . . . 104
Spring . . . 106
Autumn Morning . . . 108
Forecast . . . 110
Autumn Reverie . . . 112
A Time of Forbearance . . . 114

Chapter 7 — *The Way It Is* . . . 117

First Thing Tomorrow . . . 118
By Any Other Name . . . 120
Rural Life . . . 122
Environmental Concord . . . 124
He Always Knew . . . 126

  Free Spirit . . . 128
  Growth Industry . . . 130
  Harmony . . . 132
  A Good, Reliable Villain . . . 134

Chapter 8 — *The Great Predator . . . 137*
  A Friend Indeed . . . 138
  Maine Too? . . . 140

Chapter 9 — *Invited and Uninvited Guests . . . 143*
  The Chipmunk and I . . . 144
  Entertaining . . . 146
  "Dear Mrs. Irving . . .". . . 148
  The Mouse in the Typewriter . . . 150
  Blue Jay Bigotry . . . 152
  Balanced Alliance . . . 154
  Gulls . . . 156
  The Ideal Guest Is an Accident of Nature . . . 158

Chapter 10 — *Writing . . . 161*
  A Flimsy Business . . . 162
  People Say You're a Writer . . . 164
  The Last Priority . . . 166
  A Letter . . . 168

Chapter 11 — *Love Letters to Maine. . .171*
  The True Prize . . . 172
  Second Choice . . . 174
  Homesickness . . . 176
  Substance . . . 178
  Going Back . . . 180
  Coming Home . . . 182

Postscript . . . 185

Foreword

More and more people are seeking out islands, I read in the newspaper recently, in the hope of finding freedom from neighborhood blight, crime, atmospheric pollution, noise, and the general fears and insecurity of a troubled world. The law of supply and demand having asserted itself, the article continued, habitable islands are becoming almost impossible to acquire.

I live during the more moderate months of the year on a small island close to the coast of Maine, and perhaps I can furnish a footnote on the prizes — and shortcomings — of island life. There are some general fears and insecurity on islands too, and the fact that they involve nature rather than the mischief of man makes them no less real.

How this little island got the name of Hamloaf I have no idea, nor do I really care. Perhaps from the sea it looked like a hamloaf. I thought once of changing the name, but I discarded the notion after I found out that one had to follow a complicated procedure in changing the name of an island that was already marked on the sailing charts, and now I am a little ashamed that I ever entertained the thought. A lot of islands near me have odd names: there are Little Hen Island, Pound of Tea Island, Snow Island, and July 8th Island. What's so bad about Hamloaf Island?

At high tide, the island contains about three and a half acres; it is heavily wooded in oak, spruce, and birch, with thickets of bayberry growing in the open spaces, and with a rocky coastline to which mussels and starfish cling. There the mornings are soft and quiet, and the nights are compounded of stars and lamplight, and the silence is broken only by the chatter of the incoming tide lapping at loose stones at the water's edge. Darkness brings mystery and the smell of wood smoke hanging in the evening air. Far away, from the mainland, the sound of an automobile horn is borne on the sea wind, but it is muffled and indistinct and seems part of another and less fortunate world.

There is now only one house on the island, a second one having been recently demolished after slipping into a state of terminal disrepair. One walks down a short path from the dwelling to a small, one-room cottage which, in its more important days, served as a handyman's lodging, and later as a toolhouse. Now it has declined further in purpose, and functions only as a writer's workroom.

On the ridiculously small porch of this building, I am writing these lines. My boxer, as is her habit, followed me down the path this morning, and while I wheeled the typewriter table out so I could work in the sun, she struck out on her daily exploratory ramble of the island. She is very curious about what the tides leave on the rocks, and from time to time she brings some extraordinary prize to the door of the study and lays it solemnly there for my approval. She just brought the skeleton and head of a rotten fish, the sort of thing that may have been tossed from a lobster boat, although lobstermen are frugal people and throw very little away, expecially a rotten fish which is about the best bait there is. At least twice a day she noisily invades a rock ledge at one edge of the island, scattering the gulls resting there and causing a commotion that doesn't die down for an hour or more. I think of the rock ledge as the Beirut of the island; I doubt that I shall ever see lasting peace there.

I believe that the man who lives on an island builds his isolation without meaning to and sooner or later it begins to take possession of his soul. But it brings him a serenity and sureness, a trust in himself that he may never have known before, and he is better for it. Whether he desires it or not, he finds himself the center of his world, the arbiter between man and nature, the monarch of a miniature kingdom, the keeper of peace and the protector of lives, and the occasional intermediary in dealing with a higher power — with fretful winds and fickle seas and lightning and drought. He must be a caretaker, a carpenter, a painter, a physician, a veterinarian; on one occasion, which shall always remain green in my memory, I was called upon to lend an understanding ear to a confession of a wrongdoing.

Most island dwellers I have known are innately humble people; I have never heard one say to a visitor, "This is the greatest place in the world." I'm sure the words have been spoken, but I think rarely, and never in my presence. If you like the island, the owner is pleased; if you do not, he is not offended nor does he appear to be troubled in the least. No one knows better than he how incomplete and imperfect things are, how much needs to be done.

Islands become almost overwhelmingly familiar; every twist of the headland, every rock and indentation, is known and can be drawn faithfully to scale. During the winter when I am far away from Hamloaf Island, forgotten memories crowd in, each one separate and vivid. One July night, my friends and I were swimming and the cove was full of phosphorescence that turned our bodies to fire; more than once we would find the cove swarming with great schools of fish which the lobstermen would call porgies and which they caught in nets to use for lobster bait. And how often did I row a hundred yards or so to the rock ledge, with my towel and notebook, to lie in the sun there and jot down thoughts about the wild sweet peas that grew in the sand or the dark blue nightshade or the fat gull who sat on her eggs there despite my intrusion?

Perhaps one of the gravest errors people make is the assumption that island life is a simple life. Quite the contrary, it is immensely complicated, with every effort intricately dovetailed with another in the hope of satisfying the ultimate ambition, which is the avoidance of an unnecessary trip to the mainland. Although this island is quite close to the Maine coast — I can row the distance in ten minutes and on one occasion I even swam ashore — I find myself planning with all the seriousness of a military campaign how to manage one more day without bridging that gap between island and mainland. Of course, food and mail must be brought over regularly, although where the latter is concerned the dog demurs; this is a presumption, she thinks, not supported by the facts, and sometimes I agree.

Trips to the mainland are not casual: lists are taken, logistics are studied (the liquor store and the paint store are conveniently close togther; the post office, on the other hand, is some distance away and is visited only when stamps are urgently needed), the tide chart is consulted (lugging heavy packages up the ramp at low tide clearly reflects poor planning), and thought is given to the arrival time of the rural delivery mailman at our mailbox. There are lesser considerations, such as making telephone calls when the recipient of the call may likely be at home (remember, there are no telephones on small islands), but those must find their place in the overall pattern of the expedition and they cannot expect to exert much influence on the master plan.

Weather is an extremely personal thing to island dwellers, and occupies their thoughts in a way that mainland people would find difficult to understand. Both year-round residents and guests know that Maine makes demands, and makes them insistently. Tides rise and fall 35 feet or more at spots along the Maine coast, and some of these tidal flows create a witch's broth that can be disastrous to inexperienced sailors. Moreover, great northeasters bear down on coastal Maine in winter, lashing the villages with snow and sleet while gale winds tear at anything that is not tightly secured.

Walking out of the house, one makes contact with the elements, whether good or bad, pleasant or unpleasant. In rain, there is no taxicab or automobile to run to, but rather a wet boat which is likely to get wetter still before it reaches land. I never cease to be amazed at how quickly rainwater collects in the bottom of a boat. But one is close, too, to the bright days, to the mottled sunlight shining between the young leaves of the oak trees in the spring, and to the short, golden days of autumn when the shadows begin to slant and the water sparkles in a way that is almost blinding.

Fogs are frequent in these waters, and they don't creep in on tiny cat feet as Carl Sandburg imagined; they move in solidly and with a great show of authority and they often stick around long after their welcome has worn thin. But there is something quite pleasant about the sound of the foghorns in the channel and about that gray, opaque cloud that advances like a wall and wraps the trees and the ledges and the dock in a ghostly shroud. I have been in a rowboat when the fog came in so thickly that I could not see the tips of the oars, and then it was not so pleasant, but later, walking toward the house, and seeing the yellow glow of the oil lamps and candles through the windows, I was struck by the cheer and warmth and snugness that shone through the mist. Yes, the weather fits closely to the island dweller, almost like the clothes that he wears, and the first thing he does upon awakening is to glance at the shadows on the wall to see what is likely to be in store for the day.

Of course, sophistication and smartness have come to many islands, especially those used as weekend refuges of the wealthy. Generators supply electricity, there is color television, and one finds music at the swimming pool as well as floodlit tennis courts. I think of these places as extensions of the mainland, as spiritual peninsulas rather than islands, because the concept of insularity has not gripped the hearts and minds of the owners. I have often considered the installation of a generator here, but I have always discarded the notion because I can't bear the thought of an internal combustion engine shattering the silence that envelops this place. Total silence is nothing at all; it is no prize in itself, but it provides an acoustical background against which the sounds of nature are reflected clear and true — of water caressing the pilings of the deck in the darkness, of wind whispering through the spruce trees, of a gull squawking disdainfully as it buzzes the house at midnight. I would hate to have these sounds drowned out by an engine.

Thoughts of secession, however mad, nibble like mischievous

mice at the mind of a true islander; he knows it can never happen but he derives great satisfaction from contemplating it. I once went through a period — we were all young once — of referring to the mainland as the United States, and I thought of my shopping expeditions there as trips to a foreign country. (My foreign policy, at the time, extended to the United States a most-favored-nation status, and I was not above receiving foreign aid of a nonmilitary nature.) This only illustrates how deeply the fantasy of sovereignty resides in the islander's heart and how stubbornly the wistful dream of self-sufficiency occupies his thoughts.

I must be fair and acknowledge that the threat of loneliness is a constant condition of island life; a small concern to some and a terror to others. But loneliness is not unknown on the mainland, and unless an island is very remote and far at sea one can always go ashore to a movie or a tavern or to whatever one's heart draws one to that will fill the emptiness.

Some nights, when sleep comes slowly, I will lie awake watching the yellow shafts of moonlight as they probe the corners of the room, and occasionally I will get out of bed and go into the living room and stand at the window, looking across the cove to the lights of Cundy's Harbor in the distance, and wonder why, like stars, they dance and flicker. And sometimes, across the cove in the darkness comes a faint bar of music, like an unfinished scrap of conversation, that hangs for a minute in the air and then disappears, leaving in my ears only the sound of small waves stirred up by a fresh breeze in the cove. Occasionally there is an ominous sound, a sudden jarring noise that brings a warning growl from the dog, and I seize the flashlight and go out back, and in the beam of the light I see a raccoon beside the overturned garbage can, its eyes gazing with sullen resentment at me, its midnight snack thwarted. I am not the only resident of the island; just the only human.

For some reason that I cannot explain there is an *intensity* to life on an island; beauty is exaggerated, is felt more deeply. A few days ago I put on foul-weather gear and went down on the rocks to welcome a late-summer thunderstorm. It was tremendously exciting to stand on the windward side and watch the sky darkening to a dull gray, and to feel the rush of warm, wet air that precedes the arrival of rain. The wind rose quickly, whipping up small whitecaps in the cove, and scattered drops began to fall. They were big and they shook the leaves of the trees violently and left large spots on the rocks, but in a few moments the patter had become a wall of rain, which beat against the rock on which I stood and which searched out, successfully, a dozen cracks in my oilskins. Gusts now tugged at the trees and the bayberries behind me and built great troughs in the sea. Lightning flashed wickedly, followed by instantaneous thunder that rolled across the sky, booming and echoing until it faded away. But soon the strength of the storm weakened, and the thunder moved further and further into the distance. The clouds still hung low and scudded across the sea, but all violence was spent and a gentle rain remained. In a little while I could see light in the western sky, and a shaft of sunlight appeared, bathing the island in a weird, yellow-green light. The summer storm was over.

On clear winter nights, the temperature plunges and the whole country along the Maine coast seems to be lying frozen in the moonlight; only the sound of ice expanding and cracking on the ponds and rivers breaks the stillness. But the icy grip of winter weakens quickly in the spring, and the coast comes alive in an explosion of lilac and lupine and sunlight.

Lupine is my favorite flower. I have tried to grow it for fifteen years on the island, and I have met with indifferent success. Nothing really grows there very well, except bayberry, juniper, spruce, pine, and a few wild blueberry bushes whose roots are entangled in the mussel shells and rocks above the tide line. The island is heavily wooded, and although the forest is softened and blurred with the rains of spring, it becomes a beautiful thing in summer, especially when the slanting rays of the sun shine through the trees in the late afternoon.

The thought of owning an island is perhaps the most romantic concept left to humankind in the twentieth century. On an island the corrosion of progress is as great as the owner will tolerate, and no greater. That fragment of land, floating in the sea, offers such rare prizes as remoteness, privacy, silence, and above all the opportunity to create a small world of one's own. On an island you dress as you please or you don't dress at all if that is your choice. You can sunbathe nude, a privilege that has all but disappeared along our overcrowded coasts, or you can sit on a rock in foul-weather gear and watch a summer storm sweep across the sea.

I have discovered that islands soon take on the character of their owners, much as dogs do. They can be lonely places or centers of enormous gaiety, depending upon what is wanted or required of them. One islander may wish to spend an evening stargazing, alone and content, while another may go off to the mainland in pursuit of more familiar diversions. But more often than not, the appeal of an island is to a person's hunger for tranquility, which is why he separated himself from the mainland in the first place.

Author's Note

These pieces were written over an eight-year period, and no effort has been made here to offer them in the chronological order in which they were written. If small contradictions seem to appear in this arrangement, it is because they have been moved about at random, and the reader is urged to overlook these flaws. Moreover, the Portland Jetport has emerged from its slumber since the piece was written, and the statue of the Maine Lobsterman has been sent on to Washington, but the situations described here prevailed at the time. If the reader stumbles over a statement that seems out of place, I can only say it was in place at one time.

1

Progress Here and There

Demolition

My neighbor's son from the mainland is demolishing an ancient dwelling on this island, and although I am paying him to do the work, I have come to regard the whole demolition project with a great deal more uneasiness than satisfaction at having an eyesore removed. The fact is that every time he swings the sledgehammer, he is uncovering ghosts that a man at my time of life would be better off not having to face. The old house is stubborn and is giving way to the blows much less compliantly than either my neighbor's son or I anticipated. In truth, there are times when I think he is making no progress at all. The house was built at a time when Maine builders took great pride in their work, and on the main studs the nails are spaced no further than an inch apart. I wandered over to the demolition site this morning, and was surprised to find that my sympathies, strangely enough, have shifted over in support of the house. My neighbor's son is an ox of a man, with biceps that I couldn't wrap my two hands around, and I saw him fetch a section of siding a blow that would have knocked a modern split-level ranch house over on its cute two-car garage, but the old wall shook and nothing more. The youth was stripped to his waist and perspiring wildly, but there was a quiet serenity to the old building; it gave off clouds of dust, but no encouragement.

Walking back through the forest, with the sound of the sledgehammer still ringing in my ears, my thoughts took a strange leap, one of those soaring journeys that at first promises to extend the spirit of a man but which later turns out to be nothing more than the erratic pursuit of whatever theme was already at hand. I thought of the barnyard of the Children's Zoo on Fifth Avenue in New York City, a place to which my attention had been first drawn a few years ago by a chap standing there making some uncomplimentary references to the city of New York. He described the city with a string of bad words and said he would think of more later, and sensing that I had struck his bait, he began to reel me in slowly. "Come over here, neighbor," he said, jerking his head in the direction of the zoo. "Here on a spot of ground no bigger than a postage stamp is the only bit of reality in this whole damned city. Take a look at it." Embracing the invitation, I walked over to the wall and gazed at the zoo. There were the barn, the animal pens, the odor of manure, and a sheep and a pony searching forlornly for a blade of grass in a barnyard paved with asphalt. It was not Marlboro country, but it touched a memory of another time and place, of something compounded of clean air and sunlight and a hayrick to slide down, and perhaps the promise that there really was a life, not after, but before death. After that first visit, I stopped often at the barnyard and, resting my arms on the wall, spent many agreeable hours watching nothing at all happen in front of me. Sometimes the animals were out, nudging each other in that peculiar way that animals do, and at other times — especially after dark — the yard was deserted. But that haunting odor hung in the air, and I had the feeling of slow, warm, lazy days and nights, of animals going about their business.

The old house has stirred my thoughts in the same way. I can imagine what happened there the day it was finished. The builder had driven in the last nail ("That'll hold her," he had said to himself, as he dropped his hammer to the ground and began descending the ladder) and had pronounced it complete to the owner, who was already moving furniture into the downstairs rooms. Not a prisoner of union rules, the carpenter helped the owner ease the heavy kitchen range into place, while the wife fussed a bit with curtains and said that sooner or later another closet would have to be built in the back bedroom. (The neighbor's son had as much trouble knocking down that later closet as he did with the rest of the house.) The wife cautioned the men about scarring the Victorian love seat as it was brought through the front door, a caution I ignored when, in my wasteful twentieth-century way, I took it out a few weeks ago and burned it on the mud flats at low tide. The sturdiest item in the heritage left by that former owner was a tall woodbox of tongue-and-groove pine, triply reinforced at top and bottom, which my neighbor's son took one look at and gave up in despair. "It'd take me a week to break that thing up," he conceded. "Why don't you give it to somebody?" That night, long ago, after the kerosene lamps were lighted and a fire had been started in the new fireplace, it was no longer a house; mysteriously, it had become a home. Knowing Maine island dwellers, I suspected that a dog had stretched out on the floor in front of the fireplace that night and concluded that, all things considered, this wasn't going to be a bad setup.

The continuing resistance of the house fills me with sadness because I know houses will never again be built like that. Today's house is built to outlast today's mortgage by a few days only. And at my supermarket the other day I noticed that a razor manufacturer was exhorting me not only to throw away my blade after one use, but to throw away the whole razor; the disposable razor is the shave of the future, I was assured. I've been brooding about these things a lot lately, and seeing that old house go down — in its own triumphant way — didn't help a damned bit.

Stake Out

Now that the days are short and the nights are long, that period between dinner and bed becomes important by giving a man room to turn around in and offering the only time of the day that he can get his thinking done. (My dog disagrees; in her view, the period between dinner and bed is limited to the time required to walk from the kitchen to the living room and climb up on the sofa.) One night recently I spent the time reflecting on the cloying cuteness of America, on the hundreds of ways it has of spelling barbecue, on boats with names like *Gra-Cee*, on the thousands of motels named Rip Van Winkle and El Rancho, on the suburban plots named Justa Small Farm and Dun Rovin, and the hundreds of "country stores" that have sprung up across the land selling stick candy, T-shirts, and Pennsylvania Dutch signs for the decoration of kitchen walls. I am afraid the highest praise one can bestow on the general public taste is to say that, at its best, it is lamentable. The reader will notice that I have glossed over bumper stickers, a separate genre distinguished by the fact that it occupies the point of deepest depression in style, wit, and substance.

Since my battle with public taste is a long one with the end not in sight, I have turned most recently to fireside examination of a set of plans for the construction next spring of a new dining room. Plans for a new room contain almost everything the rural heart desires; in their way they are as rich and promising as a seed catalogue, since they set the heart to soaring on the same sort of journey into fantasy. To get one's money's worth out of making an addition to a house, I have learned, it is important to put some distance between plans and actual construction. This period of time is long on dreams if short on activity at the site. One can hold the plans in one's lap for several months, brooding beside the fire, and detect flaws of a minor nature or ideas for possible improvement that should be discussed with the builder. Tonight's discoveries may be torpedoed by tomorrow night's revelations, but that's the sort of shifting situation that gives the whole thing an air of excitement and the illusion of accomplishment. In the long run one goes ahead with the original plans, but one has enjoyed to the fullest this period of imaginary change and pleasing confusion.

In my own case, I see the completed dining room when I gaze at the plans. Moreover, I see myself at the head of the table presiding over family and guests, perhaps explaining, as I pour, that I wish them to sample a minor Mosel that has intrigued me with its spicy aftertaste. "Mosels come in green bottles," I point out in passing, "and Rhine wines come in brown bottles." I say this in a kindly way, of course, since these are my guests and I do not want to appear in any sense patronizing. The late afternoon sun, shining through a sliding glass panel that constitutes one wall of the new dining room, touches the bottle and ricochets in a dozen directions. From the living room comes, on a subdued note, the driving energy of Mozart's G minor Symphony, while on the sideboard behind me the turkey awaits carving. I have a little story to tell about the creamed mussels, which are the first course and which I first encountered in the dining room of a small hotel in Zurich, but that can wait. The sun drops out of sight, and I move to the door behind me to touch the light switch when I recall suddenly that the light switch is beside the kitchen door. The reverie shattered, I reach for my memo pad to make a note for the builder: there *must* be more light switches within reach.

Some homeowners like to stake out, with string, the outlines of new construction as though the project acquires substance by drawings and on-site measurements, but I have little taste for this sort of thing. During the fireside phase of planning, the less one has to do with the actual construction site, the better — in my opinion. Actual measurements and the location of studs tend to hamper midwinter dreaming. I'm all in favor of plans, but I don't want them restricting my mental vision of the completed work. That misplaced light switch, for example, gave me a nasty start.

This dining room of mine, while connected to the house by a small hallway, will have three glass walls and will be surrounded on all sides by forest. It was conceived by a friend of mine who lives on the mainland, a man of flawless taste and soaring imagination. Together we paced it off, and at that point I turned over to him the matter of details while I retained all rights to fireside fantasies. It will be a light and airy room, and it is well suited to fanciful and airy daydreams. I can see it now on a summer evening. The air is soft and moist, a hazy beauty settles over the forest, and . . . .

New Room

My neighbor came over to the island to check up on the construction of my new all-glass dining room, and I could tell by the expression on his face that he disapproved of the whole thing at first sight. There is a certain artificial smile, a tightening of the lips, that is an unmistakable symbol of his disapproval, and this took possession of his face when he walked through the forest and saw the half-finished structure. If a man must react to things as he moves through life, I suppose it is good that he displays his feelings in some way, perhaps a bit better than good.

"Now where in hell did you get the idea of building a glass dining room?" he asked almost angrily, coming directly to the point. "Don't you know that people can look right in on you? You won't have the privacy of a pig in a ditch." I waited, to let a little uneasiness, a little uncertainty build up in his mind over whether or not he had offended me. I could see where his thoughts were wandering, and I allowed time for anxiety to ripen. "You are completely wrong," I said. "It allows me to look out and see everybody. When I am in that dining room, the rest of the world won't have the privacy of a pig in a ditch."

This reversal of things startled him; I could see it in his face. He took out a package of cigarettes, removed one, and began to tamp the end on his thumbnail. This was a stalling device with which I was familiar. "Who are you going to look out at?" he inquired, lighting the cigarette. "There's nothing on this island to look at except maybe some raccoons. You see one raccoon backing down a tree, you've seen them all." I knew I had him then, and he knew it too, but I couldn't resist giving the winch a cruel half-turn. "Then who's going to look in at me?" I asked. "Raccoons? Should I worry that the raccoons will be embarrassed at my table manners? Are you trying to tell me I won't be able to finish a bottle of wine because one raccoon will say to another, 'Look at old Stinnett, he's really got a snootful tonight'? Is that what you're saying?"

I think I look forward to these conversations with my neighbor, and it may be that I even need them. They sharpen my resolve when I'm trying to put together the unmanageable dream. My neighbor is a tart Mainer, and I seriously doubt that he has ever left the state, yet his mind wanders freely and his opinions often startle me with their flexibility of spirit and reason. He still refers to certain models of automobiles as "coupés," a term that has been lying for years in the attic of my memory, and, when his spirits sag, he insists he has the "blues." Thus, while one foot lingers in the twenties, the other is probing a wilder shore.

As we wandered back to my wharf, after he had completed his inspection of the new room, he asked if I had gotten used to the addition and accepted it as part of the house. I knew instantly what he meant. A house is a basic reality of life, although some are reluctant to admit it. It remains the foundation of our emotional security, even for dreamers. A new growth on an old dwelling is exciting, but at the same time it is alarming because it shatters the comfort of the familiar. A stranger has arrived, and we aren't sure of its intentions. Moreover, it destroys old habits, and habits on an island seem much more solidly anchored than those on the mainland; an island is a small world offering few choices, so existing paths are heavily traveled. Already I have discovered this. Where I used to cut around the southwest corner of the house a dozen times a day on some errand, I now find this new obstruction, and within a matter of a few days a certain hostility has grown up between us. When I go down to my study or to the sauna at the end of the island, I now have to circle around the new dining room and its connecting hallway, a maneuver that is not at all to my liking. Although I arise guiltless from a two-hour nap in the afternoon, the extra five minutes a day that I spend skirting the new room are given with a reluctance that borders on outright resentment. This is a whimsicality of man's nature, and I have no apology for it. I mention it now not as some recondite discovery, but rather to point up the perception of my neighbor in bringing up the subject in the first place.

I pushed his boat away from the dock, we both waved casually, and I watched the widening ripple of his wake as he moved toward the mainland. Then I trudged back up the path to the house and walked around to take a fresh look at the new room. The sun was dropping low in the west now, and a shaft of sunlight struck the glass and made it glow like a sheet of fire. I don't know how other people would have reacted, but to me the new room suddenly became beautiful and awesome. It was a dramatic sight and I bloomed with pride. I am sorry that raccoons come down from the trees and stir around only at night; I would like for them to see that wall of gold. It would be anybody's guess then as to who had drained that bottle of Burgundy.

A Little Electricity Never Hurt Anybody

I have a daughter who is ecologically aware. When my other children come to visit me in Maine, I paint and repair and see that everything glistens and looks its best; when this daughter comes, I find myself feverishly tearing things down. I have trouble meeting her gaze when she comes upon something that she considers a foolish concession to twentieth-century materialism, and if — God forbid — it pollutes the air or sea in any way I prepare myself for the dressing-down I suppose I deserve.

My daughter spent her childhood in coastal Maine, and the relatively unspoiled beauty she encountered in her daily life — in a small village north of Rockland — undoubtedly prepared her poorly for the slothful ways of the outside world.(This reference to the "outside world" is a minor conceit shared by all of us, I'm afraid, who live in Maine. In a way it is like the Nantucket schoolboy who started his historical essay off by writing: "Franklin D. Roosevelt, thirty-second President of the United States, was born off-island.") When my daughter last visited me, I took her around the place and pointed out some of the improvements that had been made since her previous visit. I was vaguely aware that most of the enthusiasm being displayed was on my part, but it was not until I pointed out the new water pump that supplied pressure to the hot-water system that I sensed the chill which had settled in. "Makes quite a bit of noise, doesn't it?" she asked. "How long do the exhaust fumes hang in the air?" The glassed-in sunporch brought an indifferent shrug of the shoulders. "Sort of defeats the whole purpose of a porch," she observed, disapproval lying extremely close to the surface. When I protested that I could hardly sleep under the spruce trees in a sleeping bag, she brightened for the first time. "I would," she said, "if I lived here."

My daughter came to mind today when I received a letter from her, promising to visit me in Maine next summer. The letter was written from Anchorage, Alaska, where she is now living, and I could detect that there had been no softening of her attitude toward the sacredness of the wilderness or toward modern man as a despoiler. "I have spent a couple of days kayaking in the area of Skilak Lake," she wrote, "one of the larger mountain and glacier-controlled lakes on the Kenai. The fall leaves were at their peak — lovely, although far heavier on yellow than Maine woods due to the preponderance of birches. The undergrowth here is what catches your eye: rain-forest green mosses with maroon rosehips and red cranberries and pink salmonberries and orange currants and purple crowberries, and their foliage a hundred shades of red and orange and brown. The beaches are uninhabitable now, though. All the salmon have died [after spawning] and washed up to rot, and the shores are littered with them. I spent one magic morning paddling and drifting down a narrow little tributary stream, surrounded by autumn foliage, and serenaded by a pack of coyotes that paced me for almost an hour on both sides of the stream, now ahead and now behind." Already I'm uneasy about that new wharf I had built last spring, and I've spent the morning wondering if there is any way I can conceal the new sauna.

The curious thing about all of this is that in my way I am as ecologically sound as this child of mine, but in following the conservationist's path I am inclined to drift a bit, taking my eye occasionally from the holy goal of the zealots. I'm seen often by my neighbors picking up trash along Route 24, but I'm also negotiating quietly with the Central Maine Power Company about laying a cable to my island so that I can lie in bed at night and read. This suggests an indolence that perhaps does me no credit, but I feel that a little electricity never hurt anybody. My daughter, if I may voice a proleptical statement in her behalf, will say that the bed light will only lead to floodlights on the dock, electric chain saws with which to cut down the trees, blenders that whir and grind, television to shatter the silence, attic fans to blow air into places it was never meant to circulate, and all of the other appliances that destroy the primitive charm of a rural environment and contribute to man's shiftlessness. I will have to guard against these excesses and my daughter will have to show some trust in my capacity to withstand temptation, although in all candor I must say that my eyes brighten a bit at the thought of a food freezer. From the freezer on the Fourth of July comes the salmon, and my daughter has just discovered what an overripe salmon is like.

What I am saying, I suppose, is that my worship of nature is not quite so monotheistic as my daughter's; my own ardor is weakened a bit by reality and a recognition of the ultimate frailty of mankind. Going to bed by candlelight is a fine and romantic thing, but it isn't always as comforting as sinking into a chair beside a strong reading light and finishing the newspaper. Mine is a double allegiance to conservation — a highly moral one that sends me out picking up trash along the highway, and a selfish one, springing from the desire to also conserve myself, a resource of questionable value to the general public but of incalculable value to me.

Plution

Progress in Maine seems determined to take place at my personal expense. If the seeds of paranoia are detected in that line, that's the way it is. I was once described by a book critic as "a man with an adventuresome mind but also a man of many crotchets." I had to look up "crotchets" in the dictionary; I knew damned well that it wasn't flattering, and it wasn't. A crotchet, the dictionary explained, is a "stubborn notion." I find that hard to accept.

My neighbor on the mainland, now, *is* a man of crotchets. Sometime during May and June of what we laughingly called spring this year, when it rained every day but three in a sixty-day period, I dropped in to see my neighbor. I found him in a toolshed, painting lobster buoys. "What's causing all this rain?" I asked, by way of greeting. He doesn't care much for formal salutation. There was a long pause, during which time he applied a hideous magenta paint to the top half of a buoy. "Plution," he said. I thought that over for a moment and decided I hadn't heard him correctly. "What did you say?" I asked. He placed the paintbrush on top of the can and wiped his hands on a rag. "I said plution and I meant plution," he repeated. "Long as we keep on pluting the sea and the air and God only knows what else, we are going to have trouble. You haven't seen anything yet." The threat of the apocalypse is always within easy reach of my neighbor. He looks forward to doomsday with relish. There was a moment's silence between us. "This cove is full of the red tide, and you can't even dig clams here any more," he said, tossing the rag on a shelf. "You know what red tide is, don't you?" I thought for a moment. "Plution?" I asked. "You better believe it," he said.

What started me off on this train of thought was the realization a few days ago that almost every time I go to town, there have been some improvements made since my last visit and they all result in inconvenience. Years ago, when I first came here, my supermarket had a fine men's room which I invariably visited before heading back to the island. This year there were handsome improvements made in the supermarket, one of which stunned me. A sign on the men's room door said Reserved for Employees Only. Now I have to cross the street to Burger King, loiter around, shifty-eyed, while I study the menu on the wall, then bolt to the men's room when no one is looking. Sooner or later, the manager is going to intercept me on the way out, and ask me to step into his office for a little talk. I haven't felt this way since I was in school, and the teacher said, "The principal would like to see you in his office at three o'clock." Frankly, I would like to get caught soon and get it over with.

I don't know whose idea it was to improve the shopping mall by removing the two telephone booths, but there is now a bench where the telephones used to be. No one sits on the bench, which is something that could never be said about the seats in the telephone booths. I've wasted some of the best hours of my life there, waiting for some youth with a terminal case of acne to finish talking to his girlfriend. Once, last summer, a teenager was holding a portable radio to the mouthpiece, playing rock music to his Loved One. I tapped impatiently on the glass with my dime, and he threw the door open and said, "I've got it turned up as loud as I can, and if you can't hear it, I'm sorry." But the two telephones served a purpose. I now have to drive nearly three miles to find one, and I suspect its days are numbered. It's in a restaurant which I've been told is to be modernized and improved this winter. I have the feeling that next summer I'm going to be looking around for another pay phone.

I now have to pay the filling station for my gas before I even know how much the tank will hold, my bank has notified me with poorly concealed glee that if I lose the key to my safe-deposit box it will cost me eighty-five dollars, the letter carrier is displeased with the tilt to my mailbox and has placed two threatening messages in it, and my automobile insurance company, which refers to me impersonally as 0194402390110900642501427008, has instructed me to pay them every six months instead of once a year, and has hinted that if I don't, I'll soon be driving an uninsured car. I feel as though the doors to the Ark are being slammed in my face.

I don't know what to say about improvements that have been made in vending machines, cash registers, and banking equipment in the past few years, other than that I am highly suspicious of them and have the feeling that whatever all that whirring and clicking is, it isn't in my best interest. Now things go on that, I must admit, unnerve me. Yesterday the cashier at my bank punched so many buttons in registering a modest deposit that for a fleeting second I felt like I was coming to the rescue of the Bank of England. "What's all that for?" I asked timidly, after he had finished his keyboard work with a flourish. He smiled at me. "Don't worry," he said cheerfully.

Well, I do worry. All of that whirring and clicking and storing up of information creates plution, and you better believe it.

Chic

This is the time of the year, of chill winds and uncertain skies, when a sensible person does his reading and thinking, and I would estimate the ideal mix would be about half of each. I put aside a fashion magazine a few nights ago — at this time of the year I would read the Shreveport, Louisiana, telephone directory if that was all I had within reach — and fell to musing about the compulsion of so many people to be fashionable: to wear fashionable clothes, to eat in fashionable restaurants despite the quality of the food or the arrogance of the waiters, and to be seen at fashionable beach and ski resorts although they may loathe swimming and skiing. Snobbery, of course, is the unthinking acceptance by some people of the ad hoc judgments of those they admire, surrendering their honesty, intellect, individuality, and personal identity as part of the transaction. Stifling one's own taste and superimposing that of someone else on top of it is bad enough, but too often the motivationalists and trend setters set up caricatures instead of the real thing, and then we are all in for a rough time of it, because the spurious and atrocious can't be junked overnight.

The admiration of Americans for Perrier water, a product of France, has run its course, I have been told, and the fashionable new water is Poland Spring, a product of the State of Maine. I know a lady on East Fifty-Sixth Street in Manhattan who won't even water her plants with Perrier, so certain is she that Perrier has slipped in the chic world of mineral waters. Poland Spring water has been around a long time, and is both healthy and tasty, but I am a little disturbed to learn that it is now putting on airs. I liked it better when it was honest and unfussy.

Of course the fashion magazines have long regarded the American woman as a type and not an individual, and they have decked her out in some truly hideous clothes, the most awful in recent memory having been the "hot pants" of a few seasons back. But in the magazine that I put down a few nights ago, I was a little startled to discover that an unforgivably obsolete term had somehow crept into its pages — there was a reference to an "in" restaurant. This term crested in popularity long before Perrier water, and I couldn't understand how a fashion magazine, which lives in the future as though no present ever existed, could make such a mistake. I have no idea what elemental and mysterious processes banish a term from respectable currency, but I assumed that fashion magazines knew these things if anybody did. But "in" is now so old-fashioned as to be almost quaint, and in pointing this out to a fashion magazine I feel almost as though I were telling *Better Homes and Gardens* how to lay flagstone.

It was perhaps five years ago and my mind was on other matters when a lady from New York, sitting on my sundeck, admonished her boyfriend for making some reference to backgammon as no longer being "in." "That expression 'in' is now out," she informed him tartly. "It's out even further than backgammon." These proclamations falling from the sky, so to speak, upon a Maine island, are gathered carefully and preserved, and it was only the next afternoon when I ducked into the country store that I encountered the opportunity which would invest me with prestige for possession of such knowledge. The storekeeper's wife, a pleasant lady who rather prided herself on keeping up-to-date, had apologized to a customer for not having a certain brand of cigarettes. "It's hard to keep them in stock," she said. "Everybody seems to be smoking them. They're really in." Normally I would let such a remark pass, but it now served only to stir my blood; the drunkenness of high adventure was in the air. "The cigarettes are in fashion," I said exuberantly, "but the expression is not." The storekeeper's wife looked at me steadily, her eyes narrowing. "Who says?" she asked.

There, of course, she had me; the unanswerable question. If she knew that her finger had been placed at the strategic point to shut off all further discussion, there was nothing in her manner to suggest triumph. Soundly trounced and deflated, I slunk from the store, muttering something about having left my motor running. I was guilty of one of the oldest follies of mankind: of knowing all the answers except the final one. But I had one fragment of truth to sustain me, one noble ray of hope. I knew that right now, all over the world, follies were — I'll put it this way — in.

Withholding Consent

There's not a person in Maine who hates controversy and contention more than I, but every now and then a man has to have a little chat with his local government, not only so each can get to know the other better but also to remind both parties that their insights may be a shade devalued by a narrow view of what are thought to be the facts. In this country, government operates with the consent of the governed — a fragile notion that has been badly shaken at the national level —

and I would like for the folks at Augusta to know why I am withholding my consent on the matter of building a certain bridge in my township, the need for which seems to have divided us. It is a small bridge, but the principle involved is large. If it were not, I wouldn't hold the government at bay like this.

Before getting to the matter of whether this bridge is needed or not, I'd like to kick around the principle a bit. The so-called nationwide taxpayer's revolt which now appears to be a fairly solid political reality is, in my opinion, a wholesome trend and an inevitable one. Governments tend to get bigger; citizens tend to get smaller and more inarticulate. Often the voice of the latter becomes so muted as not to be heard at all. In the broad sense, this is unfortunate and does very little to secure further the blessings of liberty to ourselves and our posterity. Here in New England, the individual has not drifted down the road to anonymity quite so far as those of other regions of the country, possibly because he is rather cantankerous and independent-minded to begin with, and also because his institutions and background equip him for a somewhat different role and point him in a different direction. The famous New England town meeting, while it may not be the flawless exercise in democracy that the late Norman Rockwell pictured it as being, still exists, and the voice of civil disobedience that was Henry David Thoreau's still echoes in the woods of Massachusetts and Maine. What Thoreau offered was strong medicine. "There will never be a free and enlightened State," he wrote, "until the State comes to recognize the individual as a higher and independent power, from which all its own power and authority are derived, and treats him accordingly." When put in jail for not paying his poll tax — a refusal based on unwillingness to support a government that tolerated slavery — he was visited by Emerson. "Why are you here?" inquired Emerson. "Why are you *not* here?" replied Thoreau. A heritage like that isn't tossed aside overnight.

I am now coming to the point. Politics is a profession, and the politician, once elected, finds himself or herself the possessor of power often never before experienced. Power is a heady thing and incites more often to recklessness than to caution. Without hesitation, an elected official would be inclined to say pave that road or build that bridge when contemplating the expenditure of public funds, but when shopping for the family at the supermarket he would search carefully for a cheap cut of meat. To suggest to him that perhaps the bulldozers should be stored away during a period of great inflation and financial uncertainty is to suggest the unspeakable. This is a denial of the fruits of victory.

My opposition to the new bridge is based upon the old-fashioned and possibly obsolete concept that the present bridge is adequate. The state government is not going to get my consent to construct a bigger and more resplendent bridge as long as I find that the existing bridge does all that one can expect of a bridge, which is to provide the means for safe and prompt transportation across a body of water. I am not happy to be put in the position of defending the present bridge because it is not an attractive span at all but, in truth, is rather tacky. It's the sort of bridge that one can cross without even knowing it, which probably is all to the good because it fits well into the landscape it serves: typical Maine coastal country, with a country store here, a small marina there, and a modest cluster of dwellings along the highway. One day toward the end of summer I parked on a shoulder of the road and walked across the bridge to get the feel of it, so to speak, and it was exactly as I had always imagined it to be when I crossed it. Small, a little run-down-at-the-heel, but functional — the right bridge in the right place.

I have heard a variety of costs mentioned in connection with this project, each estimate higher than the other, but I know from the expansive and handsome way governments look at these things that a footbridge over a mountain stream or a tidal gut can't be built for less than a million dollars. I would like to see that million dollars spent on something really needed, or if nothing comes to mind, not spent at all. I'm not a New Englander by birth, having migrated here only ten years ago, but ten years in Maine have taught me that a little money in the bank never hurt anybody.

Over My Head

The small building, in which I am writing these lines, is a one-room cottage which was converted casually and with scant adornment into a writer's workroom. But it possesses a fine view of the sea, if I don't let the bayberry bushes grow too tall, and it gives me an unobstructed glimpse of a rock ledge which can be reached at low tide by my dog, who takes considerable pleasure in going there despite the fact it is the one spot on the island where she is forbidden to venture. Not only does she return from the rock ledge covered with mud, but sometimes she doesn't return at all; the tide comes in and cuts her off, and I have to go fetch her in the skiff. We have had more than one unpleasant exchange about this which, I'm afraid, has only sharpened her curiosity about what is on the rock ledge, and perhaps added a touch of adventure to what otherwise would be a rather dull ramble. Boxers have a fine sense of stealth, and it's pretty obvious now that she considers it the high point of any day when she can outwit me long enough to get to the rock ledge before I discover her missing. I don't want to exaggerate the gravity of a writer's problems, because writing is a shaky business at best, but writers usually like to get to the end of a paragraph before pausing, and by that time the dog is usually standing on the rocks looking at me, her face wreathed in triumph and mud.

Yesterday I took direct counteraction and, it being a sunny day, moved my typewriter out to the tiny porch of the cottage, where I had a panoramic view of the mud flat she has to negotiate in order to reach the rock ledge. But the porch trembled violently when I started to type, and a quick examination revealed the foundation had rotted beyond repair. Within seconds I had given up writing for the day to devote my full time to the far more pleasant job of constructing a new porch. From the boathouse I brought up some boards and a bag of tools, and after some preliminary measurements — a steel tape measure lends the luster of professionalism to even the most amateur undertaking — the sound of saw and hammer shattered the silence of the forest. The dog wandered up some time later, covered with mud and crestfallen at my indifference, but I was too deeply involved in carpentry at that point to do more than ask her to please not sit on my chalk-line. When a man is constructing something with tools he is in a state of almost total concentration; in his mind's eye he already sees the completed job, and anything that stands in the way is not to be tolerated.

I wish I could say that construction of the porch moved right along, and I wish I could provide a wealth of illuminating details on foundation stresses and the laying of tongue-and-groove planking. The truth is I'm over my head — in more ways than one — just hanging a picture, and it soon became apparent, even to the dog, that I was spending far too much time looking and measuring, and almost none on actual construction. Carpentry has destroyed my spirit on more than one occasion, and I think my worst moment came when I once called in a local builder to help finish some repairs on my wharf and he said, as kindly as possible, "What do you say we take this down and start all over again." One would think a few unnerving experiences like that would cause me to hesitate in getting out the tools, but dreams die slowly, and the vision of self-sufficiency, of man keeping his own house in repair, is the most stubborn of all.

It was several hours later that I rowed over to the mainland and called the builder, it having become clear to me in the meantime that the construction of the porch was destined to take its place in the mosaic of my carpentry failures. Further humiliation was in store for me. The builder said he was busy at the moment, but would send his son right along, a youth who had just turned thirteen. The boy shook his head when he saw what I had done — a casual gesture I would as soon have been spared — and he set to work promptly. I went to the house and made myself a drink, hosed off the dog, and when I wandered back to the study, the boy was wiping his hands on his trousers and collecting the tools. "I think that'll last," he said, smiling. I didn't smile back.

Implausible as it may be, this will not mark the end of my carpentry work. I have what automobile mechanics call a fast idle, and the moment I see a loose shingle or a rotting board I am swept up by the excitement and nobility of the challenge. I was once asked by a well-meaning friend — a friend now once removed — why I didn't buy one of those handy books which identifies termites and other enemies of the homeowner and which describes in simple terms how to make home repairs. Well, right now I know who the enemy is; it's that smart thirteen-year-old son of my builder. He could have taken a little longer, and it didn't have to be so perfect. It's hard to like a competent kid like that.

In the Name of Progress

Is there anyone else in the room who, like me, is beginning to worry that Maine is trying to become like everyplace else? If there is, I wish he or she would kindly raise a hand. I would like to know if this is some personal anxiety of my own or whether it may be a growing uneasiness shared by others.

The charm of Maine is the charm of a song, fitful, mysterious, whimsical, and it has no more substantiality than a slanting shaft of sunlight shining momentarily through a canopy of oak leaves to light up the forest floor. I am not a person to describe this contradictory thing that is at once fragile and yet possesses the strength of anchor chain; it surely is a job for a poet. But I know where some of the dangers lie, and they are invariably along the yellow brick road leading not to Oz but to that other gleaming mirage known as Progress. To describe progress in other than the noblest of terms sets a man up as a target for scorn and ridicule; few people have the courage to acknowledge that what we had in the first place was pretty good and that a great deal of its goodness was lost in the process of improving it.

A few days ago I saw a highway sign that I have been trying ever since to erase from my mind, but it lingers there annoyingly like a cinder in the eye. The sign said Left Lane MUST Turn Left; there was a nasty, New York sort of bossiness to it, a dictatorial tone that caused my resistance to stiffen instantly. Drivers are human and they occasionally wander into the wrong lane, and there is no reason why a simple mistake should cause them to be shunted off into some direction far from where they want to go. I know it is fashionable in these days of superhighways and cloverleafs to let a driver know that if he missed his exit he is out of luck because the next one is Cleveland, but I would like to think that this is not the Maine way of doing things. A Maine sign, I think, should give a man a little leeway, a little slack, some room to turn around in. At least, it has in the past.

I'm a prompt man where my mortgage payments are concerned, but I travel more than most people and when I get back from an unusually long trip I stop in my bank and explain that I've been in Egypt or Greece and apologize for being a bit late. My banker takes the payment cheerfully, inquires how the weather was in Egypt, asks me if I've gotten this year's calendar, and we part on the best of terms. But I've just noticed a stern warning on the monthly mortgage reminder that a "late payment penalty will apply after ten days," and it has just occurred to me that the bank doesn't give calendars anymore. I feel like an old friend has moved out of the house next door and that the new occupants feel they would do well to keep an eye on me. It makes me uneasy.

A few years ago I discovered an unnoticed little road that gave access to the highway when I departed from my shopping mall, and over the years it has brought me a great deal of happiness in that it saved the the frustration of two traffic lights. Traffic lights, as any driver knows, crush the spirit and destroy man's dream of the celestial highway leading off to the stars. Leaving the supermarket the other day I discovered that my secret road had been abruptly blocked off at the highway. As is the custom nowadays there was no explanation, but none was needed. I recognize an act of Progress when I see it.

My county police officer told me the shed at the end of my dock on the mainland should be kept locked, and I asked why in view of the fact that the shed contained only ½ pint of two-cycle outboard oil, an ancient sponge that I used two years ago when I last washed my car, a red chair with only three legs, and a June 8, 1976, issue of *Time* Magazine. He shrugged his shoulders, a way of saying take all the risks you want but don't call me after you've been robbed.

Nonetheless, I got a lock but I expect any day to find it forced; the lock seems to imply there is something inside worth locking up. A few days ago I unlocked the door and looked inside; the oil, sponge, chair, and *Time* were okay. I breathed easier, but in my heart I longed for the old days when the shed not only was unlocked but the door frequently flapped open, especially when the wind came from the east.

My dog can't go in the barber shop with me anymore, but I don't know why because she curled up by the door and minded her own business until I got out of the chair, when she would gaze at me in astonishment, wondering how I had changed so much in just a few minutes. The sign now says, Sorry, No Dogs. The word *sorry* is pure hypocrisy and I resent it; it gives off a hollow ring like a spurious coin when tapped on the counter. My barber, whom I have called Nick for the past twelve years, has informed me that he is now a stylist, not a barber, and that he would appreciate it if I would call him Mr. Nicholas in the future. I'm looking for a new barber.

My lumberyard waved me off a few days ago when I stopped by to pick up a couple of two-by-fours, saying they now handle only builders' accounts, and I can no longer find kerosene for sale anywhere. A new tavern has opened up down the road called Chez When, which isn't even funny the first time you hear it. I should be more tolerant about these changes because a man can't ask time to stand still, however appealing that may be in the giddy atmosphere that now prevails. Maine is both a wonderful and an implausible place, and any lessening of its wonder or its implausibility stirs me not to wistfulness but to something very close to dread. Especially when the refinements are brought about in the name of Progress.

New Hope

I stopped worrying about the free world's destiny a few evenings ago when my eye caught a headline in my Maine newspaper that said, "Hope Seen For Hadley Asparagus." Even before I read the article, I felt better. Here was a news story that didn't make me edgy; it had nothing to do with wars in Beirut or the Falklands, or assassination attempts upon the Pope, or new mischief stirred up by Fidel Castro. If there was not much hope for the end of the arms race, there was hope for Hadley asparagus. Perhaps I felt better than the situation warranted, but it had been a long time since I was soothed by what I read in a newspaper.

I suspect that the Hadley asparagus story was largely ignored by the American press, and, if that is true, it's too bad. As I read the article, I realized it was nothing more nor less than the continuing unfolding of the human struggle against natural onslaught, this one in the form of the fusarium fungus, which destroys the system that carries nourishment to the sprouting stalks. But I cherished the news story because it carried me off briefly to another world, a world far removed from suffering and weariness and conflict and treachery. Thinking about the Hadley asparagus problem reminded me of my youth when my father would give me five cents to clean the vegetable garden of potato bugs. The bugs clung to the underside of the leaves, and I scraped them of with my fingers and dropped them into a can half-filled with kerosene. I haven't picked a potato bug in some time, but I doubt that I have lost my skill. The potato bug episode leaps to mind at this time because, in retrospect, it was an experience compounded of carefree days, of the rich odor of earth, and of the fresh, cool air of a sunny summer morning. There are very few things in the natural world that cannot be controlled by nature, including that instrument of nature that takes the form of a small boy with a can of kerosene.

For some reason — the human mind is a skittish and unpredictable thing — the Hadley asparagus story reminded me of another news story that I clipped from a Manchester (England) newspaper a few years ago, when I was spending some time in London. It remains to this day my favorite news article, and, a few minutes before writing these lines, I removed the clipping from my desk drawer and reread it with undiminished delight. The item — one of the great news stories of all time, in my opinion — told of the failure of Margaret Hunter, a sixty-four-year-old Manchester lady, to pass her driving test. Reporting the story with the crispness that is characteristic of the British press, the Manchester paper declared that Miss Hunter had been taking driving lessons for twenty-five years, but that "she flunked her driving test again today, *as expected.*" The italics are mine.

Miss Hunter, who was pictured as a frail, white-haired schoolteacher, took the test against a background of unsettling events, which included a collision, the creation of a monstrous traffic jam, and the cowardly resignation of a driving instructor who was described as "having fled for his life."

According to the paper, Miss Hunter set out from her home with a friend in a borrowed car to take the test. After thirty minutes at the controls, she surrendered. "But the car is not damaged," she pointed out triumphantly. "I thought I had done quite well." Miss Hunter told reporters later that she actually didn't expect to pass. "I shall take the test again when I have had a little more practice," she said. It was then that Miss Hunter revealed she had been taking instruction for twenty-five years and implied that one couldn't expect results overnight.

The Manchester paper suspected that Miss Hunter's test was a possible news event when, a few days earlier, her instructor had leaped from the car crying, "This is suicide!" The following day, she took her car for a practice spin but got only a hundred yards before she collided with a truck. On the day preceding her test, she hunted up another instructor — one who was said to have few dependents — and took the car on the highway again. When she finally pulled off onto a side road, she had twenty miles of snarled traffic behind her. That lesson, her forty-second, left her full of confidence, and she asked permission to take the test.

"I've not looked at the form to see why I failed," Miss Hunter said when it was all over. "My thumb is a little sore from the accident, and that probably affected my driving. But I'm quite confident now, and I am sure I shall pass when I next take the test." Her instructor was somewhat less optimistic, and refused to be drawn into a discussion of whether or not he would continue as Miss Hunter's teacher.

Well, Miss Hunter's spirit seemed to maintain a small but significant lead over the piston engine, just as the Hadley asparagus is beginning to move out in front of the fusarium fungus, and, in times like this, that's all you can ask. I would like to reaffirm my faith in both of them, and I shall skip over the war news hurriedly in the future, hoping to find the real news — Miss Hunter and the Hadley asparagus — somewhere in the back pages.

Goodbye, Central

Well, the *New York Times* found the news about the shutdown of the Bryant Pond hand-crank telephone system an item that was fit to print, and they had one hell of a time with it. Not since the Monhegan Island referendum on a telephone cable has the *Times* had so much fun. In my mind's eye I can see the excitement in the newsroom when the first flash came up on the computer terminal, and an editor ripped the print-off from the machine. "OK, Chief," he says triumphantly, placing it on the news desk, "those Down East rubes have come through again. They've been made to shut down the last hand-crank telephone system in the country." The news editor's eyes glow with excitement. "This is on the level?" he asks. "On the level," he is assured. An excited group assembles around the news editor's desk. "It's worth two columns in my opinion," says one grizzled copy editor, a veteran of the Monhegan story. The news editor shoots him a look of contempt. "Two columns?" he says derisively. "This is a three-column story if I've ever seen one." He pauses, and knits his brow in contemplation. "Take this," he barks at an assistant. "Make it three columns: 'Goodbye, Central; Crank Phone Dies.' " He gazes at the group, a smile of satisfaction playing about his mouth. The group dissolves slowly, several shaking their heads in wonder. "It's easy to see how the Chief got to be Chief," one whispers to another as they make their way back to their desks.

There's something about Maine that appeals enormously to the *New York Times*; they view it as a sort of time warp, a place where progress collides with the status quo, where things remain unchanged from our childhood. Just as the *Times* classifies California under the heading of Nuts and Cranks, it categorizes Maine as Nostalgia. The *Times* is happy when things are pinned down, all neat and tidy.

In my opinion, which is not a humble one, there is more to the telephone than meets the eye of either the *New York Times* or of Elden Hathaway, who used to run Bryant Pond's hand-crank system. The telephone is the stuff of dissonance, of creating false emergencies, of shattering tranquility, of inducing nervousness, of threatening isolation by breakdown. In short, it displays an unceasing will to dominate our lives, and I, for one, hate its guts. A few years ago when I had submarine cable laid from the mainland to bring electricity to my island, I was farsighted enough *not* to include a telephone line. I am familiar with the master-servant relationship which springs up when a telephone is installed in a home; the telephone rings and someone races to answer it, fearful of being too late and missing the mysterious visitor. People wait patiently in line at stores and doctors' offices and banks while cashiers and receptionists give priority to telephone customers, a mutual realization seeming to prevail that some kind of inexplicable emergency attends a telephone call, that once silence settles on a line no sound will ever be heard from it again. This, of course, is the purest nonsense; if the receptionist told callers that she was busy with customers who had taken the trouble to come in and that she was unable to handle telephone requests at the time, the earth would not tremble. The fact is that the telephone is a bully in all respects; it threatens loudly, instilling fear by implication, yet subsides in impotence when ignored.

There is a kind of dreaminess in an island society, a peacefulness compounded of silence and such sounds as spring from nature itself striking the nail much harder than was necessary. "Know what I think?" he asked. I did, but I lied and said I didn't. "I think it's a lot of damn foolishness," he said.

I rowed back to the island and threw the newspaper away. If it wasn't going to trouble my neighbor's dreams, there was no need for it to trouble mine. A government committed to the notion of growing lobsters in individual pens is a government dwelling in darkness, because any successful aquacultural farming, in my opinion, has got to somehow manage to preserve and convey a feeling of the sea and its tides and its currents and all of the subtle checks and balances that Nature has placed there. The floor of the Gulf of Maine is not the floor of a henhouse, and the sooner the government finds that out the better off it will be.

The only comparable item I have encountered recently also concerned lobsters. It was the lament of a writer in one of the home magazines over her inability to find the proper stuffing for lobsters. She had tried shrimp and flounder and a special kind of anchovy paste, and nothing seemed just right. Well, search no further, lady, because I've got the answer for you. There is *no* stuffing for a lobster that is anywhere near as satisfying as that which the good Lord put there in the first place.

Passage

There is something very comforting about a kerosene lamp, and I've spent considerable time trying to figure out what it is. I know there's something aromatic and peaceful in a room where a lamp burns, something that suggests warmth and comfort and the cyclic rhythm of life itself. It marks the end of a day and, perhaps even more important, the end of a day's occupation. Body and mind adjust more quickly to stimulating things than to those that soothe; the process of winding down takes a little time and a bit of doing. Nature has provided some assistance to those who will open their minds and hearts to her help: the sound of the surf breaking on a sand beach; the steady patter of rain on a roof; the whisper of wind passing through spruce and pine trees; and the steady, golden glow of a kerosene lamp burning through the night, its wick trimmed low and its sweet odor penetrating every room in the house.

The matter of kerosene lamps is very much on my mind these days because I have just had a submarine cable laid to bring electricity to this island, and yesterday I gathered all of the kerosene lamps into the wheelbarrow and carried them down to the boathouse, an act which I knew would send them into exile forever. What I had thought would be a very gala ceremony ended up being quite solemn. As I placed each one of the shelf, I mused over its own peculiar eccentricities, wondered about the conversations it had overheard, the city guests who had turned the wicks too high and smudged the chimneys, the nights they had burned in sickrooms to bring comfort to the uneasy, the ones which, for some reason, always flickered a little and smelled of raw kerosene. There was one, a small brass lamp with a squat chimney, that had an enviable miles-per-gallon rate; it had skipped a lot of refillings although it was used constantly. I suddenly saw the lamps as old friends, friends who had stood by me during the ten years I had been on the island, and I knew that the coming of electricity was separating us and hurtling me into a new era. Nothing here would ever be quite the same again.

Electricity is a nervous energy, and its ganglia should be buried under a city's streets, not under the placid waters of Card Cove. I'm concerned about what it will do to the quality of life on a rural island, yet the decision to introduce electricity here was not an impulsive one. To be honest, I have had it in the back of my head for the last five years, but it was only last winter that I realized that somehow the decision had already been made and all that remained was determining when to do it. I could still dine by candlelight, I told myself as I searched for reassurance, and I could still put out all of the lights and doze after dinner in the glow of the fireplace. I would be the master of the new intruder, I decided with a resolution I didn't always feel; I would keep it firmly under control. There would be no television or blenders or other appliances that would whir or growl, and there would be no attic fans blowing air into recesses where the Good Lord didn't intend for air to circulate.

Years ago I had dismissed out of hand any notion of installing a generator, which would have cost only a fraction of the cable, because I couldn't even contemplate the presence of an internal combustion engine shattering the silence of the cove. The boxer often heard sounds in the night that I didn't hear, and she would raise her head and growl in warning, but I would hear the lonely cry of a loon calling to its mate or the squawk of the blue heron as it landed on the mud flat to fish at low tide, and these sounds to me were part of the symphony of the island night and I loved them. The Intruder — as I came to regard the electricity — would be permitted to diminish nothing.

The switch has not yet been thrown as I write this, but the electricians are drilling holes in the walls and floors, and tonight or tomorrow or the next day a light bulb will suddenly glow, and a curtain will drop and a way of life will pass. Autumn is the enchanted season on the coast of Maine, the days are warm and golden, the nights cool and tranquil. I want to hear the high autumnal tides slapping on the rocks beneath my window and I want to see the path of gold as the moon rises above the trees on Yarmouth Island and I want to smell the balsam in the dark forest and the juniper growing in the crevasses of the rocks. I want the pattern of summertime undisturbed, and I want the crisp mornings of autumn to lure me out of bed so I can stand on the high rocks and breathe deeply of air that is cold and invigorating, and I want the springtime to continue without end. All of these things must be saved; they are infinitely precious. The Intruder will let me read in bed at night and will warm my bathroom on cold evenings and will take the darkness and dampness out of my workroom on days when the fog wraps itself around the island, and that is all it can be permitted to do. I will hold back the years. I am still in charge here. But I don't know why my voice is rising.

The Great Breakdown

I think this unhealthy infatuation with computers is likely to get us all in trouble, and I'm waiting uneasily for The Great Breakdown. It will come, sooner or later, and already the forerunners have appeared. The other day at my bank I had to wait over twenty minutes for verification of my balance before I could get a check cashed; the teller just shrugged his shoulders and said, "Our computer is down." To him it seemed a perfectly adequate justification for a delay, as though some natural phenomenon had occurred over which man had no control. But I fretted impatiently, drumming my fingers on the glass shelf where I thought I had every right to expect my money to be. I had not committed my funds to a computer, I had placed my money in the care of a bank. In dealing with a computer, one is supposed to feel he or she is looking to the infinite sky, to the Almighty Himself, for results, not to a faulty and fickle package of colored wires and silicon chips.

When I inquired of the teller why the bank didn't possess some kind of backup system to care for its customers when the computer went dead, he glared at me in disbelief, feeling, no doubt, that such an expression of agnosticism had no place in a public location like a bank lobby. It was as though I had disrupted a religious service or had spit on the flag. "The computer is more reliable than I am," he said haughtily. I thought that over for a moment. It was meant to be an Olympian remark, a warning to set me back on course, but my patience was wearing thin from the wait. "I suspect you're right," I said, nodding toward the slumbering giant, "but I'm surprised to hear you admit it." I was rather pleased with this retort, especially when it drew a hearty laugh from the lady waiting in the line behind me.

Computers may perform some functions in an economical way, but one pauses to wonder if our reliance on them is not on too broad a scale. Human imagination and insight are wonderful things, and some people — I am among them — feel they are irreplaceable when a situation gets to where the rubber meets the road. During the weeks before Christmas last year I went to several linen specialty stores in the various shopping malls of Maine, searching for a set of gray sheets upon which the heart of my daughter was firmly set. Everywhere I found only incomplete sets, a totally chaotic selection, and I inquired of one of the managers if I could speak to the buyer of sheets. Struggling to keep the patronage out of his voice, the manager told me that the requirements of the linen department were reckoned by a computer, that there was no buyer. When I pointed out that a king-sized bottom sheet and a twin-sized top sheet may make a snug nest for a computer but they were not likely to please my daughter, he smiled condescendingly and walked away. Clearly I was one of those customers who couldn't understand modern retailing.

I recently bought a book in a Maine bookstore, and was startled to see the cashier punch thirty-two buttons in ringing up the sale. It took quite a while, with the cashier searching the book for telltale marks and figures and then hesitating over his keyboard as if fearful that lightning would play across the skies if he touched the wrong keys. Purchasing a book suddenly became a memorable occasion, exceeding the importance of the book itself, and I fell to wondering if anything of a spectacular nature was expected of me as this scene was played out. When he completed the transaction, nervously biting his lip as he punched the final key, I asked what all of the keys accomplished, what mysterious information they provided the machine and what in return they demanded of it. "I could see you punching a key for the amount, another for the sales tax, and another for the total," I said, "but what do the other twenty-nine do?" He looked over his shoulder cautiously, and lowered his voice. "I haven't the slightest damned idea," he said, "and I don't think anybody else here does either. They tell me it feeds information into a computer, but what the computer does with it beats hell out of me."

I worked in a small grocery and dry-goods store one summer

between college terms and I was "B" on the cash register, a sensible machine that asked nothing more of me than that I ring up the total, push the "B" key to identify myself with the transaction, and proceed to make change. A bell clanged when the cash crawer slid open, a signal alerting the owner of the store to the fact that someone was monkeying around with the cash register, legitimately or otherwise. So far as I could tell, the cash register did all that one could expect of it, and did it quickly and cleanly. I could ring up a sale, make change, and push the cash drawer back with my stomach in less than thirty seconds. It wasn't necessary to feed any ancillary information into a computer; Mr. Maupin did the buying, and he knew what was needed.

No, the computer is the hula hoop of our time, but it has become a little terrifying to reflect on the changes in our social order that our addiction to it is bringing about. And on the day when The Great Breakdown occurs — when traffic doesn't move and planes don't fly and stores don't open and banks can't verify a depositor's balance — I'm going to take a book outdoors and lie under a tree and enjoy myself. And you can guess what the book is going to be — the one that required thirty-two punches to tally up. I hope it's a good book because it may be the last one I'll ever be able to buy.

2

Unexpected Treasures

Gifts from the Sea

Anything that happens on an island is important. It is such a compact world that the slightest loss or gain throws things momentarily off balance. When the flood tide during the night leaves a fine spruce log stranded on the rocks, it is examined in minute detail the next morning by the dog and me; we speculate on where it came from, why it was sawed precisely in that length, and what was its purpose. It is then hauled up beyond the high water point and will be sawed into fireplace lengths. The bounty of the sea, like that of the land, is accepted with gratitude. The dog's curiosity exceeds mine. She is excited, or pretends excitement anyway, over the white plastic bottles that are forever floating around coves and coastal reaches. I draw the line there.

Early yesterday morning when I stepped outside to rub the sleep from my eyes, I saw on a scrub-covered ledge about a quarter of a mile away what appeared to be a beached skiff. A skiff, beached or otherwise, is a thing of tremendous importance in coastal areas, and to fail to investigate one that has slipped its moorings is, at the very least, a sin against Nature. At that hour of the morning it was fairly still, with a trace of a breeze springing up from the southeast, and I decided to bail out the rowboat and row across to the ledge. (All rowboats need to be bailed out; I wager there is not a rowboat along the entire coast of Maine at this moment with a dry bottom.) When the dog and I reached the ledge, I saw it had been a skiff but was now a total derelict. Its bottom had been mostly stove in, the transom that had once held an outboard motor was gone, and the flaked paint on the sides mutely testified to the disuse that the boat had long ago fallen into. It was destined to end its days precisely where it had now arrived: on a rock ledge where its remains would bleach in the sun, where it would accumulate its final cargo of sand, and where it would disintegrate completely in the next storm, or certainly the one after that.

If there is anyone around who can leave a rocky point unexplored at six-thirty on a summer morning, it must be a person who can be neither excited nor instructed. Leaving the skiff at the burial spot of its own choosing, we struck off across the point, climbing from the rocks to the higher reaches where bayberry and juniper managed to cling to the sandy soil, and where one stunted oak tree had entwined its roots around rocks and was fighting what appeared to be an uneven match with the wind and the sea. Over hundreds of years, man has achieved brilliance in the arts and has unlocked many of the secrets of science, but none of them seemed quite so impressive as the fresh beauty and the awesome perfection of nature that existed on that point of land. At this hour the landscape was wholly without man; peace flowed over us — the dog and me — a peace compounded of blue water, the breeze, the warming sun, the silence. A fish leaped, and we were both startled.

Higher up, away from the flood-tide level, wild sweet peas bloomed in profusion, their roots extending great distances from the plants, barely stitched into the sand with tiny filaments. Huge clumps of nightshade, with deep blue blossoms, grew almost knee-high; the virulence of their poison greatly exaggerated but still not a plant to pluck or fondle. Further on, we came upon an enormous wild rose, its branches still hung with the scarlet hips from last year's blossoms that are supposedly a prime source of vitamin C. I broke one off and bit into it; the hip was pulpy but not unpleasant.

The waterline was littered with all of the strange objects that get swept up by an undiscriminating sea, transported for great distances, and then cast adrift upon a shore that accepts them either temporarily or permanently, depending upon circumstances that involve either a profound law of nature or mere caprice. There was a small wooden box half-buried in the sand, a rubber boot, a white and orange lobster buoy, the bleached skeleton of a lobster trap, a part of a door with a rusted key in the lock. I noticed the door was locked and I had to hammer on the protruding bolt with a rock to unlock it. I was filled with distaste at the notion of a locked door; it struck me as totally contrary to the freedom of a summer morning and the ageless innocence of a world governed by the seasons and the sea.

I sat on a log on the highest point of the ledge and blinked into the sunlight, while the dog searched the reeds and the marsh grass. The breeze trembled the leaves on the stunted oak, but it was warmer now that the sun was stronger. Wild ducks flew by; it seemed early, and I couldn't decide whether they were coming or going, but it didn't really matter. Nothing mattered at that moment but the majesty and mystery of Nature, and the contentment, peace, independence, and solitude that it brings.

Refuse du Jour

I got up early this morning and walked out on the sundeck. The sun had not yet gathered its strength, but it was going to be a warm day; it was that hour of the morning when dew still clings to every surface and the smell of the sea, coming in on the moon tide, continues to bide its time and fill the air. I walked down to the wharf and got in the rowboat, not having the slightest notion where I was headed. At the last moment, the boxer jumped into the skiff and took her customary position in the bow; last night's moon apparently hadn't gotten to her as it had to me, and her thoughts were still on the delights of the warm blanket she had just left. I aimed for a forested section of the mainland, and after a short pull, I beached the skiff and started walking along a shoreline littered with the detritus of a moon tide. The dog's interest picked up immediately; a finicky eater in the kitchen, she finds nothing else so appealing as the *refuse du jour* she encounters at the water's edge. My eyes drifted across the usual litter stranded by a high tide: the chunk of styrofoam, a lobster buoy painted red and black, the wreckage of a lobster trap half-buried in the sand, an assortment of white plastic containers, a piece of ladder, a boot, a length of knotted rope. And then I saw it — a long, slender box with rusted hinges, the kind of thing an expensive rifle may come in, or a fishing rod, or some other piece of equipment of strange contour. It was empty; a small quantity of sand had managed to work its way into the box while it was being tossed about the beach by the waves, but otherwise it contained nothing. I tossed it beyond the high-water mark, finished my walk, took an overripe crab away from the dog, and rowed back to the island.

    I wish I could say that was the end of the episode, but I can't. I had finished my breakfast, and had brought a second cup of coffee out to the sundeck when I realized that something was nibbling, like a mouse, at my mind. It was the box. I certainly didn't need a box like that, I had *never* needed a box of that shape in my entire life, yet how could I leave that box on the sand dune to rot away or to drift back to sea on the next moon tide? Granted, it was an awkward size, but didn't that make it all the more valuable? When a box that size was needed, it was needed badly.

I sought to put the whole subject out of my mind by telling myself that this was a Maine reaction, the attitude of a frugal New Englander, and that I was a Virginian by birth and a Mainer only by adoption. I really didn't need to clutter up my boathouse with unnecessary boxes of odd shape and limited use. New England frugality, I reminded myself, was traceable to the hardships of the Massachusetts Bay Colony, as well as those of Rhode Island and New Hampshire, where colonists had to make their own household products because there was no choice. They grew grain, and their horses and oxen and sheep furnished food and transportation. They made their own meal, cheese, candles, and soap. They grew their own wool and flax, and in the winter the wool was cleaned, carded, combed, spun, woven, and dyed. The dye came from hickory or butternut bark. They made their own shoes, even tanning the leather. But I didn't come from this stock; my forebears in the Jamestown Colony were neither frugal nor flinty. They relaxed, and grew tobacco, and played lighthearted games with the Indian girls. I definitely did not need that box.

It was a day for answering mail and writing checks, and I wandered down the path to my workroom, where the morning passed easily enough and the stack of letters achieved an impressive height. But there was an unmistakable lateral mobility to my thoughts, moving from the letter at hand to the box on the dune, and I don't think any of the letters got much more than a fraction of my attention. An obsessive neurosis functions in this manner, I suppose, with the most compelling thought refusing to take its place in the mosaic of the mind, but intruding constantly instead, like a drunk in a nightclub.

I sawed some wood (the saw wouldn't fit in the box and, besides, the saw hung on a nail in the boathouse), I painted the oars (the box was too short for the oars, even if the time ever arrived when the oars needed being stored away), I cleaned the brushes (who would lay paint brushes end to end in a box?), and finally, late in the afternoon, I built a fire in the sauna. I'm not sure exactly when, but sometime while I was stretched out on the bunk of the sauna I gave up the fight. I didn't grow tobacco, there were no Indian girls on the island to play with, and my quixotic Virginia ways seemed to have departed and left me emotionally, as well as physically, stranded in New England. The transformation was now complete. As I write this, the box is resting on a shelf in the boathouse; the sand has been cleaned out and the hinges have been oiled. I'll think of a use for it tomorrow. Or, most certainly, the day after.

3

The Boxer

The Myth of Protection

There is a feeling around, and I suspect that it has existed for some time, that every Maine family living in the country should have a dog "for protection." What the dog protects the family against is a subject that's usually left up in the air; protection is a powerful word and few people are inclined to question its use. My household includes a fawn boxer bitch, and she is most certainly there for protection, but up to the moment of writing these lines I have done all of the protecting. If a thief broke into the house during my absence, so delighted would she be to see him that she would lead him directly to where the silver is hidden. To my knowledge, the only time she has ever growled in anger was when a county police officer stopped by the island one day to inquire if everything was all right. We've had a number of consciousness-raising sessions, the boxer and I, in which I've undertaken to give her a better understanding of her position and function in our relationship. During the last one, when I sent her on an attack-and-destroy mission, she didn't come back and I later found her asleep in the sun by the boathouse. This is inherently a peace-loving animal, and I can't escape the conclusion that if there is ever trouble on the island I'm going to have to grapple with it single-handedly. A strange Labrador retriever once swam over to the island, and I watched with interest to see at what point the boxer's territorial imperative would assert itself and she would attack. Quite the contrary; hardly had the Labrador shaken himself dry when the boxer led him agreeably down the path to the house where, presumably, I was supposed to set out lemonade and cookies.

One night I was awakened by a strange and ominous jarring sound. I got up, seized a flashlight, and commanding the dog to follow, went outside, where I found a porcupine had knocked over the garbage can. Not wanting the dog to tangle with the porcupine, I turned the beam of the flashlight in all directions looking for her, but the dog had disappeared. When I went back to my room she was lying on my bed, where she decided to remain until morning, the night being as troubled as it was. I think it was then that I realized the boxer felt her mission in life was somewhat loftier than my concept of it.

Some nights when the moon is full, she will trot down to one end of the island and strike up a dialogue with some dog on the mainland, and then she is full of threats and wastes no time in idle conversation. One would think she was a veteran of a thousand campaigns, so great is her contempt for the mainland dog and so merciless are her plans for him if they should ever meet. After she has described in terrible detail his final agony, she will trot back to the house, occasionally throwing a final insult or two over her shoulder but these are mostly for the record. I'm sure the other party in this moonlit colloquy is the Labrador retriever, but I haven't the heart to tell her. Anyway, it's all a fantasy, a dream spun out of moonlight on the trunks of white birches and the sea wind whispering seductively as it moves through the brooding grove and shadows.

I had an unsettling experience with another boxer many years ago when I acquired from the War Surplus Agency a manual on teaching dogs to guard and to attack. The manual, the text of which had been stolen from the Germans, had been left over from World War II, and after I gave it a trial, it became very clear to me why the Germans lost the war. I was living in a small town in New Jersey at the time, and carried out the basic training sessions in the front yard. One day I was teaching the boxer an exercise from the manual entitled "Following Your Master Under Fire," which called for both me and the dog to crawl on our stomachs along the gound while imaginary enemy rifle fire went harmlessly over our heads. I had proceeded perhaps twenty feet when my neighbor, a man named Harris, placed his elbows on the fence and after observing me a few moments, asked: "Pulling a sneak on the Little Woman?" I said no, I was training the dog. "What dog?" he asked. I looked back. The dog was on the front porch, scratching at the door.

Many Maine dogs sleep in doghouses, and I think their nighttime barking is not so much protective as it is accommodating; they know that's what their owners want. Any owner who wishes to invest his dog's nocturnal howling with heroism can do so if it pleases him, but it's my conviction that the dogs are pulling a fast one. Hundreds of thousands of years ago when dogs first realized that man was a soft touch and could be relied on for a solid meal once a day, they promptly moved into the cave and joined the family. A little night barking is a small price to pay for a first-class setup.

The Case for the Dog

I would like to write a piece about dogs, or rather a sort of appreciation of a particular dog, but to lay it right on the line, I'm afraid to. I'm afraid that I'll fall into one of those fatal traps which lie there waiting for the unwary writer, especially the writer who is foolish enough to write about dogs. Dogs aren't human, and there's the problem in a nutshell; writers tend to describe them in terms of human behavior and the first thing you know what started as a well-meaning piece has turned suddenly into something cute and cloying.

I'm willing to give dogs their due, but no more. It's obvious to anyone that in some respects dogs are far superior to humans, certainly insofar as basic morality is concerned, and in their distaste for duplicity and treachery. I don't think many dogs would cheat on their welfare checks, if the situation applied to them, or would be a member of OPEC or some other extortionary group, nor do I think they would rob their neighbor's house. In the first place, they know what their neighbor would do to them if they were caught, and that's reason enough. Reality, cause and effect, and action and reaction are the strong threads in the fabric of dog society. Political oratory would be laughed out of town; that sort of nonsense cuts into sleeping time.

This dog of mine, a female boxer, possesses some characteristics that I envy very much, although they have little to do with nobility or even sensitivity. For one thing, she adjusts to situations in a matter of minutes, while I'm likely to fool around, brood for awhile, weigh one thing against another, and finally come to an uneasy conclusion. Early this spring, after having been away from the island during the winter months, I got my neighbor to take me across in his lobster boat for a quick visit so I could make some measurements for a planned alteration. The boxer jumped out of the boat, sauntered up to the house as though she had left it yesterday, and was waiting for me at the front door when I arrived. The house was shuttered, dark, and uncomfortably cold when I opened the door, but she wandered from room to room to check on things and then jumped up on the sofa and stretched out. Things looked all right to her, she was back home, and what's for dinner? When I come up there to open the place, it takes me a week to settle in. It shouldn't, but it does.

The Boxer

Once, several years ago, on my first day back on the island I was moving some fireplace logs and found buried under the leaves a hammer for which I held a high regard and whose loss I had taken badly. I remember picking it up, polishing the handle with my glove, and taking it lovingly down to the boathouse, where I wiped away the rust with an oily rag and hung it on the wall between two nails. That same afternoon, the boxer discovered in the forest *her* favorite toy, a badly chewed styrofoam lobster buoy, and after tossing it around a couple of times to satisfy herself that it was as it should be, she trotted off with me to bring some packages up from the dock. She saw no need for an elaborate ritual of discovery, nor time dedicated to restoration and gloating. She will have a lot more free time in life than I will.

Perhaps the characteristic she possesses that I envy most is her patience. I have what is known as a very short fuse, but the boxer is infinitely patient, not only with me but with everyone. I've seen her frightened, but I've never seen her irritated because things weren't going well. She insists on her dinner at a reasonable hour, but I can't blame her for this because she is unable to get it for herself and she has a right to petition for a redress of grievances if I get involved in something else and forget it. Besides, that's hunger and not vexation.

Boxers are extremely dignified and proud dogs, and her pride gets in her way sometimes, but that usually strikes me as more amusing than cumbersome. At low tide she can wade from the island to an adjacent point of land on a mussel bed, and we've had some unpleasant encounters over this because she gets preoccupied over there and can't get back when the tide rises again. On two occasions I've had to get the rowboat and row over on a rescue mission. Knowing I am displeased when she wanders over there, she is too proud to bark for help when she is cut off by the incoming tide. The last time it happened, I had looked all over the island for her and it was only by accident that I saw her on the ledge. I looked at her through the binoculars and I could see terror written all over her face, but her jaw was firmly set and I knew that drowning was a more acceptable choice than calling for help.

I find a certain exhilaration in challenging a storm, in going over to the mainland when there is a strong chop in the cove and the wind is driving rain in my face, but here I am speaking for myself alone and not for the boxer. To her this is one of those inanitions cherished by certain human males who should have a net thrown over them before they do some further damage to themselves. If I go to the mainland in a storm, she will come along, but the necessity for the journey will always remain unproven in her mind.

Upper Hand

I'm a sucker for an animal with a hard luck story. The relationship between man and animal should be the simplest thing in life — a friendship based upon mutual forbearance — but it sometimes manages to develop into something as complicated as anything country life has to offer, and the discovery of this comes to each of us in his own fashion. My dog, an elderly boxer of enormous dignity and a matriarch to the core, somehow got the upper hand as she emerged from puppyhood and she has strengthened her grip steadily throughout the years. She knows me, I must confess, even better than I know her; my weaknesses were discovered by her years ago, and she is so sure of her ground now that she has given up probing for the soft spots in my authority, testing the water to make sure the time is right for a move, scrutinizing me carefully for telltale signs of impending rebellion. No, she calls the shots now, sometimes giving me a little leeway in order to retain my pride but always ready to set me back again on course if my new freedom causes me to lose my head and do something foolish. A boxer is a very bossy dog to begin with, and the females can't stand to see authority lying around without grabbing it. Whether this goes back to their German heritage, I can't say, but there is a definite Prussian presence in their distaste for disorder of any kind, in their conviction that there is a right and a wrong way to do things, and in their contempt for incompetence. It isn't easy to live with a boxer if you are inclined to be a little loose in your habits, a little untidy. There will be changes made, and soon.

If there is one thing my boxer can't abide it is getting in a wet boat and going to the mainland in the rain, and she does it only when she is convinced that I am going anyway and God only knows what kind of trouble I would get into if I went alone. But she goes grudgingly, and takes no pains to conceal it. Even when we get back, and I have dried her off with a towel and lit a fire in the fireplace, she is inclined to sulk throughout the afternoon. What bothers her the most, I think, is her belief that the trip was brought about by bad planning; whatever we went to town for should have been brought over to the island on a clear day. Plan ahead, she is forever preaching, but, hell, I sometimes forget.

But to get back to the matter of animals with hard luck stories, I would like to erase from my mind the memory of the chipmunk who despised rain and whom I permitted to come into the house during storms, only to have it move in as a permanent guest. Even cloudy days would have it scurrying through the doorway, usually in the direction of the kitchen, where it made a diligent sweep of the counter to see what was for lunch. Then one day he, or more likely she, marched in followed by five children, and I had to rethink my entire policy in regard to chipmunks. I solved the problem by scooping them up and taking them to a nearby island, where I turned them loose in the forest with a dozen doughnuts and a pound of Oreos to tide them over until they could gather together whatever food chipmunks eat when not on welfare. But the doughnuts and Oreos didn't buy for me the freedom from guilt which I expected, and to this day I carry a residual burden of unease that I somehow mishandled the situation. The four baby field mice that I rescued from the sauna chimney also seem in retrospect to have been the victims of my bungling, although I fed them with an eye dropper three times a day, and with a sturdy formula consisting of milk and bourbon whisky. They passed away on successive days, but their passing seemed painless, possibly because in desperation I stepped up the strength of the formula. The skunk that showed up on the island one day was left to his own resources; I suppressed the impulse to set out some scraps for him around the boathouse, where he had set up headquarters, and I'm glad that I did. After a couple of days living off the land — which on a small island is slim picking — he departed by whatever means he had arrived. Of all the animals that dropped in, I was perhaps least hospitable to the porcupine which greeted me sullenly one day from the branch of an oak tree just outside of my study. Whatever virtues porcupines may possess, flexibility and the ability to make quick decisions are not among them; I finally had to saw the limb off the tree to get him to the ground, and then he disappeared in some crevices in the rocks by the shore. I kept the boxer in the house for two days before I was convinced the porcupine had decided the island was not to his liking, and had departed.

Some friends of mine in Vermont have sold their place and are moving to Georgia, and I approve of the way they did it. The husband left first with the dog, the two of them driving south to set things up for the rest of the family who were to follow in a month or so. This struck me as a sensible and perhaps even inspired arangement; the man and the dog becoming familiar with the new setup, putting things in order, making new friends, and being on hand to greet the late arrivals. No mooning or wistfulness is wasted on the old place, no exploring the past; the dog would be more excited than the husband in showing the family the new place, in the warmth of the welcome. I set down these remarks because I think people are inclined to underestimate the role which animals play in their lives. My own awareness has by now become instinctive; if you live long with a female boxer you are not allowed to lose sight of her influence for a second. Not if you know what's good for you.

4

Minor Grievances

My War with the Outboard Motor

I possess an admiration for the man of coastal Maine, but of all of his talents the one I admire the most is his understanding of that seventy-five-pound package of inert metal, tubes, wire, and general mischief known as an outboard motor. I despise these things, even those that have not yet been built, but a man who chooses to make his home on an island has to learn at least to live in peace with an outboard motor. A person with an unreasoning fear of elevators should not take an apartment in the top reaches of a skyscraper, and I tell myself this when the air turns blue with profanity at the end of my dock. But it doesn't help; nothing helps except my neighbor, who starts the damned thing with a gentle tug of the pull cord.

If it were just one motor that caused me trouble, I would junk the thing and start with a new one. But over the past twelve years I have had at least a half-dozen of them, all of them new, and whatever that mysterious current is that passes from the human arm to the motor and starts the combustion of gasoline, it seems to be lacking almost entirely in my case. I have seen twelve-year-old kids jump into half-filled boats on rainy days and start, with one pull, a patched-up motor that looked like it belonged in a marine museum. On other occasions, I have seen lobstermen untie their lines and push off from docks, then casually draw the pull cord without even looking at the motor. They take off instantly, all the time finishing a conversation with someone being left behind. I wouldn't dare untie a line until I had the motor going; I've rowed back in embarrassment and tied up a boat with a silent motor too often to try that again.

When a man's claims to fame are as few and as slender as mine, he may as well make the most of them, so I have let my reputation build in the neighborhood as a person for whom an outboard motor refuses to operate. Once last June, while I was drifting idly in the cove hoping to hook a flounder, a neighbor put out to tow me in. "I thought you were having a little trouble," he said, pulling up beside me. He was a kind man and slightly embarrassed to discover that I didn't need help; the implication, I'm afraid, was clear. "Come back in about half an hour," I said, "when I try to start up." We both laughed, but the laughter had a hollow ring.

Several times a year I manage to jerk the pull cord out of the motor, and this requires professional help and a trip to the repair shop. I have been told by the repairman — and I hope the reader will observe that I'm trying to keep the bitterness out of my voice — that I have a greater incidence of broken pull cords than any other customer he services. I explained that this is due to the fact that I have to pull the cord so often to get a stubborn motor started, but I could tell by his expression that he felt not all the facts in this story had surfaced.

My neighbor, who is a lobsterman and clammer by trade as well as by nature, appears to know everything there is to know about an outboard motor, regardless of its age or make. He disregards brand names. "They're all alike," he says, taking the cover off the motor and eyeing the compact mass of machinery. "If a spark gets to the gasoline, it'll run." His hands know what they are doing; they follow a wire here, a tube there. The spark plug is disconnected, wiped clean, and capped tightly. The bulb on the gas line is squeezed. He pulls the cord gently and the motor springs to life. In his presence it invariably runs like a demonstrator in a dealer's showroom. My dislike for it increases.

"Your trouble," my neighbor said one day when I had rowed him over from the mainland to help get me started, "is you think there is some trick to starting an outboard and you don't know what the trick is. It's just a piece of machinery. The Devil isn't in there." Of course he had put his finger on the problem; I regarded the operating manual, which I had read a dozen times, as fiction. It explained the motor in technical terms but it perversely omitted the real key to successful operation, and that is the rapport between owner and machine. I approach an outboard motor as an adversary, a mortal enemy, whose defeat is necessary if I am to enjoy any standing in the community. The motor responds; if I want trouble I'll get trouble.

The fact is, I don't really think I'm alone in my attitude toward outboards. Exact knowledge seems pretty scarce, and despite what they say I notice that my neighbors have a limitless assortment of metaphysical aids which, it seems to me, they tend to rely on with more faith than they put in a direct approach to the motor's vital organs. I've seen a kick on the gas can accomplish some enviable results, and I once saw a youth unscrew the gas cap and spit in the tank. I was not aware that human saliva possessed any high octane catalytic properties, but something brought the motor to life because it took off with a few scattered explosions and then settled down to a reassuring rhythm. The ideal outboard owner should be half mechanic and half witch doctor; I'm convinced that walking both sides of the street is the only sensible thing to do.

My most recent motor, purchased only a short time ago, has been the most stubborn of all in starting. The dealer, moved by my complaints of having been sold a faulty motor, brought his best mechanic over to the island one day recently to check the motor out. Before removing the cover, the repairman pulled the cord experimentally and the motor took off instantly, purring like a Rolls Royce. They left, casting uneasy glances backward. It's been a long battle — this war between the outboard motor and me — and I'm afraid the end is not in sight.

Cloying

It is my experience that New Yorkers need to be reminded almost constantly as to what they should like and admire. Being snobs by nature, they are mostly incapable of making qualitative decisions and rely upon those whom they admire and imitate to make such decisions for them. One publication which seeks to perform this function is *W*, a newspaper not easy to describe but one that clearly assumes its destiny to be the ultimate authority on what is fashionable and stylish. A few nights ago my eyes were roving idly across the pages of *W*, a copy of which had been left behind by a guest from New York, when suddenly I saw something that caused me to sit bolt upright. Under a listing of "Things With Style" (*W* fancies the catalog approach) there were the Connaught Hotel in London, Harry's Bar in Venice, Harrod's Food Shops in London, Fauchon of Paris, the Concorde, and L.L. Bean. *L.L. Bean?*

While L.L. Bean has been fashionable with me for a number of years (how can you be indifferent about a store that will sell you a bear trap at four o'clock on a Sunday morning?), I was stunned to learn that it had been embraced by the jet set, and this stirred anew a free-floating anxiety I have possessed for some time. Is Maine becoming chic?

Take the matter of that word "Vacationland" appearing on Maine license plates. Many years ago, E. B. White, one of Maine's most distinguished residents, wrote with considerable indignation on that topic, claiming that it made the people of Maine appear to be drones. A license plate, in my opinion, is no place for a promotional slogan. It's to give you a clear reckoning on the identity of the person knocking you down, and under circumstances prevailing at such a time no commercial message is going to make much impression. Most license slogans are idiotic, but few are as bad as "Vacationland," unless it is that of Rhode Island, which calls itself the "Ocean State." One feels more like weeping than jeering in the face of slogans so poorly conceived.

I have been watching too, with some uneasiness, the growing cuteness of some Maine towns. Carmel-by-the-Sea in California and New Hope in Pennsylvania were once towns of considerable charm; now both have cases of what urban planners call "terminal cutes." Both towns possess such a cloying Hansel and Gretel atmosphere that one departs from them with a queasy feeling, as though there had been an overindulgence in marshmallows. Boutiques are now outnumbering the shops in a lot of Maine coastal villages, and I notice with dismay the proliferation of coy names for gift shops and restaurants — names like The Noisy Earthworm and Your Father's Moustache and The Damn Clam and The Pier Group. Nothing to warrant any action yet, but enough to flash the red alert. A straightforward name like Mike's Fried Clams would be a welcome sight, and I pledge it my business right now.

Before I became a resident of Maine I came here often, but not to eat at The Damn Clam. I came to sit beneath the lighthouse at Pemaquid Point, and to watch the Atlantic beat against that massive rock, and to smell the salt air that was sweetened by spruce and balsam. It is still one of the best shows in Maine, and I recommend it highly to visitors. Moreover, it's complete in itself. It doesn't need an adjoining ice-cream parlor with heart-shaped chairs nor a Barbary Coast bar with red velvet draperies and sleeve garters on all the bartenders.

It's my contention that Maine is the only state on the eastern seaboard to preserve its character and remain unspoiled. The Maine village is still intact, serving as the scaffolding of a social order that shows every sign of enduring, and it's reassuring to see that the customs and speech of Maine are stubbornly sticking around to see if the twenty-first century is going to provide something better. But no one can say for sure whether or not the independence of Maine people is sufficiently blight-resistant to hold off the horrid smartness that has engulfed other states and regions that happened to lie athwart the tourist path. The presence of L.L. Bean on that list in *W* has me worried.

There's Been Enough Talk

In 1975 an unexpected frost struck Brazil's coffee plantations, and by the summer of 1977 a cup of coffee in the Portland airport cost forty-nine cents, a price that diverted me to the airport water cooler. The coffee disaster in Brazil may be real — certainly the Portland airport's cost squeeze is real enough — but I'm not so sure; it possesses too many of the elements of the "manipulated shortage," that new enemy that we are all very slow in learning to cope with. First there was the sugar shortage, then the toilet paper shortage, then the oil shortage, all of which sent prices skyrocketing until the public learned that no shortages really existed, certainly not in corporate profits, and prices retreated to more reasonable levels. Last winter, television viewers witnessed the distasteful sight of Florida citrus growers rubbing their hands in delight and smacking each other on the back as frost coated their orange groves; their eyes were aglow with the prospect of shortages and higher prices. But they had momentarily fogetten about the California crop, which in the long run put a rein on the ambitions of the Florida growers. Brazil has a deplorable balance of payments problem, and when a 132-pound bag of coffee rose from $40 in 1975 to $400 in $977, things got brighter for Brazil and darker for the Portland airport coffee shop. I dislike leaving the Portland airport holding the bag, so to speak, in this matter but I have a balance of payments problem of my own and it is more real to me than Brazil's.

Now that I have brought out into the open my feelings about that forty-nine-cent cup of coffee, and while I'm in a somewhat petulant frame of mind, I'd like to catalog a few other minor grievances. Why, for example, don't Maine radio stations give the time more frequently? I live on an island, and for an island dweller there is nothing more important than time. I need to know constantly where I stand in regard to the passing of the day, but instead of the time I get another one of the Top Forty. The song "Margaritaville" doesn't suggest to me that it's time to stop painting that boathouse and start sawing wood. "Margaritaville" only suggests that perhaps I should turn the radio off.

There are more islands off the coast of Maine than anywhere else on this continent and few have electricity. Why is it, then, that chimneys for oil lamps are almost impossible to buy and when they are found they are invariably of only one size and shape? Breaking a chimney in my house is almost as calamitous as breaking an arm. I've conducted intensive searches throughout country stores along the coast of Maine and aside from the standard chimney with the beaded top there is nothing. Even more rare is the Humphrey mantle for gas lights; coming upon one in a hardware store is almost like stumbling upon a Winslow Homer painting at a garage sale. I have one in reserve, kept like a pricelss jewel in a safe corner of my shirt drawer. The Humphrey mantle is an indescribably delicate contrivance, and its extrication from the box requires the nerveless fingers of a surgeon. More than one has collapsed into nothingness in my fingers at the moment of lowering it over the gas jet. Only the owner of a gaslit home appreciates the gossamer nature of the Humphrey mantle and understands the care with which it must be handled.

I see by the papers that the Administration is going ahead with the development of the neutron warhead at a cost of many billions of dollars, and I wonder if — in a popular referendum — the people of the United States would not prefer that a small fraction of that sum be spent in the development of a workable repellent against black flies and mosquitoes. My vote is in the bag for the repellent people. A lobsterman told me a few days ago to eat an onion every day. "A mosquito won't go near you if you eat onions," he told me with great authority. "Just one onion." I ate onions for three days with results that can only be classified as poor. Then I read in one of the medical journals or possibly *Reader's Digest*, that thiamine was the thing. Take thiamine regularly, readers were told, and leave your windows and doors open; mosquitoes and black flies despise thiamine. I have a large bottle of thiamine tablets available for anybody who wants to give it a second try; my own experience indicates thiamine is just what an adult mosquito craves. I've tried cigar smoke, citronella, the commercial repellents, and — following the advice of an elderly neighbor — rubbing kerosene on exposed surfaces. Nothing works, but I have high hopes that someday the true repellent will be discovered and I say let's get on with the research, even at the cost of one neutron warhead. Odd as it may strike the government, I am more interested in killing black flies and mosquitoes than I am in killing people.

Only one complaint remains. As long as I've been in Maine I've never heard anybody say, "A-yuh." Is that too much to ask for a man who has chosen Maine as the state he prefers to live in for the rest of his life?

Who Says It's Vacationland?

I woke up in a contentious mood this morning and before my normal disposition returns I want to discuss once more that cretinous slogan, "Vacationland," which my state expects me to display on the front and rear license plates of my car. The passive acceptance by the citizens of Maine of this foolishness is disheartening; it shows either disinterest in the individual's dignity or concurrence in the notion that the slogan in some way improves the State of Maine and makes it a more desirable place in which to live.

I do not consider Maine to be a vacationland, if I know the meaning of the word. Las Vegas is a vacationland and so is Walt Disney World and so is Yosemite National Park, but Maine is home to a million people, most of whom make their living by farming or hauling lobster traps from the sea or cutting timber or — to cite the hardest work I can think of — by writing, as I am doing at the moment. My neighbor, who is now hauling 700 lobster traps, comes in the cove around five o'clock each afternoon, ties his boat to a mooring and rows to shore, an exhausted man. I am not going to ask him if he thinks he lives in vacationland, although I think his answer would have some bearing on this matter in a blunt and profane way.

Placing ridiculous slogans on state license plates is a tired and tiresome fad that should have run its course by this time. It was never far removed from the cute bumper sticker, or the tote bag with the cunning legend, or the T-shirt carrying a message that was meant to be hilarious. The last bumper sticker that I saw said "I hate bumper stickers," which, in an odd way, I consider a step in the right direction. I saw a tote bag in a gift shop the other day that said only "Bag," the cryptic, final backlash of a fashion that has expired. T-shirts, I notice around the house here, are now being used for washing the car; their final fate is perhaps their noblest. Only the license-plate slogan is hanging on, dismal, humorless, and often completely misleading. Rhode Island license plates proclaim that state to be the "Ocean State," although there are eighteen other states bordering the Atlantic and Pacific oceans, most of which have far more ocean littoral than Rhode Island. This is the worst public relations idea I have heard since a few years ago when a midwest promotion man came up with the idea of establishing a Hall of Flame for distinguished firefighters.

I don't see why Connecticut is the "Constitution State" since I know for a fact that all fifty states possess constitutions, and Florida's contention that it is the "Sunshine State" didn't set too well with me last winter when I spent five days trudging around Key West in the rain. Most puzzling of all, of course, is New Hampshire's challenge to "Live Free or Die." A lot of the more sensible people of New Hampshire considered that to be cheap sloganeering, causing the United States Supreme Court to ultimately rule that the First Amendment gave people the freedom of silence as well as the freedom of speech, and that it was not illegal — as the state claimed — to cover the slogan with adhesive tape. I have twice covered "Vacationland" with tape, but Maine weather and the state's promotion people don't work in tandem, and this particular vacationland's winters are hard on tape; in February you're lucky if it stays on two weeks.

I don't know if fire trucks, ambulances, and hearses have to carry "Vacationland" on their license plates or not. I rang up a local funeral parlor the other day to inquire if they would be interested in a special plate saying "Earthly Vacationland" and I was told they did not feel such a distinction was necessary.

Massachusetts has no slogan on its license plates, but I gather this is because most Massachusetts plates are so badly crumpled that it is difficult to read the numbers, much less the fine print. If Massachusetts is toying with the notion of adding a slogan to their plates I would like to suggest that "Collision Capital of the World" would be appropriate. However, I'm just thinking out loud, and if Massachusetts doesn't like that, I may come up later with something better.

But getting back to "Vacationland," I wonder if anybody — anybody in his right mind, that is — believes that the slogan has brought one person into the state who wasn't coming here anyway. I ran a quick test on myself this morning and I offer the results to the folks in Augusta with no strings attached. The results were negative. "Vacationland" is too much like Oz; there isn't any such place.

Where There's Wood Smoke

This is a day of hazy skies and dire predictions. I have just read in the morning newspaper that the Maine Department of Environmental Protection is concerned about the pollution from the 460,000 wood-burning stoves in the state. "If everybody converts to wood burning with airtight stoves," a spokesman said, "we could expect a substantial increase in the dust particles in the air from wood smoke." I would like to depose that I, for one, am not terribly alarmed about pollution from wood smoke even if the Environmental Protection people think I should be. I deal with an authority that possesses better connections all around than the DEP, and that is a force known as Nature. Long before men inhabited this planet and set about to destroy it, there was wood smoke. It came from forest fires touched off by lightning and by volcanic ash, and very likely from some other natural causes that I'm overlooking at the moment. If wood smoke exists in nature, I'm not terribly worried about it. All nature isn't benign, but it's a damned sight more benign than man.

Moreover, there's something very comforting about wood smoke in the air; it's pleasing. I don't feel that way about the blue haze that comes from diesel trucks or the choking exhausts of oil or gasoline combustion. But a little wood smoke, floating in the air at twilight, welcomes a man home from work and causes him to quicken his step in anticipation of a cheerful blaze in the hearth. If too many sparks fly from the chimney I worry about them setting fire to the leaves, but I don't worry about them choking me to death.

That's part of the story; the other part is that I don't trust that figure of 460,000 woodburning stoves because I think I was one of the people polled in the survey and I took a somewhat antic attitude toward the whole thing. I not only thoroughly dislike polls but I like even less the substitution of poll results for good judgment. I was coming out of a store at the Cook's Corner shopping mall last autumn when a lady forced a card into my hand and inquired if I recognized the names of any of the woodstoves printed there. She held a clipboard on the crook of her arm, and she had the manner of a woman who worked the *Londay Sunday Times* crossword puzzle in ink. I held the card out at arm's length to accommodate a minor visual flaw having nothing to do with age, and glanced at the names. "None of these names are familiar to me," I said, glancing up. "However, I don't see anything about Kennedy and Carter. Don't you want to know. . . ?"

"Is there any one stove here that you would not like to use?" she asked, checking a form held on the clipboard.

"No," I said. "I'd try any of them, especially if you have in mind giving me one as a sort of sample. But if you want to know what kind of stove I think Carter or Kennedy. . . "

"Have you ever used a woodstove in Maine?" she asked.

"No, but I use a fireplace all the time," I replied dispiritedly. "Don't you want to know about my 2.4 children and my median income of. . . ?"

"Using Maine-grown wood?"

I answered affirmatively. "I own 1.8 automobiles," I offered hopefully, "which projected on a. . ."

"Do you prefer a fireplace over a woodstove?"

"Can you list me as undecided?" I asked, pleased at the chance to show that I knew my way around the categories. "And if the election were being held today, my vote would. . ."

"One final question," she said, her pen poised over the clipboard. "For either fireplace or woodstove, which kind of wood do you prefer?"

"That involves a comparison," I said, "and it needs clarification. Do you mean by geographic region? By marital status of the user? By size of household? By occupational status? By socioeconomic group? By sex? By age? By education, aged ten and over? By home ownership? By urban or suburban. . . ?"

She took the card from my hand and turned away. "Wait a minute," I said. "You didn't mention provisions for variable stability and control characteristics. What about qualitative ratings? Conceptual measurements? It isn't fair to just ask a few questions and wander off."

But she had already handed the card to another man.

"Public opinion polls reach everyone in America from the farmer in his field right up to the President of the United States, Thomas E. Dewey," humorist Goodman Ace once remarked. You remember Thomas E. Dewey. He defeated Truman in 1948. The polls say he did.

Backsliders

The storekeeper started me off on the wrong foot this morning when I went in to buy some nails. "I have some that size," he said, "but I'm not going to sell them to you because they are no good. They won't go through hard wood. It's hard to get good nails anymore." It set off a train of thought that was hard to derail as I drove home. The memory of the lightbulb that lasted sixteen days came to mind, then the burnt-out clutch on my almost-new automobile, then the three outboard motors I had purchased in the past four years. Other items with notable shortcomings crowded in: the vacuum cleaner that broke down the first time it was used, the razor blades that cut skin but not whiskers, the padlock that refused to open, the calculator that couldn't be trusted not to capriciously add three zeros to the total, the shirt which lost a sleeve the first time it went to the laundry. Is this why Japan and Germany are calmly dividing up between them the American market for automobiles, cameras, televisions, electronics, and optical goods?

A few days ago I was reading some essays by Henry David Thoreau, and the old New England meddler and troublemaker seemed to foresee what was lying down the road and he hastened to heap scorn on it. Nature, of course, was Thoreau's major preoccupation, but there was hell to pay when man's folly and depravity crossed his path. The state of America's productive genius in the closing years of the twentieth century must have flashed into the old prophet's mind when he wrote that men believe that "they could safely slide down a hill a little way and would surely come to a place, by and by, where they would begin to slide up again. . . but there is no such thing as sliding uphill. The only sliders are backsliders." Thoreau feeds our faith and pulls no punches. If our castles in the air tumble into fragments it is because they should be secured to heaven's roof, and he tells us so in blunt language.

Thoreau saw nothing but sublimity in nature, and the cities and shopping malls and landfills and golf courses stretching unbrokenly across the land would have suffocated him as it began to suffocate Rachel Carson many years later. Nails that wouldn't drive into wood would cause him to have contempt for the man who made them, but if the song of the thrush no longer rang out in the forest this would reflect a folly of such magnitude on the part of twentieth-century man that Thoreau would certainly have stalked off into the woods denouncing as a lie the myth of the golden age. The voice of Thoreau today would be called the voice of the escapist, the eccentric who wants to block progress, and I can't delude myself that very many of my neighbors will pay any attention to my own protests that more emphasis is being placed on "shelf life" than on quality. The key word in the whole discussion is that stubborn but mystical thing called pride. A nation without pride is a nation foredoomed, and I'm beginning to wonder how long pride can be sustained in a society incapable of making a nail that can penetrate an oak board.

At high tide the other evening, my neighbor beached his lobster boat, and the next morning when I came over to the mainland, he and a helper were working on the engine. Bits of machinery were lying exposed everywhere, as was my neighbor's exasperation. "Look at that junk," my neighbor said, gesturing to the pieces of the engine. "That stuff was made to last three months, and not a day more." My neighbor is a resourceful man and given the time he can fix anything, but a lobsterman whose boat is on the beach is a lobsterman who is not making any money, and this doesn't sit well. I suggested he might need a new engine and he snorted in disgust. "A new engine wouldn't be any better than this one," he said, "and most likely not as good."

My neighbor has been told that he inhabits the greatest nation on earth, one whose technology regards no problem as insoluble, yet he sits idly there beside the internal organs of his boat, which fall apart after three months' wear. He is angry and frustrated, and I don't blame him. Thoreau may have been an eccentric, and I undoubtedly am, but my neighbor isn't. If the lobsterman and the storekeeper think we are backsliding — that the seeds of degeneration are in the wind — it's time to start listening.

Tilt

My rural mail carrier is greatly displeased with the tilt that my mailbox acquired over the winter, and I am equally displeased with the slow delivery of mail. We are at a Mexican standoff in our separate resentments, although I don't hold my particular mailman responsible for the fact that it takes a first-class letter four days to reach Boston, which, any way you look at it, is only a three-hour drive away. The fact that the United States mail service has become something of a joke is not my mailman's fault but is the result of new ideas of mail collection and distribution in the mail service's Washington headquarters, ideas that in my time have caused overnight delivery of mail to go from the thirty-five-cent Special Delivery to the $9.20 Express Mail.

Although I have exculpated my mailman completely, he still holds me personally responsible for that slant in my mailbox and is grieved that I don't give him a clean right angle to the ground. The printed note which he left in the mailbox a few days ago struck me as a rather feverish reaction to a minor delinquency. My own complaint is of a graver, more encompassing nature, and in our exchange of notes I sought to place my charges on a higher and more dignified level of debate. The carrier's note called my attention to the fact that it was my obligation to maintain the box at a proper height and stability and warned that my failure to do so could result in delays or abandonment of my mail delivery. His use of the word *delays* provided me with the opening for which I had been searching, and I lost no time in pointing out that I had been experiencing delays for the past five years, a period during which my mailbox was standing straight and tall and beyond all reasonable criticism. In expressing my dismay at the slothful habits that the mail service had fallen into, I made it clear that I disassociated him from this retrogression and, indeed, went out of my way to assure him that he had performed at the highest level of the snow-and-rain-and-gloom-of-night tradition.

The responsibility of the government is to make life easier and more secure for its citizens, but frequently it makes life harder. A college graduate with a reasonably nimble mind finds federal tax laws so complicated that he or she has to go to a tax lawyer or an accountant for protection against the baffling requirements of the tax form — something every individual should be able to fill out without perspiring unduly. Moreover, the government threatens its citizens in a way that brings to mind more the manners of a bill collector than a benign wardenship. The post office, for example, says it will refuse to handle letters or post cards unless they are of a size and shape to suit them, and to hell with what people want to mail. I'm content to go along with the standard-sized envelope, but I would like to think that if overtaken in a fey mood on a spring day I could drop something irregular into the mailbox addressed to an understanding friend. What I am trying to say is that we seem to be moving distressingly away from the concept of government with the consent of the governed, and into the sinister area of government by bureaucratic direction. I'm getting uneasy.

My family tells me I'm old-fashioned and set in my ways, and that I should forget about that thirty-five cent Special Delivery and become happy and content with the $9.20 Express Mail folks. It isn't that I'm not trying to keep up to date, it's just that I'm concerned with the hypocrisy of it all. It seems like only yesterday that President Ford was urging me to wear a Whip Inflation Now button on my jacket lapel, yet I can't see anything more inflationary than an increase from thirty-five cents to $9.20 in a class of mail service.

The tilt to my mailbox is undeniable — the government has me there — but in my opinion it is rather rakish and gives the place some panache and style. The other boxes in the cluster are all sturdy and upright, thoroughly regimented and in line, but I am somewhat suspicious of uniform practices. A man who follows his neighbors' footsteps too closely loses a certain pace to his stride which he may never regain. I see myself in this situation as the abrasive grain of sand that produces the pearl, the anti-aesthetic that bestows grace upon the conforming.

A silence has prevailed at both ends of this dialogue for a week now, with no further extension of remarks by either the carrier or me. Perhaps he feels, as I do, that both sides have been given an airing and the matter should be laid to rest. The authority of the government has been reasserted, and the indignation of a citizen has been vented.

Frankly, I don't think the mail service is going to get any better, but one day soon I'm going to take a post-hole digger out to the highway and straighten up that mailbox. Not *entirely* straight, because I have some pride, but enough to let the government know I'm willing to meet it halfway.

This Isn't Massachusetts

I'm writing this in great haste, as though I am late in getting to the airport to catch a plane, because I have an obsessive desire to get down on paper a fear that has been building up in my subconscious mind for some time and has just now — not thirty minutes ago — broken through to the conscious level. I am afraid that Maine drivers are becoming like Massachusetts drivers, who consider the observance of any motor-vehicle law as an indication of cowardice and moral weakness. The fear itself is enough to drain the color from a sane man's face.

Boston is the only city I know of where a pedestrian crossing a one-way street has to look in both directions. A Massachusetts driver will do anything, or at least attempt anything. He doesn't park his car; he abandons it. If there is a parking place, fine; if not he will leave the car anywhere and face the consequences upon return. But the greatest danger of the Massachusetts driver, of course, is in the total disregard of all rules of safety while in motion. It isn't an accident and coincidence that Massachusetts has the highest collision rate in the nation as well as the highest insurance premium rates. It may be unkind to mention that one deserves the other, but since kindness is a word not understood by the Massachusetts driver I do not feel pressed by the need for compassion.

Late this past winter I drove from Key West to Boston. During the long journey through Florida, Georgia, North and South Carolina, Virginia, Maryland, Pennsylvania, New York, and Connecticut the trip was uneventful. But suddenly I felt the world had gone mad: cars were crossing median strips, the scream of brakes shattered the silence, horns were blowing belligerently, drivers were moving in and out of traffic in a suicidal pattern, left turns were made from right lanes, every traffic law ever made was being violated. I had crossed into Massachusetts, where, in the minds of Massachusetts drivers, laws are suggestive only. Charles Morton, the late Boston humor writer, once observed that the Boston driver started blowing his horn before he turned on his ignition, and while this may be fanciful, I know that once the driver has pulled away from the curb his ambition is to see that no other driver is permitted to do so.

The cause of my immediate disturbance is the coincidence this morning of three cars in succession pulling out of side streets onto the main highway without pausing, as though the drivers were quite certain that side-street-traffic had the right-of-way. In all three cases I was forced to brake quickly to avoid a collision, and I expected to see Massachusetts license plates on the cars, but to my surprise all were Maine cars. My mind began to race in all directions, as though a fence had collapsed. I remembered the two cars racing on the Maine Turnpike last week and I recall that they were both Maine cars. Then there was the car stuck in loose dirt as it attempted to cross the median strip near Brunswick; its wheels were spinning wildly as the driver sought to extricate himself before a police car arrived. It was a Maine car. And there was the car, with Maine license plates, that swerved in front of me in order to achieve a belated exit from Route 1, narrowly avoiding a grander exit on a more cosmic scale with me as an unwilling companion. Drivers should never forget that they, as well as the car, can be recalled by their Maker.

A thought that now sticks in my mind is the matter of contagion; Massachusetts is too close to Maine. A Maine driver seeing a Massachusetts driver break highway laws with total disdain cannot help but wonder if he, too, can't get away with this sort of thing. The outlaw is almost always envied; his free-and-easy way of life exerts a strong romantic appeal for those whose lives lack hardihood and robustness. It is not inconceivable that the Massachusetts malignancy could metastasize into Maine; the invasion of cars from out of state grows into an impressive volume in the summer, and Massachusetts is separated from Maine at one point by a scant ten miles of New Hampshire. It is a perilously frail buffer zone.

In Boston I was once startled to see a truck of the New England Telephone Company proceeding complacently on a one-way street, headed in the wrong direction. Private cars, I thought, could get by with this indiscretion, but a plainly marked corporate vehicle wouldn't dare attempt it. But I was wrong; the driver of the truck saw other vehicles breaking laws and he probably felt it was more of an accomplishment than a wrongdoing. This is an interesting bit of reasoning and clearly a dangerous one.

For what it's worth, Massachusetts highway and insurance executives all agree that the recklessness of the Massachusetts driver is traceable to the fact that highway laws have never been enforced in this state. In four generations of drivers, the individual has been left unencumbered by any sense of responsibility to anyone other than himself. This has produced a breed of aggressive, inconsiderate, reckless drivers that feel thwarted and frustrated by the sight of a traffic light or a No Parking sign. This obsession with self strikes me as an unhealthy thing. I hope it doesn't come to Maine, but I'm worried.

Stay Tuned

About this time of year I become suddenly aware of the letters from readers complaining of my excessive affection for the State of Maine, and wondering if anyone so prejudiced can be trusted to draw an accurate portrait of the state and its way of life. I am seen, I think, as a chap living high on the *cochon* in some coastal hideaway and coming home each night with a whiff of the tavern on his breath; certainly not the type who can be relied on to send out monthly bulletins in which readers can put any trust. The essays appearing in this space reflect only my own feelings about this tiny corner of the world, and not one was written without a little residual anxiety that in displaying affection there was always the likelihood of the killing side effects that often accompany sponsorship. The chief symptom of this, of course, is the loss of content resulting from any missionary enterprise.

You can be sure that an introduction like this leads to something, and in this case it paves the way for some critical comment on Maine and its folkways. Maine isn't California, where the season is usually spring and where man's imagination tends to soar in an intemperate sort of way, but it seems willing, if not eager, to adopt some of the latter's least attractive customs, and I am referring here specifically to what has come to be known as the "yard sale," the "garage sale," or the "porch sale." They are all the same, and it is now impossible to drive five miles on a country road without encountering one. Several years ago I thought the "yard sale" mania had about run its course in Maine, only to discover last summer that it had drawn fresh breath and was off again. Most of the items offered for sale on these occasions are broken, sprung, or thoroughly useless articles that in saner periods were destined for the township dump or used as fill in gullies washed out in the lower fields. Now they are labeled "collectibles" and placed out for sale on boards supported by sawhorses. A cardboard carton is flattened out and YARD SALE is scrawled on it with a magic marker, and this is nailed to a tree or a post bordering a highway. Usually, but not always, a housewife presides over this collection of trash, and as nearly as possible she attempts to give the impression that parting with the articles will bring pain, but the children must be educated. I stopped at a yard sale on Route 1 last year, at the request of a guest from New York, and among the clutter was an old post card showing the beach at Asbury Park, New Jersey. The post card had been mailed on July 10, 1922, and carried the message: "Dear Sibyl: We will be here until Aug. 10th. Love from us all. Mary T." Why this post card could be of interest to anyone other than Sibyl puzzled me, but the proprietress, seeing me examine the card, offered to part with it for fifty cents. Her manner indicated it would be like parting with her golden retriever.

So much for yard sales. Now I would like to make a few remarks on the subject of Maine frugality, and if cynicism tinges these remarks I can't be blamed. The men and women of Maine are personally thrifty, perhaps tightfisted, but a surprisingly broad streak of profligacy seems to be woven into the political fabric of the state. No fight is being picked here for the sake of creating controversy, but the Maine taxpayer who gets his full money's worth is one who examines public construction from a critical point of view rather than suffocating on old beliefs. Every day that I drive to town from my mainland landing I now have to cross a temporary bridge, while beside it a handsome million-dollar span is being constructed over tiny Gurnet inlet. A nimble jumper could almost leap across the water at the point where this new bridge is being built, but for reasons that seem to confound most of the residents in the area, the state highway people have yielded to a fascination for overkill and are constructing a monument on the site. A bridge, in my not-so-humble opinion, should provide safe and convenient conveyance from one point to another, and nothing more. The old bridge, which has now been demolished, did just that in a disheveled sort of way. But the point is that it performed its function, and it kept a million dollars of the taxpayers' money in the bank — where it belonged, I am tempted to add.

The newly renovated Portland airport is a magnificent facility, but I also think it is about three times too large for the area that it serves. The two airlines using the terminal have their check-in counters at one end of the huge building, leaving the rest vacant and gloomy. Signs on the first floor wistfully advertise space for lease. In that wondrous moment of discovery, after the renovations were completed, I felt a warm glow of pride as I walked through the new building, but now, like one sobering up from an excess, I am inclined to grumble over the long walk from arrival gate to the baggage carousel. Someone either lost his head completely in expanding the airport terminal or else knows something about the future of air traffic that has been concealed from the rest of the industry.

The only other thing I have to complain about now is the weather.

I have said some extremely uncomplimentary things about Maine weather in the past few weeks and I have the feeling that I'll think of some more later. Stay tuned.

Burglary

Autumn is a golden season in Maine, especially for a certain number of Maine teen-agers whose favorite recreation is breaking into and looting summer cottages. Most summer houses are shuttered and padlocked now, with the owners back in cities showing their color slides and wondering why they brought the starfish home with them, but Maine youths are busy checking on the better-looking places and organizing themselves for the wave of burglaries that is about to begin. Not all of the vandalism and crime is committed by teen-agers, but most certainly the bulk of it is, with professionals hovering in the background to buy, at absurd prices, the more valuable appliances and other articles that the youths steal. It is a dreary and shameful ritual, and one that badly taints the reputation of the State of Maine.

Although I have lost several outboard motors, gasoline tanks, and even a rowboat to thieves, it was only two winters ago that my house was robbed. I paid a visit to the place one New Year's Day, and my heart sank when I approached the house and saw the front door open. Snow covered a large part of the living room floor, but it could not conceal the huge mound of my possessions that had been heaped into a pile in the center of the room and then abandoned as being either of questionable value or too difficult to fence. Mattresses had been ripped from beds, books pulled from shelves, and human feces decorated the rug. But all major appliances had been taken: a record player, radio, rifle, cameras, binoculars, clocks, and a number of expensive *objets d'art* I had brought back from Europe and the Far East. "Most definitely the work of kids," said the deputy sheriff, who a short time later toured the looted house with me. "The fact that they committed a nuisance on the rug is the signature of the teen-ager. They think that's very smart. Also your liquor was untouched. Very young kids don't know what to do with liquor, but professional thieves will take it." The officer was sympathetic but could not tarry long; another summer house nearby had been looted and he had to check on that one also. "If we locate a cache of stolen stuff," he said, "we'll contact you and see if you can identify anything of yours. But that's our only hope, and that doesn't happen too often."

In many Maine high schools, especially in coastal towns where summer houses are more likely to be concentrated, word is passed around as to the identity of local fences, the older professionals who take possession of stolen goods and pay cash to the nervous teen-agers. Occasionally a youth is caught at the scene of a looting, but because of his age is treated tenderly and more often than not continues to break into vacant houses, secure in the firsthand knowledge he possesses that nothing serious is going to happen to him.

The National Sheriffs Association, working through the sheriffs of Maine counties, has launched the Neighborhood Watch program, which is designed to call the attention of homeowners to precautions they can take to lessen the likelihood of their houses being looted when vacant. Whether this self-help program will do much to diminish Maine's teen-age breaking-and-entering problem is questionable, but it can be applauded as a step in the right direction, if only a weak and faltering one. The Cumberland County Sheriff's Department has mailed out to homeowners pamphlets listing the sheriff's emergency toll-free number and twenty-one things that can be done to help prevent burglaries. Also listed are the names of the four area patrol deputies, and presumably a mailing similar to this has been undertaken by the sheriff's departments of other Maine counties.

It is the opinion of this writer, though, that a far greater deterrent would be teach teen-agers the majesty of the law, something they now appear to respect very little. It would seem that a youth worldly enough to plan a robbery and successfully fence stolen goods is a youth who is capable of assuming responsibility for his actions, and the harsh application of the law in a few cases would undoubtedly set off a chain of uneasiness in Maine's teen-age communities. The alternative to this is not pleasant to contemplate but is most certain to happen. As robberies continue to increase, homeowners are going to become more stubbornly protective of their property, and sooner or later an intruder is going to be shot in the darkness by an aroused owner. Parents who now go into court and lie to protect their children would do well to study this possibility. The Maine Criminal Code specifies that a homeowner "is justified in using deadly force upon another" when he reasonably believes it is necessary to prevent or terminate the commission of a criminal trespass under a variety of circumstances. This could easily become the ugly conclusion to a situation that neither Maine teenagers nor their parents — nor even the judiciary — seems eager to face.

Frustration

There is not now and there never has been a fireplace screen with a pull arrangement that didn't jam, and jam badly. I've seen new ones and I've seen old ones and I've never seen one that functioned properly. The vacuum cleaner that will pick up a thread from a carpet has yet to be made. Is there any reliable and foolproof way or has any paper ever been written on the subject of how to get into a fresh package of bacon and get a few slices for cooking? Why does any repair to a camera, however slight, cost almost as much as a new camera? It's been twenty years now since the milk carton replaced the milk bottle, yet in all that time the makers of the carton have failed to develop a product that can be readily opened once it's sealed. I do not know why the pages of the *New York Times Magazine* stick together, and I cannot believe that legal language is more precise than clear English grammar. It is a language that lawyers use in speaking to other lawyers, and it was meant to exclude the general public for perfectly obvious reasons. There was a time — I recall it clearly — when automobiles were called Ford or Chevrolet or Buick, but they aren't anymore. Now they are Sabre or Cutlass or Fury or Holocaust or Something Truly Menacing, and you have to get the hood up and look at the engine mount to find out the real name of what hit you. It is impossible to cut a tomato skin with the edge of a fork, so forget it and leave the salad alone. Weather reports are no more reliable than they were fifty years ago, which seems to say that the science of meteorology isn't going anywhere. However long you think it'll take a first-class letter to get from one point to another, you are in error; double it, and you've hit it right on the head.

    This catalog of frustrations is printed here not as a comment on the world and times in which we live, but as an introduction to what I have come to regard as the ultimate frustration. This is a dilemma which I share with the State of Maine, a dilemma possessing some of the engagingly innocent character of a Kafka plot written in the style of "Dynasty." I say I share this problem with the State of Maine, but that isn't strictly true; Maine, so far as I can tell, has washed its hands of the matter and implies the problem is mine alone. For an insoluble problem it is extraordinarily simple. Engaged as I am in the flimsy business of writing, I find it necessary to travel a great deal, and my trips sometimes involve an absence from Maine of a month or even more. This sounds routine enough, but wait; on two occasions I was gone so long that when I returned, my car's inspection sticker had lapsed. Both times I tried to sneak back into the state and get my car inspected at the first available station, and both times I was nailed. Since neither Massachusetts, New Hampshire, nor Vermont could give me a Maine inspection sticker before entering the state, my options were bleak: sneak in under cover of darkness and hope for the best, or sell the car.

The first time I was arrested, I had confidence in the rightness of my position and I pulled over to the shoulder nonchalantly and undisturbed. The arresting officer walked slowly up to me, exuding rectitude in all directions. But even as I explained the situation, he took out his pad and began writing me up. "Your inspection sticker has expired," he said flatly. "I don't care what your reasons are." I stepped up the tempo of my protest, but I was whistling in the wind. Once the pad went back into his hip pocket, I knew I was finished.

On my second arrest, I tried a new tack. I had been in Europe for six weeks, and I whipped out my passport to show the officer that there were official stamps certifying that I had indeed been there during the period claimed. The passport was less distracting than entertaining. Holding out the photograph at arm's length, he gazed first at me and then the photograph. There was some similarity, but one couldn't be sure. Was this a forged passport? Was I wanted by Interpol in every capital in Europe? Suspicion was written on his face, and he unhesitatingly did what all police officers do when suspicion takes over. He reached for his pad.

I would like to say that both officers were narrow-minded men with complete faith in the rightness of their own arrogance, yet I know this is not strictly true; their responsibility was not to make judgements. It was perfectly true, they conceded, that neighboring states could not grant a Maine inspection sticker, but it was equally true that once I crossed into Maine, regardless of how quickly I was making my way to an inspection station, I was subject to arrest. There was no way out; the law was precise. I asked one officer if I should have my car *towed* from the state line to an inspection station. I asked the other officer if the only solution was to give up a career as a writer and go into a business that did not require me to travel. Both shrugged off the questions as manifestations of petty irritation on my part.

Frustration is an edgy and exhausting state, and since I was brought up to believe that a legal solution exists for every civil entanglement, I am finding it difficult to adjust to the reality presently facing me. Slowly my faith is being squeezed out of me, like dentifrice from the mouth of the tube, and I am now craftily trying to plot my way out of this, like an imaginative opportunist who turns at last into an outlaw. It's Maine against me now, and may the best man win. I'm going underground, but there are those who know how to reach me.

Lament

I am occasionally visited by friends from New York who wish to see for themselves if I have disappeared into rural circumstances with all of the contentment which I claim. Since I lived in New York for nearly twenty years, my defection puzzles my friends because they honestly believe there is something odd about a man removing himself from his natural environment. (New Yorkers persist in thinking of Manhattan as a "normal environment"; it's one of their more piquant characteristics.) A few days ago a trio of New Yorkers were seated on my sundeck making what I suspected was a field investigation into my mental health, when they fell to chiding me about the unrelieved lyricism with which I wrote about the State of Maine. "No place," asserted one man, a magazine editor who had lived in Manhattan all of his adult life, "can be what you describe Maine as being. You have no credibility."

After they departed — New Yorkers can't stand fresh air for too long a period — I began to wonder if perhaps my friend was not right, that I had invested Maine with such a plenitude of virtue that it seemed I had won mankind's eternal quest for the unattainable. The State of Maine is far from perfect, I realize, and I should catalogue its shortcomings as I praise the prizes it bestows.

In the first place, there is that matter of constant low tide. Don't try to tell me there are as many high tides in Maine as there are low tides, because I know better. If high tides occur, they sneak in late at night when I'm in bed asleep, and by morning the rocks and mud flats are exposed again. When I'm bringing something heavy to the island, something like propane tanks, for example, it's not only low tide but *dead* low, and I have to drag them over slippery rockweed and across yards of mud before I can beach them on solid ground. And when guests arrive it is inevitably low tide (tides are influenced not by the moon but by the arrival of planes at the Portland Jetport) and they have to climb up the ramp of the wharf that possesses an incline as steep as a ladder. Often I catch them glancing apprehensively over their shoulder toward the mainland, wondering if there is yet time to correct what appears to be an unfortunate mistake.

I've been told that the most merciless mosquitoes in the world can be found in Alaska during the summer months, but I consider this report to be pure nonsense. During the hour before twilight on a quiet evening in Maine, mosquitoes emerge from the marshes and forests that would strike terror in the heart of an Alaskan. Working in my study a few evenings ago, trying to complete some correspondence before dark, I saw fluttering against the screen some mosquitoes of a size that caused me to disregard the folded-up newspaper beside me and, instead, to eye the rifle hanging on the wall.

I would like to say a few words at this time about red squirrels, appealing-looking little animals that can penetrate a Sherman tank if they have reason to believe the tank contains something flavored with chocolate. When the ice broke up this past spring, I rowed over to my island to see what damage had been done by the great February storm. There was considerable damage, including the total demolition of my wharf, but it all seemed trivial compared to the state of the kitchen, where, apparently, a family of red squirrels had operated a lively commune during the winter months. My immediate reaction was to just seal off the room and build a new kitchen; this would have been the easy way out.

Anyone seeking to earn my gratitude can easily do so by explaining why it often rains along the coast *only* in boats. I have seen brief showers sweep across the cove, giving off a momentary patter on the roof, and later found my skiff half-full of water. The water cistern received not a drop, the flowers remained parched, the leaves on the oak trees were dry — only the boat was sitting low in the water, the bailing can afloat.

The caprice of Maine's weather is too familiar to evoke much comment one way or another; studying it is futile and time-wasting. Every morning I listen to the weather report as broadcast from the Bath radio station, and the news is almost always bad. Passing the home of the news director of the station the other day, I stopped and pinned a note to his door. It said, "If you don't offer better weather, I'm going to switch stations." I signed it "A Listener" and felt the matter then was in his hands.

I have only one other small complaint, and it is of such a minor nature that I hesitate to bring it up and do so only to gain back a small amount of the credibility I am told I have lost. It has to do with extremely poor quality of the profanity I have encountered in Maine. There is no body to it, no richness; it lacks timing, cadence, and imagination — the basic ingredients of good profanity. I am told that in southern Maine, where some Massachusetts people have begun to settle in, there has been noticeable progress in this regard. They have a lot to swear about in Massachusetts, and I have great hopes that this improvement will spread north promptly.

5

Memories

First Trap

Every man's mind is an attic of sorts, and we all have a pretty good idea of the chances of involvement we take when we close our eyes and start rummaging around up there. We stumble over the best stuff first, possibly because it's stacked near the door where we can easily get at it when times are bad. I remember well the first time I drove the family Overland alone; I was trembling like an aspen leaf when my father stepped casually out of the car after starting the motor and said, "Take her around the block, son, but go light on the accelerator." (Cars were always "her" in those days and sometimes "accelerator" was called "exhilarator.") And somewhere in that dusty file of memories, easily retrievable — as the computer people are fond of saying these days — is a period piece that today's young people could not possibly understand: the day that I received my first Western Union telegram. A man from the railroad depot brought it to our house on his lunch hour, and I recall him telling my sister, who answered the door, "Telegram for Caskie Stinnett. He must sign for it *personally*." I put down the book I was reading and swaggered to the door; one didn't walk to accept something as important as a telegram. And there was the first time I kissed Alma Ferguson; it was in a swing on her front porch about dusk one Wednesday evening. I know it was Wednesday because her parents were at Baptist prayer meeting and, to my everlasting shame, I had that fact in mind when I sauntered up and inquired if I could help her with her Cicero translation.

Things now move with lamentable speed, and I often wonder what memories, if any, young people, here in Maine — and elsewhere — are storing up to soothe them in later years and at quieter times. A young chap I know, he must be about twelve, just got a handsome

Memories

new motorcycle, but he didn't seem as excited as I thought he should be when he showed it to me the other morning as I was walking back from my mailbox. But I witnessed something this morning that set everything right again. I know the achievement of a dream is still a bright and warming thing.

What happened, stated starkly, is that my neighbor's son put out his first lobster traps this morning. I watched from my sundeck, where I had been having an early breakfast, and although I possessed a tinge of guilt for witnessing a tableau that was as passionately private as an act of this kind could be, I couldn't take my eyes from the momentous thing that was occurring in the boat a few yards from the edge of my island. I knew that the boy had gotten his lobster license, and I had seen a half-dozen crudely painted buoys — a vivid orange and white, with considerable orange paint dripping down over the white — drying in the sun on the dock when I got in my boat on the mainland yesterday with an armful of groceries. But these, and other feverish preparations, had slipped my mind until the motorboat came to a halt this morning in the lee of the island, and the first trap went over the side. I watched in awe; as the world grows more complicated, an episode of great emotion and total simplicity, such as this, takes on increased fascination.

The boy was accompanied by his friend, an out-of-state visitor, and I was uncertain whether the latter was his new partner in the lobster business or whether he had just come along, pleased, as children often are without knowing what they are pleased about. But my neighbor's son was master of the boat, no doubt about that, and while I couldn't hear what he was saying, I gather that he was either giving orders or demonstrating how it was done because there seemed to be considerably more conversation than action in those first few crowded moments. There was a slight problem with the first trap; it wasn't weighted heavily enough and it stubbornly refused to sink. The boy pushed it under water with his hand several times but it popped disappointingly back on the surface, and the two of them hauled it aboard again, where they loaded it with some more rocks, which they had brought along in anticipation of just such a problem. The boy waved his friend aside and pushed the trap over the side again, and I was greatly relieved to see it sink. After the trap settled on the bottom, the boy picked up the buoy and the slack rope and tossed them into the water. The gesture possessed everything the heart could yearn for: dignity, a casual disregard for trivial details, finality, and recognition of a job well done. At that moment, the boy became a lobsterman.

There was some discussion as to where the next trap was going, the motor was started up, and the boat moved out of sight around the end of the island. I took my seat at the table and poured a fresh cup of coffee. The morning was filled with pleasant sounds, the sun was warm, the sky was blue, and I felt strangely excited. What I had just seen may not stick in my mind beside the recollection of that first spin around the block in my Overland, but I know that episode is destined to live forever in the memory of my neighbor's son.

Bahnhofangst

A very thin line, in my opinion, separates anticipation from dread, exultation from despair, pain from pleasure, and, for all I know, heaven from hell. I say this in the midst of preparations to depart this island temporarily for another one, far to the south, where the midwinter temperature is a bit more to my liking, where I will have breakfast out-of-doors, where after lunch I will take a slothlike snooze in a hammock strung up between two coconut palms, and where, when boredom sets in, I'll put on a mask and swim around the coral reef that lies only a hundred feet or so offshore. This would seem an enviable prospect to most people in Maine, whose driveways are filled with drifted snow, and in the abstract it is to me too, yet there is a strange reluctance to go. I first dismissed the uneasiness as some kind of guilt over a cowardly withdrawal in the face of adversity, but this theory doesn't hold up well under scrutiny. I'm a writer, and I can work as well one place as another (this isn't strictly true, but it serves my purpose to state the principle here), so I can't be accused of abandoning my responsibilities when the weather turns unpleasant. The Germans would say I have a moderately severe seizure of *Bahnhofangst*, that vague anxiety which besets travelers on the way to the train station, and I suspect this is probably true. In the hours before departure, familiar household possessions have suddenly taken on fresh value; I am conscious of the affection felt for these odd things whose only real distinction is that they have existed under the same roof with me for the past twenty years or so.

Lying in bed this morning, sleepless, my thoughts clung stubbornly to Maine. Several times I tried to soar off into magnificent daydreams of the tropics, of swims before breakfast in warm, green water, of tennis games in the cool of the afternoon, of a dark rum on the rocks, spiced with lime peel, sipped in a deck chair as the sun drops beneath the rim of the sea. I couldn't swing it. Who would report fallen wires in case there was a bad sleet storm? Who would bring the firewood over to the island after the wood man unloaded it at my mainland wharf? What would happen to my mail after my rural mailbox filled up? I lay still in the dark, listening to the rustle of the leafless branches of the trees outside the window. I was sorry I had ever planned the trip in the first place.

Winter before last, when I took this trip south, it was snowing hard when I left, and snow had begun to drift across the highway on the way to the airport. Then, as now, I felt the whole adventure was a mistake from the beginning. It's strange the way trivial thoughts stick in one's memory. On that occasion my free-floating guilt attached itself to some Saturday night baked bean and brown bread dinner that I had committed myself to, and now would have to miss. *Bahnhofangst* is something that a man who travels a lot doesn't need; it's excess baggage. The heart can't be in two places at one time, and if you are going to get your money's worth from a trip, the heart has to go on ahead, not linger behind.

In retrospect, I think I have always been uneasy about leaving home, of going beyond the reach of familiar things, yet I possess a certain kind of wanderlust and I have certainly traveled far more than most people. It has just occurred to me that last year I was in Africa three times, a circumstance made all the more remarkable by the fact that I really do not much care for Africa and would not be the least disturbed if I knew I was not ever going to set foot on the continent again. Show me a compulsive wanderer who is also a chronic victim of *Bahnhofangst*, and I'll show you an active battlefield. It's like a Puritan with a strong Cavalier drive, an accident on the way to happen.

When I was a small boy in Virginia, my mother wakened me early one morning since she was going to drive to Washington for the day and I was to accompany her. Although I was no more than ten at the time, I recall very clearly my anxiety at the breakfast table and the feeling of doom that, for me, surrounded the whole trip. Nothing happened that day, nothing disastrous anyway, and I guess now that was probably my first attack of *Bahnhofangst*. Uneasy symptoms have followed me on every trip I've taken since then, a path that would ultimately lead me to the conclusion that I am crazy, except for the fact that once the trip actually starts, I enjoy myself hugely. I like to travel; it's just that I don't like to leave home. If you think that's puzzling, I have to agree with you.

I will go to the tropical island despite the *Bahnhofangst*, and if it persists after I get there, I know already what I'm going to do. I'm going to sit in that deck chair and watch the sun go down, and if the first rum over ice with lime peel doesn't do the job, I'll have a second.

You've got to whip these anxieties on their own ground.

Morality

I suppose a man can't expect the world to stand still. What is a shocking excess to one generation is merely quaint to the next one, and the supreme challenge, I suppose, is being able to swing with the fast-shifting landscape of morality and not to lag too far behind that group referred to by the rest of us in an enviously accusing sort of way as "consenting adults." I'm not sure what a consenting adult is, but I have grave doubts that I am one of them. I was told straight out by a young grandson last summer that I was square, and for a fleeting moment I thought he was complimenting me. He was speaking affectionately, but I could see by the way he was shaking his head that he considered me a museum piece that he was glad to have around if only for its quaintness.

Morality standards are revised all the time, but it seems to be always downward. Even as I write, impatient citizens are waiting in the streets to see the newest porno movies, whose very titles I would hesitate to write in an essay struggling for a family readership. Young girls, who a scant fifteen years ago were concerned about the predator-prey ration, are now filling singles' bars, on the prowl, and it's anybody's guess as to who is predator and who is prey. At a cocktail party in New York last winter, I heard a woman say to her husband, "I don't think he's a homosexual at all. I think he's just social climbing." I have tried to dismiss this remark as a bit of surrealistic froth, but as you can see, I have failed. Is my grandson right in regarding me as possessing some faded charm not unlike a handful of long-forgotten sepia prints that have lain undisturbed in an attic for years?

Maine has never been a leader in social or moral upheaval — a distinction for which New York and California have been locked in combat for years — but change sweeps across the land in a way that disregards state boundaries. Some of the new cable networks now being formed, according to an account in my newspaper, will have porno channels which will permit a citizen to sit in his living room and watch a film the mere possession of which a few years ago would have brought twenty years in the slammer. I don't know if this is good or bad, but it sure as hell is different from anything I am used to.

Is there anyone here who remembers the movie *It Happened One Night*? My mother — a woman of unassailable piety who nevertheless had a taste for the risqué — went to see the film and upon returning home called my sisters and me into caucus and announced that none of us were to see the movie, which she described, with ill-concealed satisfaction, as "leaving nothing to the imagination." I was fourteen at the time and, naturally, went to the matinee the next afternoon. It was dark in the theater but not so dark that I couldn't recognize both of my sisters sitting three rows away. The shameful episode came late in the film, when Claudette Colbert and Clark Gable shared a motel room with only a sheet strung up on a wire to divide the space and provide two bedchambers. Leaving the theater, I had to admit to myself that it was a real sizzler. This adventure is being cited here for two reasons: one, to demonstrate how far we have drifted in coming from *It Happened One Night* to *Deep Throat*, and, two, to suggest that I have not always been the square that my grandson suspects.

I will skip lightly over such shockers as *The Sheik*, although I would like to pause long enough to point out that when Rudolph Valentino let his nostrils flare while holding Vilma Banky in his arms, it was a sure thing that the film was going into what was known at the time as a "dissolve" — a fading of the scene into a gray nothingness. Here the imagination — which my mother felt was the logical key to the whole matter of cinematic morality — took over, for better or for worse. My mother's imagination, I have every reason to believe, was as lurid as the next person's, because she would frequently come home from a movie shaking her head and saying she didn't know what the world was coming to, showing such filth in public. Nevertheless, she would often go back the next day to see the film again, just to make sure it was as destructive to public morality as she had first thought.

The World's Fair of 1939, which took place in Flushing Meadow just outside of New York City, took an attitude toward nudity in its amusement area that to my mind was too carefully hedged to bring any credit to the Fair management. The ruling was that one female breast could be revealed, but not both, a straddling of the issue so blatant that it led Mr. E.B. White to comment acidly at the time that the "ladies exposed one breast in deference to the fleet and kept one concealed in deference to Mr. Whalen." Grover Whalen was the Fair's chairman. The theme of the Fair was "The World of Tomorrow," but I think it unlikely that anyone wandering around the honky-tonk area looking for a glimpse of the future ever suspected that within forty years New York, Boston, and San Francisco would be licensing theaters staging not just topless shows but bottomless ones as well.

I try to keep up to date, despite the opinion of my grandson. Confidentially, when I come out of the sauna on the wooded end of my island sometimes late in the afternoon, I take a quick plunge off the rocks *au naturel*. What about it, fellows? Don't I get any credit for that?

6

The Seasons and the Elements

One Man's Island

First Day

There is something as exhilarating about opening a summer house as there is sad about its closing. One pushes open the shutters, and the light fills not only the corners of the room but also the corners of the heart. A breeze rushes through the open window as though it were filling a vacuum; the curtains flow inward, an unframed photograph is blown from the dresser, a door suddenly slams shut. They are the reawakening sounds and motion after a long winter of stillness.

A few days ago I experienced again the ritual of opening a house on a small Maine island, and it left me with a light heart and a fine sense of life's renewal. I pulled the boat well up beyond the high-tide line and, leaving it unloaded, struck out through the spruce forest for the house. It was a gray day, misting lightly, and tiny patches of snow clung stubbornly to the floor of the forest, giving the impression more that winter had withdrawn than that spring had arrived. Water dripped from the trees and the odor of last fall's moldering leaves rose from the wet ground. Everywhere my glance fell I searched for signs of change. The dead pine tree that had been perforated by woodpeckers was still standing sturdily, and I was surprised and pleased; I had no idea it would survive the snow and ice storms of winter. Along the ledge I came upon a yellow and gray lobster buoy that had broken loose from a trap and had washed up on a winter tide and lay imprisoned in the marsh grass. I hurled it as far out into the sea as I could, thinking it might wash up on the mainland and eventually be recovered by its owner. An immense log, turned silver by the sea and the sun, was still lodged between two rocks; last summer I had planned to free it but somehow had never gotten around to it. I had hoped the high autumn tides would be more effective than my good intentions. Two blue jays challenged me raucously from a branch high in a birch tree, the overture in the symphony of spring. There were no leaves yet on the birch tree but there were ripe buds which said the long siege of winter was broken.

The house appeared before me, and I stood for a few moments at the edge of the clearing, almost as though I were approaching a holy place. In this house I had come to think of life as life and not as existence. I knew every board in it; I knew which of the shutters stuck and which windows opened easily, and where the rain from northeasters seeped in around the fireplace chimney and moistened the great stones. When the wind blew, I knew which windows would rattle, and I knew the sounds of the floorboards when one walked on them, and I recognized the peculiar sound that each door possessed when it was opened or closed. Sometimes during the winter when I was far away from Maine, when I was in Switzerland or South America, and I would hear a sound that was similar to one I was accustomed to on the island, it would transport me back and for a fleeting moment I would be there again, listening to the water lapping against the dock in the stillness of the night or hearing a gull squawk as it winged over the house or marveling at the mournful sound of the foghorn when the heavy mists settled in.

It was cold and wet, but spring was part of the promise of that fretful southerly wind, and I threw open the windows and opened all of the doors and let the moist air blow through the house, and I put a match to the kindling in the fireplace and a Mozart record on the record player and I was suddenly at home again. Without my being aware of it, the mustiness had disappeared and the house had been retaken from silence and darkness. Everywhere there were reminders of last fall: a faded swimming suit left to dry on the rim of the bathtub, a book on the coffee table that I had searched for all winter in the city, a letter I had written and stamped and, in the confusion of closing, had abandoned on the table beside the front door.

I walked down the path through the spruce forest to the boat and began to carry the packages to the house. The mist had disappeared and the sky was lightening; the sun would be out later. A chipmunk scampered across the path and disappeared in the leaves. I lowered a bag of groceries and got out a couple of slices of bread and placed them beside the path. It had been a hellish winter; the chipmunks would appreciate a windfall. Back at the house, I moved the cap off the well and gazed down into the darkness. The water was high; higher than I had ever seen it. During August I would be gazing into the well with mounting anxiety, but now I could be profligate with water. I replaced the cap, and walked around to the front of the house and stood on the sundeck. A neighbor from the mainland was taking his lobster boat through the opening of the cove. He saw me and waved.

The next day my friend would arrive to help me move the float out to the end of the dock and connect it to the ramp. This was always the final declaration of the end of winter, more meaningful than the turning of the pages of a calendar. It meant that the island was no longer isolated, that ownership had been transferred back to me from the gulls and the seals and the chipmunks. T.S. Eliot said April is the cruelest month, but I wonder. I wonder.

Fickle Mistress

Does anyone, any adult in his right mind, really believe that there is any such thing as spring in Maine? I'm not talking about that brief fortnight between the last snow and the beginning of summer, that tentative pause when the streams run clear and cold again and the meadows are suddenly bare and animals come sleepily out of burrows, shake themselves, and squint into the sunlight. That's welcome after the rigors of a Maine winter, but it shouldn't be confused with a genuine spring. I suppose only those of us who love Maine can say it, but this state has only three seasons, and winter preserves the flavor of its discontent right up to the doorstep of summer. And sometimes, even then, it backs off slowly and begrudgingly.

I've read many lyrical accounts of Maine springtimes, but I know now they are nothing more than testimonies of faith, mere examples of the fantastically poetic quality with which man invests hopes and dreams. I have been bewitched by the promise of spring in Maine too often; I've succumbed too many times to the exhilaration of those first few warm days, when I've thrown open the windows to let the soft, moist winds from the sea blow through the house. I've tramped through the forests and grown excited at the first sight of the graceful, curling leaf of the lady slipper, and the dark green moss growing in the north shadow of the tree trunk where only a few days before there had been snow. And in the end I was betrayed, just as a lover is betrayed by a fickle mistress. I awake one morning to see icicles again hanging from the porch roof, and the rhododendron leaves folded back into tight little cylinders. My Maine world is clutched again in the icy embrace of winter. I won't be fooled again.

The Italian for spring is *primavera*, which means first green. It is a beautiful and evocative word, and in the part of Italy that I know and love, the promise of spring is a vow that is honorably kept. In Virginia, where I spent my childhood, spring arrived, as it was supposed to, in March, and it lasted for several months, a definite season that became a bit unreliable toward the end as it merged into summer, but that seemed to be the way with spring. Suddenly it was May, the forsythia, the lilac, and the dogwood had disappeared, the days were no longer warm but hot, and summer had arrived. There was a solid rhythm to the seasons. They came and went with astral punctuality.

Maine can be hot in the summer, which seems to surprise some summer visitors. The warmest I have ever been in my life was one Saturday in July, summer before last, when the temperature in Brunswick reached 109 degrees in the shade. I spent most of that searing day in the water, and I ate a picnic lunch in the shade of a large oak tree beside the sea. That night, even on an island where there are always sea breezes, I slept in every room in the house, searching for the coolest spot I could find. It's not that Maine is forever wrapped in a blanket of snow and ice, it's just that hot weather arrives on the heels of winter and that spring is unaccountably overlooked in the rites of passage.

My idea of a fine spring is a succession of warm days that draws one from the house with the promise of a thousand prizes. Overcoats and heavy gloves are thrown aside, porches and sundecks are swept, rotten leaves are cleaned from gutters and downspouts, long walks are taken with an eye for sagging fences and loose shingles or some other damage that has occurred during the winter and stands in need of repair. The sound of saw and hammer is heard, and the smoke of brush fires is in the air. In a warm and sunny spot behind the barn or boathouse, one is tempted to settle down for a short nap or, at the very least, a meditative rest with hat off and sleeves rolled up. And with twilight comes the shrill symphony of the tiny frogs in the swamps and lowlands, a symphony of reawakening and a pledge that the long winter has ended. As the days lengthen, the shadows shorten, and shade comes once again to the forest, replacing the mottled sunlight that filtered through the budding leaves. The first robin settles in, a little lean and ruffled from the long flight up from the south, but too busy to bother with appearances.

When I say there are no springs like that in Maine, I fully realize I will be attacked by my more zealous neighbors for my prejudices, my notions of error, the inaccurate articles of my own faith. I have long ago discovered that the readers of this magazine tolerate no dissent from their view that Maine is noble in every respect. In my defense, I say that I too am a member of the family and I see this as an admission of a minor family frailty, no more serious than acknowledging that an uncle drinks a bit too much or that one of the younger chaps is having a little trouble balancing his checkbook. We really aren't *perfect*. And one day soon I'm going to write an article, a rhapsody really, about Maine autumns. Now there's a season for you!

New Wharf

Tomorrow is Friday, and the men who are going to build me a new wharf to replace the one lost in the great storm will be coming to start work, so I must decide before then where the new wharf will be. This sort of decision can tear a sensitive man apart. The natural impulse, of course, is to build the new wharf on the location of the old one and thus avoid the need of approval from a host of governmental agencies. But in this case other factors enter the picture to seriously cloud the basic issue. My friend Rudy, the lobsterman who is supervising the work and who appears to know everything, says the wharf was always in the wrong location, that it was always exposed to the prevailing wind, and that anybody with the sense that God gave geese would move it to the lee side of the island.

The only trouble with Rudy's counsel is that I've learned from experience that what he doesn't know he makes up and offers for fact, and the coinage of his wisdom occasionally gives off a hollow ring when tapped on the counter. Nevertheless, so great is Rudy's influence around the cove that I hesitate to seek corroboration from his peers since they are certain to echo Rudy's appraisal of the situation, thus invoking Gresham's Law, so to speak. Gresham's Law holds that when a debased coinage is introduced into circulation alongside a true coinage, the latter will disappear from the marketplace, or, in other words, bad money drives out the good. Rudy, who has lived all of his life in the cove, asserts with considerable authority that the wharf was built out of sight from the mainland in the first place because it was constructed during the Prohibition era and the owners of the island didn't want federal agents witnessing the unloading of cases of whiskey there from offshore rumrunners. I must admit that this fanciful explanation so stirs my imagination that I am inclined to accept it as fact, although in my heart I harbor grave reservations about Rudy's concept of history.

There are practical considerations, too, that complicate the question of the wharf's location and prevent it from being a matter easily resolved. The old location gave access to a path that led directly to the front of the house, something that Rudy's prop,sal would not accomplish. I could, I suppose, make a new path, but in my way I'm as stubborn as Rudy, and I don't cotton to new and untried experiments, especially where something as important as a path to the house is concerned. Maine does this to a man; there's something in the air here that endows the status quo with more weight than it possibly deserves. I argue that the good Lord would not have put the path there in the first place if He hadn't wanted it there, and it is only after some reflection that I realize it was not the Lord's work but that of the fellows carrying those cases of whiskey who determined where the path would be. This affords my conscience a little more leeway but it does nothing to blunt the edge of my obstinacy.

If my old pier was swept away because it was located in unprotected water, as Rudy asserts, there is always the risk that a new pier will meet the same fate. This would not only be humiliating to me personally, but I would live with the constant awareness that I was as exposed as the wharf. I would have a hard time meeting the glances of my neighbors if this should happen.

Spring — if it exists at all — is a compressed season of frenetic activity, coming as it does after a long winter of idleness. The men coming to work tomorrow will be restless, anxious to get on with the wharf, regardless of where it is located. There are other more important things than building me a wharf. Their minds are on their own projects: clamming and mossing, repairing their boats, building lobster traps. When they arrive with their tools they will expect me to have made up my mind so they can get to work. I once displayed some doubt to a carpenter as to where I wanted a door located, and his glance grazed me like sandpaper as it passed. I won't risk that again.

For better or worse, I think I shall take Rudy's advice and relocate. I'll build a new path through the forest and — the thought has just begun to effloresce in my mind — I'll cause it to wind in such a way that it will intersect with the old path, thus claiming the best of both situations. It will mean that I will have to carry my own cases of whiskey a little further than formerly, and in full view of my neighbors on the mainland at that, but if this becomes a hardship I can always put the case down on the forest floor and open a bottle. I suspect the rumrunners did that anyway. How else could you explain such poor judgment in deciding where a wharf should go?

Summer

There are times when I am profoundly touched by the absorbingly lustrous quality of Maine, and I always think that then I am witnessing the true Maine. Whether this is true or not is really irrelevant; I believe in it as deeply as Newton believed in gravity. I have just been struck by the majesty of a late summer morning, and echoes of the experience are still ricocheting around an empty corridor in my mind. I had been awakened by some new sound — to those living on an island every sound is classified, coded, and filed away — and I rose and pulled on my trousers and a shirt, and walked, still half asleep, down to the sea. My dog tarried on the sundeck. It was unconscionably early for exploring in her opinion, but she later changed her mind and trotted down to join me. There were twelve ducks engaged in formal maneuvers just a few feet from the rocks. Gulls, herons, and egrets are common in the neighborhood but ducks are rare. I returned to the house and gathered a handful of stale rolls and came back to the rocks. The ducks were squawking strangely, a rhythmic, throaty sort of sound that came across the water like an unearthly chorus. I threw the rolls toward the ducks but recognized instantly that the gift was going to be misunderstood. They regarded the rolls as missiles, and wheeling as one they steamed out of the cove like a flotilla of destroyers. Silence settled in the wake of the ducks, and I sat on the rocks wondering why I had committed such a stupid and unthinking act.

Dawn had swept the darkness from the eastern sky but the sun was not yet in view; a rose-colored glow had settled in the cove and it was difficult to tell where the sky and the sea met. The tide was coming in fast, pushing great clumps of rockweed ahead of it, and the air was wet and heavy with salt. Across the way on a rock ledge that was fast disappearing underwater, a blue heron abandoned his watch and took off, his immense wings beating the air furiously to get him airborne. He headed for some tall pines on the mainland where he has a nest; several times during the summer when I had been poking around the area in a rowboat he had come out defiantly and sounded his own grave alarm. In encounters like this, between man and fowl or those between man and beast, I usually withdraw first on the grounds that I am better able to sustain myself, although this is most likely an egocentric and foolish point of view. Man has not greatly distinguished himself in this regard, while I know of no blue herons or chipmunks or porcupines who receive food stamps. The heron disappeared into the woodland, leaving the cove and the ledges to the gulls and cormorants.

Quite often a fickle little breeze will spring up behind an incoming tide but there was none now. The dog had gone down to the edge of the sea, and was trying to reach a floating stick. Boxers hate to get wet, and she had waded in as far as she felt the prize warranted; now she was reaching for it with her paw, but it remained tantalizingly out of reach. She backed out of the water cautiously and sat down, her eyes fixed on the stick. In a few minutes it had floated up to her feet and she picked it up in her teeth and ran into the forest with it. In many respects, dogs are smarter than men; for one, they understand the waiting game.

The early morning has always belonged to nature, it seems, and to poets. This is a shame because in many respects it is the most exciting part of the day. Twilight, which most people prefer, is an epilogue, a footnote to the day's history; the grand drama has already unfolded. But the hours of early morning are resplendent and filled with adventure; one feels that anything can happen. The light is tricky and changing, and one can never be sure he or she is seeing what is really happening on the stage. The cormorant dives suddenly, cutting the water as keenly as a blade, but when he surfaces there is no indication that the mission was a success. He may have missed or he may have devoured his prey underwater. The gulls put on a somewhat better show; when they smack the water, one can often see small fish wriggling in their mouths. And when they drop mussels on the rocks, it is easy to see their irritation grow when a shell refuses to break. I once saw a gull drop a mussel seventeen times before the shell broke. I couldn't tell whether it was a particularly hungry gull or an uncommonly stubborn one.

There is a total absence of frivolity before the sun rises; everything is to the point and strictly business. Later in the day the cormorants will line up on the rocks with their wet wings outstretched, a comic frieze contrived to permit the sun and air to dry their feathers, but now they are busy filling empty stomachs. Bluefish dart into a school of alewives and the water is churned up as the latter leap from the water. The egret's head bobs into the water so quickly one can hardly detect the motion. A lobster boat heads busily through the opening of the cove, its wake a widening triangle that leaves the buoys dancing wildly. The whole landscape is a panorama of restless motion.

The morning air is raw and wet and it chills, but in the tidelands and marshes this is part of the menace and mystery of the world at that hour. Every surface is covered with a film of moisture, every leaf drips water. Later, when the sun rises, the chill will disappear, the singing birds will move onstage, and the air will be filled with the sounds of man and his work. But in that misty hour before sunrise, nature stages its most impressive performance. I wish the ducks would come back every morning, drawing me to my seat on the rocks to witness it.

Fog

The fog came in a few nights ago — silently, unexpectedly — and wrapped a thick, gray blanket around the island. It was nearly dark when I first noticed it, and I walked down to the dock to see how thick it was. Weather is the most important thing in the world to islanders because every time one emerges from the house there is contact with it. On the mainland one can get in an automobile and drive off, but on an island one must get in a wet boat that will get wetter still before it reaches land. The mist was heavy, and I could tell it was probably one of the persistent early summer fogs that would very likely hang around long after its welcome had worn thin. Maine fogs have a way of doing that.

There is a saying among Maine coastal people that a long fog seizure will be followed by good weather. This I do not believe. I've seen one fog follow another too often to be fooled by such misplaced optimism. I believe fogs operate independently of all other meteorological phenomena, that they are capricious and errant, and that anyone who tries to chart their whimsical arrivals and departures is wasting his time. Science denies this, of course, but science and I have only nodded coolly at each other for some time now. Our final breakup occurred two summers ago when I kept a log of the accuracy of the scientific weather reports on my local radio station. In the two-week period that I monitored, the weather report was correct twice. Once the meteorologist reported it was sunny when, in fact, it was pouring rain and the wind was shifting around to the northeast. I wondered then, and I still do, why the weather forecaster doesn't look out the window.

Meteorologists classify fogs into seven groups, ranging from a thin haze to a dense mist with visibility almost zero. I've been in a boat in a Maine fog when I could barely see the tips of my oars, and it was an eerie sensation and not a reassuring one. Once, on Monhegan Island, I was walking with my little daughter through a forest when a fog blew in suddenly from the North Atlantic and in the brief span of five minutes we went from sunshine to an enveloping shroud of soft gray nothingness. If it hadn't been for the path, which I felt my way along, we would have had real difficulty getting back to the cottage. On my island, fogs arrive more leisurely but also with more determination and purpose. A three-day fog is so common as not to merit comment; anything beyond that gets a thorough discussion at the grocery store. "Seen your boat lately?" one lobsterman will ask another, and the laughter will be as spontaneous as though the question had not been asked a thousand times before.

Fogbows are not as common in Casco Bay as they are in other coastal areas of Maine, although I've seen a few and once I saw a real beauty. The sun in the west had suddenly broken through the fog bank, and in the east a white arc appeared that hung in the sky for five minutes or more. It was magnificent. When it started to fade, it disintegrated fast, and I was left wondering if I had indeed seen it at all.

While I know fogs are a nuisance to lobstermen and others in small boats who must work their way home painstakingly around ledges and shoals, I find them strangely pleasant, especially if there is no need for me to leave the island. I like the distant sound of foghorns, so faint that I have to concentrate to hear them, and the fog itself tends to isolate the island even more than it normally is. There is a snugness to the house when it is enveloped in fog, a cheerful containment. I light the lamps early, I build a fire in the fireplace, and I settle down to read or listen to music, free of guilt that I am not outside painting or sawing wood or replacing boards in the dock, all of which need doing. Fog closes me off not only from the rest of the world but also from the nagging of my own conscience; the house is pervaded by an invitation to rest, to stare into the fire, to doze, to do nothing.

Perhaps the strangest aspect of fogs is the startling way that they transport sound. Voices come with great clarity from boats quite some distance away. One night I arrived on the island in a fog and I heard people talking on the sundeck. I tied up the boat hurriedly and raced to the house with a flashlight. No one was there. I walked over the entire island, but again I found no one. Then, standing on the sundeck I heard the same voices again, this time coming from the sea slightly to the west of the island. I knew then it had been an acoustical trick played on me by the fog. Fogs can be mischievous. But if there were no fogs, I would miss them. I would miss that sharp taste of salt that they bring, the ghostly look they bestow on spruce and fir trees, but most of all I would miss that wonderful air of unreality and otherworldliness that they impart to everything that they touch.

Autumn

A winter reverie is the most dangerous of all; it can open the way to emotional involvements we would as soon let stay buried. Looking across the dismal landscape of a rain-drenched city a few days ago, my mind went back to a day in Maine in late autumn. I had awakened to the drumming of rain on the roof. It had been a dry summer and fall, the soil was parched, and the sound of rain was strange and unreal. There were recognizable shadows in the room, but the grip of darkness had not been fully broken; only the sickly light which followed positive darkness made me realize night had ended. I got out of bed and went into the living room to look at the eastern sky, and saw that it was overcast and threatening. A fitful breeze had sprung up, and was blowing the rain against the windows. I saw by the clock that it was much later than I had imagined; the cloud cover was low and thick, and we were in for bad weather. I got back in bed; there are moments when the prizes of silence, ease, and contentment become the jealous property of one person, and this was such a moment. The rain was more than just a patter now, it had gained strength and was lashing the windows of the bedroom. I drifted back to sleep, borne along by the torrent outside.

My boxer awakened me the second time by jumping on the bed to see why I was not up and doing the chores that a man should be doing at this time of day and at this season of the year. She was not at all anxious to go outside — boxers can't abide rain — but she felt a responsibility to get me on my feet and at least to start a fire going in the fireplace. I pulled on a sweater and trousers, and went into the living room. The rain was still falling heavily, the smaller trees were bending low in the wind, and a heavy sea was running in the normally sheltered water of the cove. A solitary gull was clinging to a rock ledge that had been exposed by the receding tide; she looked miserable. I crumpled up a piece of newspaper in the fireplace, threw some kindling on it, and put a match to the paper. In a moment a cheerful blaze was lightening the dark corners of the room. I opened the front door and asked the boxer if she wanted to go out. She gazed at me from the warmth and comfort of the sofa as though I had lost my mind. I turned on the radio, and the announcer at the Bath station said that the rain would continue heavily throughout the day, possibly clearing in the late afternoon, with the wind shifting to the northwest. I set about to fix breakfast.

A person who dwells in the country knows that there are days when outside work is impossible, and in his or her heart there is a secret yearning for such a sedentary day, for a chance to doze by the fire free of nagging pangs of guilt, for the chance to read something wholly worthless, to sort aimlessly through papers, or to listen to some ancient and forgotten record, the sound of which will bring back memories of a time long past. I surrendered myself into the full embrace of just such a day, and the boxer joined me with an enthusiasm that she hadn't displayed for some time.

One of the extraordinary things about Maine is that while much has changed in recent years, a great deal more has remained obstinately and invincibly the same. It is that constancy, I think, that makes it possible to savor the wonder and contentment of a stormy day; one knows nothing will have been missed, no radical changes will have taken place, the first brilliant strokes of sunlight will come racing across the horizon the next day as they have in the past. Maine storms are often followed by days of softness and great beauty, as though nature were penitent for the upheaval and stress it has created. I have seen too many storms subside into tranquillity and mildness not to be struck by the inevitability of it all.

Not long ago I raced back to Maine from India, halfway around the world, to recover from an illness that had stricken me in Bombay. The long flight back, almost twenty-four hours, was a nightmare, and when I finally got to Boston I got in my car and sped north as though my life depended upon reaching Maine. Once on my island, I made an enormous fire in the fireplace, turned on the hot water heater, and just before going to bed I took two flags out to the sundeck and placed them in their sockets. Whenever I am on the island I fly them as a signal to my neighbors on the mainland that I am in residence, but on this occasion they possessed a different symbolism. They told me that I was home at last; it was a ritual meant to reassure me, not to inform my neighbors. When I sank into my own bed, I was overwhelmed by a feeling of security, of contentment, of a curious state of utterly calm well-being. It was the same blend of qualities that I experience on a stormy day.

The rain did not abate in late afternoon as the Bath announcer had forecast. I went down to the dock before dark to check on the boats, and saw that the clouds were still hanging low, a heavy mist was drifting in from the sea, and the rain was still falling, more gently now but nonetheless steadily. I walked up the path to the house, realizing that I didn't really give a damn how long it rained. The ground needed it, and, in a way, I guess I did, too.

First Snowfall

There's something exciting about the first snowfall of winter. It is seldom more than a flurry, a brief and tentative sort of drum roll to get autumn off the stage and to raise the curtain on winter, but it does something to the spirit of man that is far out of proportion to its importance. In rural Maine, that first snowfall causes one to glance over the shoulder apprehensively at the woodpile, it prods the homeowner to bank the foundations of the house with spruce boughs, it suggests a long list of things that had been postponed during the lazy, golden days of autumn and which now must be done promptly. Those swirling snowflakes are just a warning; they aren't meant to be taken seriously, but the next, or the one after that, may mean business. Time is running out.

Last fall I was living in a cottage in a spruce forest not far from Wiscasset, and I was walking with my dog along the spine of a hill overlooking the Sheepscot River when it began to snow. I refused to believe it at first because it was a warm afternoon in November and the sun had disappeared under an overcast sky only moments before. But the flakes were real enough, and in less than a minute after I first noticed them, they were coming down fast, melting quickly on the warm leaves and rocks. I was wearing only a sweater and I moved in under the protective canopy of a spruce tree to wait it out. It lasted no more than ten minutes, but that brief span of time gave me a gentle foretaste of what was to come. I stood there entranced and learned, for the first time, that snow in a forest is not as soundless as most people think. When there are no other sounds, snow can be heard. It makes the slightest sort of rustling as it touches the spruce needles and settles on the ground. It's a hushed and guarded sound, and I later heard it many times when I came out of the house on snowy nights to check on the weather before going to bed.

Last winter was said to have set a record for severity in Maine, but I look back on it with nostalgia and pleasure. Early in December, I remember, the dog and I were forced by the snow out of the fields and woods, and we had to content ourselves with paths and the roads when we took our daily walks. This isn't the same thing at all; a path is the same today as it is tomorrow, but walking across the fields and through the forest yields something new and often exciting every few minutes. One comes upon a high rock that offers a fine view of the valley, or a dead birch tree that is being energetically prospected by a woodpecker, or a drowsy and sluggish snake enjoying the last warm rays of sunshine before disappearing in a crevice for the winter. The dog's excitement outraced mine, and she endlessly chased birds, rabbits, squirrels, and often nothing at all except what she had dreamed up in her overheated imagination.

Moving from the fields to the roads wasn't to our taste at all, but gradually the slogging became too difficult and we found the plowed-out roads the only places where we could easily move. We set off every morning for an hour's ramble despite the depth of the snow. I think we both enjoyed most the days when the snow was coming down, when our footprints were filled as we made our way back home, and when we encountered no one on those lonely country roads except an occasional farmer making his way cautiously to town or returning home, thinking only of the warmth that awaited him when the trip was over. Only once did the dog complain and hold back, and that was on a clear and bitterly cold day in January. After her first excited romp she turned around in the road and started trotting back to the house. It was obvious that she had found the cold too intense for any serious walk, and that if I intended to go ahead with any nonsense in that regard she wanted no part of it.

One morning I awoke and realized I was snowed in. I got up at five o'clock, pulled on some trousers, a heavy sweater, and boots, and went out to shovel a path from the porch so the dog could have relief. I knew at a glance that no car would get in or out of the driveway that day, so after attending to the dog I went back to bed. I awoke again at nine o'clock and the snow was still coming down heavily. It was a fine day. I cooked an enormous breakfast, turned on the radio to get the weather report from Portland, and spent most of the day reading by the fire. The dog slumbered most of the time, and seemed to share my contentment at doing nothing. At two o'clock the next morning she awoke me by barking furiously, and I turned on the outside lights to see the snowplow pushing its way through the lane, its searchlight stabbing the darkness and the grinding of its motor proclaiming freedom for all. For a crowded moment — like a paroled prisoner standing at the penitentiary door — I wasn't sure I wanted to be free.

But it's that first snow that stirs the imagination, and it is hardly any snow at all. One strikes off for a long walk, hoping the snowfall will last but knowing in the heart that it will stop long before he gets back home. It may be a couple of weeks before the next one, but by then autumn will have lost its grip and anything can happen in Maine in winter. Anything.

Christmas in Maine

Christmas goes with Maine as naturally as drawn butter goes with lobster. One somehow gets the feeling that they were *meant* for each other. Snow falls according to some high-level prearrangement, logs crackle in fireplaces, long-lost uncles show up at the last minute bearing armfuls of presents, and a feeling of good will and fellowship lingers in the air. In too many places throughout the country the National Retail Credit Association is the unseen sponsor behind the event, but not in Maine; there is a spontaneous buoyancy surrounding the whole Christmas pageant that no Hidden Persuader could invent. No, Christmas is real in Maine, a great emotional release coming as it does at the end of a long and troubled (aren't they all these days?) year.

The first Christmas I ever spent in Maine was many years ago when I was a visitor, not a resident. I had come from New York City, (where Christmas is about as artificial as it can get, with the big stores broadcasting warnings to shoplifters along with the Christmas carols), and I expected the season to be somewhat similar though hopefully on a less shrill scale in the small coastal village where I was to visit. Before leaving New York I had dutifully and wisely tipped the three doormen of my apartment building, the superintendent, the three handymen in the boiler room, the boy who delivered my groceries, the three attendants at the garage where my car was stored, the man who delivered the newspapers (and whom I had never laid eyes on), the man in the package room, and — don't question this — the two mailmen who made deliveries at my building. All of them distrusted my memory and had, overtly or subtly, reminded me of their expectations. Buying protection in New York takes many forms; Christmas tipping is perhaps the most common. It was in this frame of mind that I arrived in Maine.

It took a day or two of decompression before I could get into the spirit of the thing, and then I gleefully joined into the celebration of the finest Christmas I have ever known. There were parties despite the snow, which I seem to recall fell steadily throughout Christmas week, there was endless wassail, there was an almost reckless exchange of presents, and there was a Christmas drama in one of the local churches. I remember that drama vividly because my small daughter, then about four years old, had hastily been cast as an angel with one line of dialogue. Never before as a parent had I experienced such apprehension; there was my child on the stage before the entire world (well, two hundred people anyway) acting independent of her father. I sat there in the chill church, my stomach knotted and my palms sweating, waiting for that one line to be spoken, and when it came properly on cue, enunciated coolly and with poise, I sank back in the pew almost limp with relief and pride. What a Christmas!

Once before this, I wrote glowingly of that first Maine Christmas and I received a curt letter from a reader in Los Angeles who admonished me for linking Christmas and snow in such a romantic fashion. "There was no snow on that first Christmas," the reader reminded me sternly. "It was a day something like this, with the temperature probably in the fifties and a slight bit of overcast. I don't know why you Easterners persist in thinking Christmas without snow is no Christmas at all." The reader was right, of course, as readers so often are, but I have stubbornly resisted the truth in the pursuit of something more to my liking. In my opinion, Christmas without snow is no Christmas at all.

One chilly day last fall as I was contemplating the chore of closing my island cottage and considering whether this would be the year that I would fulfill a long-made promise to myself by spending Christmas Day on the island, my reverie was interrupted by a radio news item telling of Peking's latest nuclear tests. This is a gloomy note to put in an essay on Christmas, the birthday of the man called the Prince of Peace, but I promise you some cheer too. The day that bad news from China spoiled my anticipations of the holiday season, a squirrel was energetically scratching in the leaves for acorns and scurrying up a tree with them. The cold weather had made him nervous — not all summer or fall had he rushed around like this — and he wasn't heartened any by the knowledge that his world (my island), like ours, is small. Right then, he wasn't nearly as worried over radioactive fallout as he was over the prospect of snow, about as damaging a fallout as a squirrel can imagine. Well, the nuclear fallout never did arrive, and when I finally closed my house in late fall, snow had not yet blanketed the island and hidden the acorns. These are small prizes perhaps, but we were grateful, the squirrel and I. And now, even though winter's first snows are a fact of squirrel life in Casco Bay and mankind's future remains uncertain, the squirrel and I are grateful still for our tenuous but rewarding hold on life. Merry Christmas, *everybody!* Peace on earth, good will toward men.

Wind

I've got nothing good to say about wind, nothing at all. Most writers, I've noticed, deal lyrically with rain, fog, snow, even sleet, their hearts and typewriters beating out a sort of *allegretto grazioso* rhythm that provokes fine elemental images: fog turning a spider web into a necklace of pearls, brooks gurgling through green meadows after a spring rain, the silence of snow falling in a spruce forest. But who speaks for wind? Here the rhythm slows down to a mumur, or fades away entirely. It's not easy to be lyrical about banging shutters, broken trees, and heavy seas.

Wind is a negative element and it follows a negative pattern, and mine is not the voice to speak up in its behalf. Three or four years ago, when the tail end of a hurricane whiplashed through New England, I left my island after hearing ominous predictions on the radio, and spent the night with friends on the mainland. I awoke early the next morning and stepped outside to see, firsthand, what the weather was doing. The sky was gray, rain fell in a drizzle, and a stiff wind was blowing from the southeast. There were good-sized troughs in the cove, but nothing that could prevent me from getting across to the island. I went down to the dock, started up the motor, and cast off. It was rough and the boat took a little water, but I got across safely. I tied up securely and walked up the path to the house. But the wind continued to strengthen, and once, shortly before lunchtime, I felt perhaps I had made a mistake in coming over. The house shook alarmingly, there was an ugly and persistent rattling of the windows, and a high-pitched whine took posession of the front of the house, drowning out the radio, which I kept tuned to the Bath station to keep me informed of the storm's progress. All that I have always disliked about wind was intensified that day, and I realized — when the skies cleared and the wind died down later that evening — that wind and I would never be friends. The relationship that existed between us possessed no potential for betterment whatever; we didn't need each other, and that was that.

The question of what to do when a heavy wind is blowing is always baffling to the man who lives in the country. City people know wind only as something that sweeps scraps of paper up in the air; they get a firm grip on their hat brims while they wait for taxis, but otherwise wind is pretty much meaningless to a city dweller. But in the country, a strong wind asserts its authority over everything; what work is done must be done in a sheltered spot. Everything moves and flutters in an irritating way, and whatever is moveable must be battened down with weights. My neighbor says that a windy day is good for painting, but I have a strong suspicion that he's thinking out loud and not really speaking from experience. I've painted on windy days, and later have found so much trash stuck to the paint that I've permanently abandoned painting as a windy day activity. The paint dries quickly, but not so quickly that it doesn't function for a brief period as flypaper, openly hospitable to whatever is flying through the air.

Moreover, there is something about a windy day that sets my teeth on edge; I feel somehow off-balance, as though the horizon had shifted slightly. Europeans understand this much better than Americans. The mistral, the cold wind that blows in squalls into southern France from the Alps, is so universally accepted as mood altering that French law gravely acknowledges its effect upon human behavior. Those who commit crimes of passion when the mistral is blowing are treated more leniently than those who cannot claim the mistral as an accomplice. The föhn, a strong, dry wind that occasionally sweeps across Germany and Austria, and the sirocco, a sand-laden wind coming across the Mediterranean from the Sahara Desert, are also credited with stirring up restlessness and violence. A Sicilian after a few days of a sirocco is said to be as nervous as a fox in a forest fire. Only Americans seem to assume that a man of normal intelligence and willpower will remain essentially sane during a windstorm; I know otherwise. Furthermore, the longer the wind blows, the more fanciful one's behavior becomes.

What makes a heavy wind basically sinister, of course, is its limitless capacity for causing mischief. Mooring lines part and boats blow aground, floats become separated from docks, shingles fly from roofs, flowers are blown to pieces, and electric wires come down. These are just openers; when a wind really gets going it can find a hundred ways to make man miserable. Perhaps the worst aspect of wind is its synergistic alliance with another element to multiply man's misery. I refer specifically to wind *and* rain. Late one afternoon not long ago, rain began to fall and drove me indoors. A glance at the sky showed I was in for a wet evening, so I filled the woodbox, closed the windows, and settled in for a snug night of reading. Suddenly the wind shifted around to the east, picked up strength, and began driving rain against the windows. Water began to seep under the front door. Then it appeared around the edges of the window. Then a steady and ominous *plunk* was heard in the kitchen, which meant that the wind had found a loose shingle and was blowing water under it. It was a long, blustery, and active night, and I got very little reading done. If I describe wind as a personal adversary, I'm not — as the saying goes — whistling Dixie.

Spring

A year ago, in what I suppose now was a totally reckless mood, I wrote in this space that Maine had only three seasons and that spring was not among them. This raised the hackles of a number of readers, and I shudder to recall the underlying theme of the mail; nicer things have been said about Idi Amin. The flat assertion that spring did not come to Maine but somehow skipped the state entirely was — in retrospect — one of those judgments we all occasionally make when old frustrations and new vexations create pressures from which a man or woman simply needs release; in this case release from the icy grip of a winter that had worn out its welcome. I had looked at the thermometer once too often, and I didn't care for what I saw. The only way to get even with nature, as any sensible person knows, is to write something extreme about it, and to hell with accuracy. Poets know this better than most writers. T.S. Eliot was at the end of his patience when he wrote "April is the cruelest month," and Robert Frost, in his poem "Two Tramps in Mud Time," described the April moment when a cloud blots out the sun and the frigidity of winter shamelessly reasserts itself. Stephen Vincent Benét, fed to the teeth with winter, wrote "Now grimy April comes again," and even Shakespeare made a hit-and-run reference to "the uncertain glory of an April day." However high the fires of my own resentment against winter had been stoked, if the above is a fair anthology, I was not alone.

While I do not wish to make a full retraction of my remarks about the absence of a Maine springtime and must thread my way cautiously here between fact and a lingering sullenness, I would like to amend the record to say that there are days falling roughly between winter and summer that possess some of the promise of spring and invoke all of the hope for it. These are the days, especially in the coastal areas, when the seas are quiet, the wind dies down to a gentle brush against the skin, the sun for the first time sends shimmering waves from paved highways, and one suddenly realizes that a sheep-lined coat is too much and that a sweater is all that's needed to keep warm. Maybe — around noon — even the sweater is shed. These are the days when the sun is still too fickle to fool the lilac, but the buds are heavy and the clusters are discernible, and a few clipped forsythia branches, properly soaked, can be forced into full bloom when placed for a few days in a sunny window. A strange restlessness hangs in the air, a new look appears in the eyes of children, who sense that something exciting is about to happen. Snowmobiles stand awkwardly about, their grace and mobility having disappeared along with the snow. Spruce boughs are taken from the foundations of country houses, where they have helped to insulate the downstairs rooms from the cruel cold of winter nights, and are hauled into backyards and set afire. The first snake appears; one lifts a stone and the snake moves sluggishly away, its irritation showing. A few weeks before, it would have remained tightly coiled, refusing to move. There seem to be more birds about; starlings are building nests according to some urban renewal program of their own design, and the more adventurous robins are beginning to show up, a little tired and hungry from the long trip up from the South. They aren't entirely sure they aren't crowding their destiny a bit by arriving too soon, but they are too busy getting settled to worry about it.

Spring seems more magical to boat people, I have noticed, than to anyone else. For farmers, spring is the beginning of the year (January 1 is meaningless to a farmer, an empty date in a vacuum). But to a boat owner, spring is intoxicating, a real drunk. It is the beginning of something bigger and better than he has ever known. This will be the summer of the most adventurous voyage, this will put all other summers to shame. The chipping, scraping, polishing, and painting takes on a feverish intensity, marinas are visited, new hardware is examined and handled, new dinghies are priced, new sails are discussed and debated, new coils of rope are purchased, and on the thousands of wharves from Kittery to Eastport there is the odor of fresh paint in the air. "This year we are going to take her down to Montauk and back," a friend of mine assured me last spring, putting the brass polish down on the deck and rubbing his hands on his trousers. His eyes shone with an unholy light. I don't think he got more than ten miles from his wharf during the entire summer, but I doubt if that has diminished his dream for the summer in the least. This will be the summer for Montauk. For sure.

So the spring that comes to Maine is more a suggestion than a reality, but it performs the function of a spring, it does what a spring is supposed to do. And as the sun climbs higher in the sky each day, one soon doesn't care what it's called. One responds to the warmth, to the wonderful embrace of the sun in a protected place, to the feeling of lazy contentment that it brings, to the escape outdoors after the confinement of a long winter. Whatever this thing is that Nature bestows upon us at this time of the year, it's powerful stuff and it nudges us into beginning life all over again.

Autumn Morning

I awoke early this morning, and knowing that further sleep was out of the question, I did what any other sensible person would have done. I slipped on some old clothes and went rowing. The seat of the skiff was wet from droplets of dew, but I wiped them off with the palm of my hand, untied the line, and headed for the forest on the eastern shore of the cove, which was little more than a shadow in the half-light of early morning. There is something immensely satisfying in rowing a boat in totally calm water; the bow cuts the water cleanly, the silence is disturbed only by the sound of the oarlocks, and one can rest on the oars when lost in thought. The dog had followed me sleepily down the path to the wharf but had seemed unable to make a decision about whether to accompany me or not, so I had rowed away and left her on the float. Her feelings were definitely hurt, and now she was barking, the sound coming across the water with every note of grief and outrage amplified.

This day was going to be a model of beauty, I could see that already. The sun had not yet appeared, but the East reflected a rosy glow. The air was cool and moist, freighted with that indescribable hint of expectancy, that suggestion that some great adventure lay ahead. The birds were already awake on the island — I heard their rehearsal as I walked down the path — but here on the sea even the gulls were quiet. Gradually the trees took shape as I neared the far shore, and the grayness of the rocks emerged from the shadows. Three egrets, like small white ghosts, roosted in a pine tree. The tide was moving out fast, carrying whole islands of rockweed with it. A yellow, plastic oil container bobbed beside the boat; I held it under water with an oar until it filled and sank to the bottom. The time will come, I thought, when the entire world will be covered with plastic bottles; the coastline of Maine is almost covered with them now.

There were small gnats in the air but no mosquitoes, which struck me as an odd but welcome discovery. Unless there is strong sunlight, which mosquitoes can't abide, all coastal life is pervaded by mosquitoes, especially in the still hour before sunrise or the hour of twilight. Now the sun was about to take command of the day; I could see its first rays shining on the far side of the cove, which told me that it had risen above the trees on Pole Island. The light struck the eastern windows of a house on the mainland, and they glowed like a fire raged within. I rowed slowly long the shore in the shadow of the forest, and I could sense the coming alive of the woodland. There was an occasional scurrying in the leaves, birds suddenly appeared in the thick underbrush, and I caught a fleeting glimpse of a chipmunk racing across the rocks. The forest was black and impenetrable even in daylight, and in the shadows of early morning it looked forbidding. I knew it contained nothing larger than porcupines and squirrels, yet I would have hesitated to tie up the skiff and enter it. I came to a place where the stone palisade ended and the forest sloped down to marshland and eelgrass. It was lighter now, and the lichen on the rocks behind me stood out like highlighting against the dark background of the forest. I rowed through the weedy shallows and pockets of eelgrass, and came out again into deep water near the southern end of the cove. As I turned the skiff around, I saw the first shafts of sunlight touching my island, and I don't think I have ever seen it look so beautiful. I was perhaps a half-mile away, and I shipped the oars and sat there entranced, watching the light as it touched first the tops of the tall spruce and pine trees and then gradually exposed the entire forest. What I was watching had been going on for thousands of years, yet it seemed to me that I was watching a performance that was truly unique and which I was fortunate to have encountered. Man's capacity to accept reality is finite; few, if any, of us are fully adjusted to life on earth.

A small sliver of moon hung low in the western sky as I started rowing back to the island, but the sky was now blue. When I had left the island I had seen stars; only the East had glowed with a pale, pink light, and the morning had still possessed the feel of night. A patch of fog blocked my view of the island, but it thinned and drifted away before I reached it, and the sun was warm against my skin when I tied the boat to the float.

The dog joined me as I walked the path to the house, but she was still nursing a grudge, and she ducked out of my reach when I bent down to pat her. Forgiveness comes slowly with this dog; the worst sin I can commit is to go off without her. By afternoon the episode will have slipped out of her consciousness, but right now my shameful behavior is too green in her memory, and I must be made to suffer and repent. I know that she will reject her breakfast because she is aware of my anxiety when she refuses to eat; nevertheless I open a can of dog food when I reach the kitchen and place it on the floor. This is her moment of revenge. She walks past me without a glance at the food and goes into the living room. I make myself a cup of coffee and take it out to the sundeck to watch the lobster boats go out of the cove. It's going to be a warm autumn day and one of the loveliest of the entire year.

Forecast

Like everyone else in Maine, I am constantly concerned about the weather, and right now I am in a high state of indignation about what's been going on lately in the matter of weather reporting. Meteorology, so far as television is concerned, has become a growth industry, and my skepticism about its reliability increases with barometric pressure. Weather is a more insistent thing than it has ever been and the forecaster, tasting and greatly admiring the attention he is getting, is beginning to take some shortcuts. I am afraid things need to be set straight.

The modern forecaster is surrounded by some awesome instruments which keep him informed as to the surface temperature of the oceans, the force and direction of the winds, air currents at stratospheric levels, high and low barometric areas, and Heaven only knows what other natural phenomena that need to be recorded. But there is one instrument that I think modern forecasters have consistently overlooked, and I am referring to the window.

One morning late last autumn I turned on the television to get a weather report, and the forecaster, surrounded by those mysterious cloud-covered maps, announced with the cheerfulness that seems a requirement for the occupation that "the chances of precipitation are 20 percent this morning." If precipitation means rain, he was off only on his percentage figures. The rain was lashing the house savagely, the gutters were overflowing, and what was happening in Maine was happening along the entire East Coast as far south as Georgia. A glance out of the window, if meteorologists were only allowed access to windows, would almost certainly have caused him to think twice before making such an idiotic statement.

I have just come to realize that weather broadcasters in television stations display real enthusiasm only when Nature provides them with some sort of malevolence. This undoubtedly can be traced to their envy of the newscasters and sports announcers, who deal nightly with violence and disaster, and when there is nothing more alarming than frost threatening the orange crop, the weather reporter can't help but feel he is in a business of minor distinction. In kicking this subject around a little, it is only fair that the listener's preference also be examined. Listeners relish disaster, and if the weatherman is confined to vague low-pressure areas over the Great Lakes and mixed rain and snow in western Pennsylvania, there is going to be a lot of channel-switching to stations offering more action. The weather people know this. When they do get a hurricane or blizzard, they feel justified in pulling out all the stops and letting an enthusiastic hysteria take over. In lulls, however, a brief squall is sometimes given a bit of media hype that may not square with the facts, but weather broadcasters are human, and if this elevates their spirits somewhat, no great harm is done.

All of this is introduction to the matter of my neighbor's near infallibity in weather forecasting, a performance remarkable in that he relies entirely on the window. This isn't entirely true; sometimes he goes outside to sniff the air a bit and to get the *feel* of the weather in his bones. Once he has completed this personal confrontation, he can return to the house and tell you how to plan the rest of your day. I would say he has achieved an accuracy level of about 90 percent, which is a damned sight better than anything I've encountered on television. The reader will notice my hesitance in calling attention to the scope of my neighbor's talent, the long delay before I move him on-stage. The reason for this is that I am as tired as the next man of those stories of the farmer outsmarting the scientist, of the simple, old-fashioned procedure being superior to the modern, complex one, of the unorthodox remedy succeeding where the scientific one has failed. My neighbor is a lobsterman, and not only his income but also, on occasion, his life is dependent upon the weather and what advance warning he may have of what is in the cards, so to speak. The television man isn't around at five o'clock in the morning when he takes his boat out of the cove, and even if there were a report at that hour I don't think my neighbor would be greatly impressed by all of those maps and satellite studies. He has his own method of forecasting, and it has served him well.

One day in a downpour he came over to the island clad in oilskins to discuss a minor business matter, and when I saw him to the door I remarked that I would like to cross over to the mainland to get my mail but that I had no taste for going out in a rainstorm that was obviously going to keep up all day. He squinted up as though he were looking above the rain. "Go over around four," he said. "Maybe four-thirty." This was nonsense, and I told him so. The television weatherman had said that morning the rain would end late the next afternoon. After lunch, lulled by a deluge hitting the windowpane, I took a nap. If I said that a ray of sunshine hitting my eye awakened me at four o'clock that afternoon, I would be putting my credibility strictly on the line. But it did.

Autumn Reverie

Autumn. A strong breeze is coming out of the north, chilling the air, but in the lee of a large rock beside the sea it is warm, and the light reflecting from the miniature whitecaps is almost blinding. The dog is sitting behind me, staring off into space and lost in her own train of thought. I can feel her leaning against me slightly, which I long ago learned was her way of reassuring herself that I was close at hand while she is working something out in her mind. If I move enough to break contact, it shatters her reverie. My rock is just above the tide line, and the tide only recently pulled away, because there are still small pools of water in the crevasses at my feet, and in one of them, which is exposed to the breeze, there is a small chop running. Behind me is a steep bank rising up to a flat meadow, where a horse with a white blaze running down its nose is grazing peacefully. The dog and the horse ignore each other; it's an arrangement they worked out some time ago. Animals seldom go out looking for trouble in the way that human beings do. The bank behind me is covered by scrub growth, with Queen Anne's lace waving in the fitful sea breeze. The warm sun causes it to give off a spicy, clean odor, but I've long known to resist the temptation to bring it into the house. The first night in the vase and it sheds small white grains all over the table. Queen Anne's lace belongs outdoors.

The engine block of some ancient automobile is rusting away in the eelgrass on the opposite beach. It is a heavy, inert mass, and because of this such castoffs are valued highly by coastal people, who use them as anchors for moorings. Three goldenrods are waving above it; they are in full bloom, and they make the cylinder blocks seem strangely out of place. Junk at the water's edge used to bother me a lot, but I'm less easily disturbed by it now, and I like to think I am calmer about a lot of things than I was when I first moved to Maine. There is usually so much flotsam on the rocks and beaches of Maine that if one permitted oneself to be excited by it, one would end up in a mental state of a most embarrassing nature. Pieces of rope and discarded boots, I have decided after exploring miles of Maine's shore, are the most common objects encountered, and I am impressed by the fact that an old boot is almost totally indestructible.

The rock gets hard, and I climb to the top of the bank, but here the limb of an aspen tends to provide more shade than I care for. The leaves are falling now, which means there won't be many more warm days like this, inviting a man to put aside his work and have a little rest in the sunlight. A bee settles on the Queen Anne's lace, but the pollen isn't to its liking and it moves on. The bee's actions are hurried; it feels the pressure of winter on its back. I can hear the angry whine of a chain saw coming across the cove, and it tells the story a little more pointedly than the briskness of the bee. Autumn is a dispiriting time for laggards; there's a lot to do and not much time to do it in.

I get in the boat with the dog and row slowly across to a tiny island, where I find warmth on some rocks at the leeward tip of the ledge. Yellow mullet sends up spears out of the sand behind me, but the blossoms are turning brown, and what I am seeing now is the final performance of the season. The blue is gone from the sea heather, and all of the weeds seem burned, even the dried and blackened rockweed. Two trees, both stunted, grow in the rocky soil, but the skeletons of two others furnish a discouraging prediction of what can be expected. The only green on the little island is provided by a clump of bayberry growing behind the mullet. The rocks are covered by mussel shells which have been dropped by gulls, and in the burned grass around the rocks the purple shards of mussel shells reflect the sunlight. Even the bayberry here seems to have been burned by the autumn sun, and the ground around the clump is covered by brown leaves. I crumple in my palm a handful of dry leaves and am surprised to find they are as aromatic as the green ones.

Seasons back out as they come in — slowly, reluctantly. A herring gull soars easily overhead, gliding over the water to touch down gently on a rim of sand and pebbles — a flight of neatness, flawless precision, and grace. A gull has forgotten more about the aerodynamics of flight than man has ever known. I lie back in the dry grass and close my eyes. The sun is heavy now, and I can feel its weight against me. The whole long winter will creep by before I can lie like this in the sun again, and I want to store away the sensation of warmth and peace. It is a little too warm here for the dog, and she begins to wander. So far as I know, she is not aware of the fact that December and January are the next two leaves to fall off the calendar, and I guess she is better off for it. From the corner of my eye, I see her down at the water's edge, pawing at something she has discovered. I don't know what it is because I slip off the slope of drowsiness into sleep.

A Time of Forbearance

I awoke to a banging at the back door, and it was my neighbor's son. Like most Maine kids, he came right to the point. "Dad's going duck hunting," he said. "He wants a few for Christmas. He says do you want to come?" I pulled on some old clothes and stumbled down to the dock. My neighbor was sitting in the back of the motorboat, a shotgun in his lap. "Took you long enough," he said. I recognized it as a greeting.

The boy untied the line and the father gunned the motor. Outside the cove we met a light easterly breeze and fairly heavy swells, but the small boat slipped into them easily. We were headed toward open sea, and when I inquired where we were going, the father pointed to an island some distance off the port bow. "Shot many a duck there," he said, "and I'm bound to get some today." I'm a conscientious objector to killing animals and I refuse to do it, but I don't attempt to force upon my neighbors this point of view. In the first place, they wouldn't pay any attention to me if I did, and secondly, they usually hunt for food rather than whatever sport is involved in blowing a rabbit apart with a twelve-gauge shotgun. I have insisted that no one with a gun or any other weapon may set foot upon my island, a pronouncement that only brings laughter from my neighbors, who claim there is no game there anyway, other than perhaps a raccoon or two. This isn't precisely true, because a lobsterman told me he spotted four deer on the island last winter, but I'm quite content to let word get around that it's a waste of time to hunt there.

It was an overcast day and the breeze had a bite to it. I wanted a cup of coffee badly, and when I mentioned this aloud, my neighbor handed me a bottle of beer that had been lying half-submerged in bilge on the bottom of the boat. It was better than nothing, but considerably below even the minimum standards for breakfast. A lobster boat approached, and responding to some unseen signal, hove to. Both the lobsterman and my neighbor hooked feet over the sides of each other's boats, holding them together, and the speed of both engines went into that mysterious idle that only lobsterboats seem able to achieve, when the boats nudge each other gently and nothing more. Conversation opened on a bantering note, I was introduced by my first name, Christmas was falsely referred to as something they both dreaded, a few words were said about the weather, which was to nobody's liking, and then my neighbor inquired if any ducks had been seen around the island toward which we were headed. The lobsterman said he had flushed a covey from some eelgrass on the south end of the island while hauling traps there about an hour ago, but that he seriously doubted my neighbor could shoot one since he had often heard that the safest spot to be in when my neighbor fired was as close to the target as possible. My neighbor spat over the side of the boat; a remark like that deserved no reply.

We altered course and headed for the southern end of the island. A light mist began settling, and the shoreline of the mainland disappeared into a gray fog bank. My neighbor broke the gun and loaded it, and the boy, sitting in the front of the boat, suddenly became alert. We rounded the tip of the island, but there were no ducks. A few gulls were wheeling in the air above the eelgrass, hunting for whatever scraps the lobsterman had tossed overboard, but there was nothing else. We circled the island twice, cutting back on the speed, before my neighbor gave up. "He scared them away," he said, unloading the gun. "I would have a couple of Christmas ducks if he hadn't come in here hauling traps." He made a wide circle and headed the boat in the direction of the mainland. The boy was disappointed, but I wasn't. It was cold and the mist was settling heavily. My thoughts were on a fire, dry clothes, and some breakfast.

Years ago in Virginia I went to a Christmas party where a five-piece band performed. A large sign on the stage beside the bank proclaimed that it was provided by "Haines Meat Market, Dealers in Fresh-Killed Meat, who also wish you a Merry Christmas." I didn't like that sign, and I'm also glad that my neighbor didn't shoot any ducks in order to celebrate the birth of the man called the Prince of Peace. Christmas suggests a gentle sort of forbearance, something we can all grab hold of with vast satisfaction: the devout, the errant, the wistful, the lonely, and of course, the National Retail Credit Association. The churchman, on his way to midnight services, encounters one of his brethren making uneven progress home from the office party, a paper cup crumpled in his hand and perhaps a crimson smear on his cheek. They pass, for perhaps the only time of the year, in mutual forbearance. A strange sort of reason seems to prevail.

But in Maine, like everywhere else, the season ends and what has been called the spirit of Christmas, like the decorations, is taken down and stored away until needed again. It's too bad; it could be the warm sun around which we revolve all year. Meanwhile, I am consoling myself that there is one wild duck — maybe even two or three — that will see another spring.

7

The Way It Is

First Thing Tomorrow

When my friend, who has been living in Maine now only a year or so, told me the other day that a man with road-scraping machinery had promised to come "early next week" to level his lane, I felt very depressed. I hate to see an innocent man's expectations shattered; I know what "early next week" means, and it's bad news. It means either "I'll try to get to you sometime this summer, but I doubt it" or "I'm reasonably certain that if you keep after me and make my life miserable, I'll get to your place sometime in the spring."

It could have been worse. My friend might have been told "I'll come any day now," which any student of Maine work agreements — those who search between the lines for hidden meanings — knows is even more vague and offers very little hope at all. "Any day now" is wispy and totally lacking in substance; a workman who uses that term is — in my opinion — declining the job outright. Only the most trusting and innocent could nurse an aspiration through a situation as bleak and barren as that.

I have been waiting two years now for the electrician to come and finish wiring my house so that the new gas cookstove can be activated by an electric spark. I really require only one new outlet, which would take at most only a half-hour of the electrician's time. The last time I spoke to the electrician about this, he promised to come by later that same afternoon. I suppose the disappointment showed in my face, but I knew what "later this afternoon" meant. He is not a mean man, and when he noted my stricken look, he added, "Or first thing tomorrow." "Later today" means you haven't a chance, but "the first thing tomorrow" puts you back in the ballpark. You won't see him for months, but ultimately he will show up.

My friend whose driveway needs grading is also concerned about a house painter who last March promised to send in his estimate "tomorrow." My friend felt the estimate was a logical prelude to the actual painting, but I had to straighten him out on that. "You will get the estimate, if you get it at all," I explained, "long after the bulk of the painting is done. The painter's wife does the estimate, and it has very little to do with the actual painting itself and, in fact, should be considered an entirely independent element in the whole transaction." My friend looked troubled at this, which caused me to feel even worse about what I had to tell him next. But I bit the bullet and went on. "You will note that I said 'after the bulk of the painting is done,'" I said. "The job won't be completely finished, because the painter has promised somebody else to finish a job and that person is really putting the heat on him, and he will finally take his ladders away from your house one night and go off to finish up the other job."

My friend thought this over silently a moment. "Then he will come back and finish my job?" he asked. I shook my head in sorrow. "No," I said, "he won't. He's behind in a half-dozen painting jobs and you will have to wait your turn. You're lucky to get half your house painted."

My friend looked glum, and to cheer him up I reminded him of his success with the drywall man, who had submitted his estimate in March of 1982 and who had actually done the work in May of 1983. "That was only fourteen months," I pointed out. "Surely you can't complain about that."

When I first came to Maine fourteen years ago, I thought that workmen failed to show up because I lived on an island, and they found it inconvenient to come over on a boat with heavy tools. I've since learned that this has nothing to do with delays. In fact, it is my conviction that postponement is such an integral component of the Maine labor process that I doubt that a workman would show up for a job on schedule even if he had idle time on his hands. My neighbor, a native Down Easter, once remarked, when I complained about delays on some wharf repairs, that "You're going to have to wait until that job ripens." Apparently only a workman can sense when a job is ripe; the owner's circuits are too overloaded with emotion to make a reliable judgment.

Another friend, Art Buchwald, thinks workmen are slower to respond on Martha's Vineyard than they are in Maine, but Buchwald is a highly competitive chap and likes to think his problems are without equal anywhere. A few weeks ago he wrote that he was expecting a visit that afternoon from a babysitter who had advertised for work in the Vineyard *Gazette* in 1972. When he was reminded that his children were all grown up, he explained that the babysitter protested he had promised her the job only eleven years ago. Knowing how Buchwald exaggerates, I am skeptical about this, but I do believe my friend when he says he is so outraged that the road grader hasn't come to scrape his lane that he is thinking seriously of selling his house and moving away. Somebody has got to tell him that until the lane is scraped, no moving van is going to be able to get in to move him. He doesn't know this, but I'll bet I know who does. The road grader knows it, that's who.

By Any Other Name

The miracle of Maine, I suspect, is that those of us who have given our hearts to the place never seem to get very far from it regardless of how far afield we wander. One thing leads to another, and suddenly we find ourselves walking down an avenue in Paris or Madrid with Moosehead Lake or Pemaquid Light on our minds. A short time ago, while riding a train from Zurich to Bern, I was reading the international edition of the *Herald-Tribune* when my eye suddenly fastened on a comment about lobsters by Waverly Root, the celebrated American-born food writer who has made his home in Paris for many years. At least two-thirds of what are known as "Maine" lobsters (I am following Mr. Root's practice of placing Maine in quotation marks) actually come from Canadian waters, the writer asserted with that note of unassailable authority which food writers often adopt, while the same proportion of "Breton" lobsters are now imported into France from England or Ireland. Mr. Root didn't come right out and say so, but the implication of his remark was that something a little shifty was going on, that lobstermen and distributors were misrepresenting the waters of origin of their catches.

What qualities do Canadian lobsters possess that Maine lobsters lack, or vice versa? And those lobsters that perhaps swim across the international boundary several times during their lifetime: do they change in some mysterious way each time they cross the invisible frontier?

Mr. Root's credentials as a food writer are first-rate, there is no doubt about that. His best-known book, *The Food of France*, caused even the French to regard him with considerable respect, an accomplishment that is more than just remarkable when one considers how violently the French challenge any statement made about food, regardless of what it may be. Yet Mr. Root's comments on lobsters seem weighted with a strange sort of innocence. I suppose there are indifferent restaurants and markets which declare all lobsters to be Maine lobsters, just as too often all potatoes show up on menus as "Baked Idaho Potato," but I'm not convinced it's something we need Mr. Root to alert us to, as though some impending danger is settling ominously over the American horizon. The cold waters off Nova Scotia and in the Gulf of St. Lawrence have not yet been overfished as Maine waters have, and lobsters there are more plentiful at the moment than they are to the south. However, I know of no one, not even Mr. Root, whose taste apparatus is so sensitive that he can distinguish a Penobscot Bay lobster from, say, one from the waters adjacent to Prince Edward Island. Both are excellent, quite possibly the finest in the world, although the Breton lobster of France is also of extremely high quality, and there is no denying the fact that French cooks have a fine way with lobsters. And I seriously doubt that much more than snobbery distinguishes a real Breton lobster from a "Breton" lobster caught off the shores of Ireland. Mr. Root's discovery just doesn't strike me as very startling. There is a certain value, I am aware, of adding place names to items on menus, but often this coinage gives off a hollow ring and it's only the most naive diner who isn't aware of it. Ninety percent of the "Virginia Ham" appearing on menus across the nation has never been within five hundred miles of the state of Virginia.

I agree with Mr. Root when he says that unless some means is found soon to maintain or replenish the lobster populations of the North Atlantic, this distinguished delicacy will disappear from our tables, except those of millionaires. This is certainly true, but Mr. Root gets into trouble again when he gives the reason for overfishing as being due to the fact that "taking lobsters is child's play." I would like Mr. Root to see my neighbor bring his boat into the cove around five o'clock some afternoon after hauling traps for twelve hours. My neighbor is a strong and resilient man, and I've seen him lift and carry loads that I didn't think a man could or should handle alone, but when he ties up his boat after a day of fishing, there is a spent look in his eyes and his shoulders sag with exhaustion. He stows his lobsters in a moored car, splashes a few bucketfuls of seawater across his decks, and trudges home with the slow and deliberate pace of a man who, for the moment, has had it. He wouldn't say his day had been spent in child's play.

Paris is a fine place from which to write of the delights of *Homard Cardinal* or *Homard Grille Flambe au Cognac* or *Homard Rothschild*, but I wonder if Mr. Root isn't crowding his destiny by using that city as a base for writing about the business of lobstering. I don't know to what extent there are similarities in lobstering in the waters off the coast of Brittany and those off the coast of Maine, but I suspect there are differences, and I doubt that Paris is the place where these differences come to light.

Anyway, Mr. Root's article served a pleasant purpose. As I sped across the Swiss countryside, I closed my eyes and dwelt upon the memory of summer nights in Maine, of lobsters lifted from boiling seawater and brought to the table with small cups of melted butter, of glasses of cold beer, and of dining with friends on what is beyond doubt America's finest dish. I was sorry when I reached Bern.

Rural Life

One day last summer a friend of mine from New York accompanied me to the neighborhood dump, where I rid myself of several days' accumulation of garbage, tin cans, and wine bottles. It is a trip I take so frequently that I think nothing of it; in fact, I didn't even see the sign posted there that brought so much laughter from my friend. The sign, when it was pointed out to me, called attention to a Bean Supper the following Saturday evening to be given in a local school as a benefit for some township cause. New Yorkers laugh in derision, or contempt, or scorn, but unlike other people they seldom laugh in mirth. My friend thought it hilarious — this was a scornful laugh — that a Bean Supper should be advertised at the village dump. Since, like me, everyone in the area comes there several times a week, it struck me as an ideal spot to put up a sign, but I didn't attempt to shake my friend's grip on what he was sure was a rare specimen of backwoods humor and one that he would endlessly recount at dinner parties during the fall and winter.

Country living has always been a wellspring of humor for city folk; even country clothes are good for a laugh. I notice that overalls, the dirt farmer's traditional uniform, have been adopted in some instances as sportswear by urban dwellers, but always with the disdainful air one possesses when wearing something patently outlandish. There's rollicking good humor in playing a hayseed so long as one's neighbors and friends know it's a game. A lot of people who have fought and clawed their way out of the 59th Street station of the Lexington Avenue subway at five o'clock in the afternoon have suddenly gathered together their possessions and moved into the woodlands of New England, eager to see what quietude and fresh air are like, but their letters back to Manhattan make rich dinner conversation. "At that town in Vermont where the Millers went," a New Yorker will say, "the local supermarket puts Velveeta cheese on the Gourmet Shelf." Or "Miller sent me a snapshot, and already he's wearing a toothpick in his mouth." Nothing is more laughable than nonconformity, or more fearsome either.

It seems to me that country people dress more sensibly than those who reside in the city and I held to this opinion even when I was a city dweller. A Down-Easter, for example, is not easily thrown off balance by a salesman's pitch; he has a pretty good idea when he enters a clothing store what he wants, and he's far more interested in the practical aspects of the garment than whether or not it is cut to the latest Savile Row style. Abraham Lincoln once shrugged off criticism that his legs were too long by saying "a man's legs should be long enough to reach the ground," and I think rural New Englanders take this same attitude toward their clothes. Clothing should do what clothing is supposed to do, which means it should wear well and provide a genuinely comfortable appearance. There is a practical approach to business attire as well. A Gorham, Maine, chimney sweep, who last year cleaned over 2,000 chimneys, told the *New York Times* that he dressed in the tall hat and tails "if the household has little children, but if there are not any children around, I don't bother." This strikes me as the sort of sensible compromise one encounters almost exclusively in the country; that flapping tailcoat can get entangled in television antennas and there's no sense in adding another risk to an already risky job if there's no audience on the ground watching the performance.

There are, of course, people in the germinal or embryonic stage of rural life, city people who have resettled themselves and are trying to sink as quickly as possible into their new surroundings. Although they have acquired country clothes, an occasional sports jacket cut a little too snugly around the waist or a snappy topcoat may betray their origin. The smart newcomers know that acceptance in the neighborhood doesn't come overnight and they will let time do the job, as a newly shingled roof is weathered to blend into the background. New arrivals may think it odd that a Bean Supper is advertised at the dump, but they don't snicker about it. For them, the humor has suddenly leaked out of hayseed jokes.

There was a time when the winter loiterers, seated around the stove in the village store, cherished the jokes where the city slicker got badly taken by the rube, but those days have gone the way of the minstrel and the medicine show. The humor that amuses country people today is relatively sophisticated due to the homogenous taste level created across the country by television. The zinger that gets a chuckle in San Francisco brings one also in Cundys Harbor or Castine; the congenial vice of television, for once, is beyond criticism.

I can see now that in my trips to the dump I have been far too concerned about separating my cans and bottles and newspapers, but the next time I go I intend to look around to see what public notices have been placed there to catch my eye. The more I think about it, the more I value the location as a township bulletin board. Before slamming shut the tailgate on the pickup truck, we should all see what's happening in the neighborhood. I would even tack up a tearsheet of this little essay, just to let my fellow citizens know that my loyalty to the whole venture falls into the proper pattern and gives off an honest ring, but no one would have the time to read it. One comes to the dump in a responsible frame of mind; it isn't a carefree expedition, and one's attention is elusive. A two-line notice about a Bean Supper is just about right.

Environmental Concord

My Maine island is a total loss where agribusiness is concerned. I may as well face that fact before the hopes of spring arise. Nothing will grow on this land except trees, and I've finally choked down my regret and become resigned to the proposition that I'll never look a sunflower in the face or watch the first exciting surge of yellow come to a green tomato. I'm still holding out some hope — we were all once full of faith — that my Colorado raspberries will come through any summer now, but up to the moment of writing this report, they have shown no hint of bearing any berries or even of a lessening of their hostility. My daughter brought them from Colorado, three healthy plants, and found a nice spot in the sun where she felt they would never know that the Rocky Mountains were not on the other side of the island. It is obvious now, four years later, that they know exactly where they are and that they don't care for the setup at all. They have grown about two inches in four years, which to my way of thinking is foot dragging of the worst kind. Last summer two stunted green berries appeared; and although I kept the bowl handy, neither of them ever ripened. Last fall when I was spreading spruce slash around to protect things from the frost and snow, I noticed that the raspberry leaves had turned a sickly shade of bluish red. I don't know what that means and I'm afraid to ask.

My neighbor, who knows more about what grows in the soil and in the sea than anybody I know, advises me to forget about the raspberries, but thinks I will have a pleasant surprise next spring where lupine is concerned. I've tried twice to seed lupine, with no results at all, so last summer I set out several lupine plants which a friend of mine in Camden had dug up from her garden. The lupine feel at home in the coastal climate, and they show no disposition to be sulky and resentful over the transfer, *such as some plants that I know*. Lupine — historically the first flower to bloom after the glacier melts — is a magnificent thing, and success with lupine would go a long way to ease my embarrassment over the failure with raspberries.

My only success, after twelve years of scratching around in unresponsive soil, has been with basil, which I prize highly because it is the foundation of pesto, the second-finest pasta dish in the world. As basil plants go they were a total failure until a lady playwright who lives on Martha's Vineyard asked me why I didn't plant them in large boxes filled with soil from the mainland. There was magic in the suggestion; from the start they thrived with such vigor that I was having pesto three or four times a week, just trying to keep my head above water, so to speak. Now, on a rainy day in midsummer I imagine I can smell the basil even when I go outside the cove in a boat, but sober reflection forces me to concede it could be any one of a dozen aromatic plants spilling their fragrance on an afternoon breeze.

My daughter, who is practical to a degree clearly beyond my grasp, has lectured me patiently on what she calls "environmental concord." Palm trees withstand hurricanes, she explains, because the fronds offer no resistance to wind; a Maine birch would go down in the first tropical gale. The bottom line, she continues, is to plant only those things on the island that are in harmonious relationship with the climate. When I ask her about the unhappy raspberries from Colorado, she shrugs the question off. "That's a controlled experiment," she says, "and, besides, their future still lies ahead." I'm a literary man and I could have delivered a short lecture on that future-lies-ahead remark, but I also value a harmonious relationship within the family and I let it pass. But a few days later I went over to a narrow strip of land between the cove and the open sea and dug up some wild sweet peas, which I brought back and set out around the sauna. Knowing very little about environmental concord, they succumbed immediately. The prosecution rests.

The plants native to the island which delight me the most are the lady slippers, which come out after the last snow melts and which bloom through the early part of June. In my opinion, there is no ornament anywhere lovelier than the mauve blossom of a lady slipper, standing shyly and alone on the forest floor. I take a census of lady slippers every June, and one far more thorough and painstaking than any census ever conducted by the Federal government, just to determine where I stand. For the past five years I have counted twelve of the plants, which seems to suggest a fairly stable population level. I lost one two years ago, a real beauty, but one which stubbornly insisted upon coming up every year in the middle of the path leading to the dock. In desperation I tried to move it to an isolated end of the island, but I think it was DOA. I watered it and kept up a cheerful bedside manner, but it remained limp on the ground and in a few days it turned brown, which I correctly diagnosed as the end.

My neighbor came over one day last summer and solemnly proclaimed that, aside from lupine, my only hope was bulbs. "They'll grow anywhere," he said, looking critically at a handful of soil he had scooped up. "Maybe even here." I didn't have the heart to tell him about the fifty dollars' worth of bulbs that had been buried there twelve years ago and which had never been heard from. Or the fact that my hopes for flowers were now interred as deeply as the bulbs.

He Always Knew

My neighbor has broken his leg. I called on him yesterday and took him a bottle of bourbon, acting in the belief that he would be bedridden and bored and under those circumstances may as well possess a little glow. I'm not at all certain how the injury occurred since during the course of my visit he gave me three different accounts, none of which agreed in even the most trivial details. This didn't bother me in the slightest; I have long admired my neighbor's ability to reconstruct things until he hits upon something that is to his liking. Like a nightclub comic working with new material, he feels out his audience until he gets the response he is looking for, and then he knows he has it right. Facts are troublesome; they can clutter up a good story and drag it down. My neighbor regards facts with poorly concealed distaste, and usually discards them on the grounds of irrelevance.

When I arrived he was seated at the kitchen table, with his trousers leg pulled up to expose a cast with which he was obviously pleased. The cast was new, white, and businesslike, and my neighbor kept glancing at it with satisfaction. "Broke it in two places," he said proudly. "Doctor said I'd be laid up four months." I accepted the statement that the leg had been fractured in two places, but I told him

I didn't believe he would be laid up for four months. "Bones heal more quickly than that," I said. "No doctor told you it would take four months." My neighbor considered this rebuttal with distaste for a moment. "Maybe he meant four weeks," he said. "Anyway, I'm going to give it four weeks. What's in the bottle?"

In his way, my neighbor is one of the most admirable men I have ever encountered, and I am constantly amazed by the neatness of his life. He can fix whatever needs fixing, which in itself sets him apart and gives him an independence that lesser men can never hope to achieve. Over the past decade I have probably rowed to his house a hundred times seeking his help in getting an outboard motor started, or securing the float on my dock, or inquiring about the proportion of concrete to mix with sand in getting a quick-drying mix, or any one of several other requests which he must have thought were foolish but to which he cheerfully responded. When we are discussing serious matters, conversations which usually take place at the end of my wharf over a couple of bottles of cold beer that I have brought down to prime the pump, I find that he is always on the side of common sense, and that he has a deep contempt for what is obviously foolish. His self-reliance is a matter of continuing satisfaction to him, but he buries it carefully and chooses to pretend that he is merely riding his luck. Like all lobstermen, he complains bitterly about the growing scarcity of lobsters, the high cost of bait and gasoline, and the lack of competent help, and when I asked him bluntly one day why he didn't stop hauling traps and get a job in town, he stared at me in astonishment. "When I'm on that boat," he said carefully, as though he wanted to put me in my place once and for all, "I don't have a boss except the good Lord, and that's the way I've got to have it. I haven't had a boss since I was in the army, and I don't expect to ever have another one. So I'll probably be fishing for lobsters the rest of my life." My neighbor doesn't tell himself lies; he judges things calmly and hates the guts of any man who tries to mislead him.

Where politics are concerned, he talks like an anarchist but I suspect him of being basically conservative. He sees all layers of government as corrupt, some worse than others, and all politicians as self-serving and opportunistic. I doubt that he votes, because I think he would consider this a quest for the unattainable, and therefore a waste of time.

One day last fall, shortly before I closed up the island for the winter, he tied up his boat and accompanied me to the house, where we had a couple of beers before the fire. Upon leaving, he glanced at a large oak tree and informed me that during the winter it was going to fall on the house. It was a solemn pronouncement, and although I disregarded it at the time it stuck in my mind and worried me all winter. When I opened up the house this spring the tree was still standing, to my vast relief, but on my second day on the island I asked him to come over with his chain saw and fell it away from the house. Before starting the saw he suggested that I point out the spot where I wanted the tree to fall, and I asked if he could place it between two small trees at one side of the kitchen. He didn't answer, but in a few minutes the oak tree was lying there snugly, and he was sawing it into cord lengths. "Where did you learn to cut down trees?" I asked him. It was the work of an expert woodsman. "I never learned," he said with no hint of conceit, "I always knew." I suppose this is called the sense we are born with, although I have always been skeptical about this sort of thing.

Quite often my neighbor passes close to this island when he heads out of the cove on his way to tend his traps, and when I wave to him he always gives me an exaggerated, almost comic wave in return. I understand this; a wave has to mean something, and since our relationship is built on banter, he feels more comfortable keeping it on that level. He likes me in the way that I like him, although I don't know exactly when I learned this. Perhaps, I always knew.

Free Spirit

I don't know if we fear to face the news because it is so appalling or so trivial. At a psychological association meeting in Atlantic City a paper was read on the subject, "Do Frogs Prefer Blue?" and at a Playboy Club on the West Coast orders were said to have gone out that no guests could be served well-done steaks. Frogs *do* prefer blue, it develops, and some people prefer cooked meat, but we live in an age of fashion and we must adjust; the frog to green, man to rare steaks. People of an earlier period, I suspect, took a more sensible view of man's basic rights and were less inclined to see them corrode away. I can't imagine a Bunny telling Thoreau that his steak must either be rare or else he would have to have the sweetbreads. Thoreau was more than willing to meet issues of this kind, and I'm sorry he isn't around any longer.

But not all of the news was gloomy. A letter from Mrs. Ruth Heiser, of Cundy's Harbor, asked our help in getting a statue of a Maine lobsterman erected on Maine Avenue in Washington. This would be the first statue in Washington to be dedicated to a state or an occupation, despite the fact that monuments in that city are as prolific as spruce trees in a Maine wilderness. As any school kid who has made the spring pilgrimage to Washington knows, the most common statue around the capital depicts a patriot doing what he seems to do best, which is talking. The lobsterman statue, if it finally finds its place in the thicket of Washington statuary, would be unique in that it would reflect an occupation of the hands. Maybe Washington isn't ready for any such freakish concept; a departure so bold may be unsettling.

Mrs. Heiser sought me out because, as she put it, "I understand you are a writer." This expression of faith in someone engaged in the flimsy business of writing was as poignant as I am afraid it was groundless. A writer lives in an airy and illusory world; he likes to think his contributions are substantial without much believing it. Heartened by Mrs. Heiser's confidence, I talked to her on the telephone and promised to do what I could to help her project provided it did not mean that the statue of *The Maine Lobsterman* would be removed from the tip of Bailey Island and sent off to exile in Washington. I visit that statue during the summer months almost weekly, while my out-of-town guests are wandering through the gift shop or taking photographs on the rocks, and I've not only become immensely fond of it but I notice that my neighbors here in Maine also seem to have a high regard for it. One Sunday afternoon last August I saw an old man studying the statue with stoical reserve, and I recognized almost instantly that he, too, was a lobsterman; there was an ingrained understanding between the two. I glanced at the old man's face when he at last turned away, and the spectacle was exhilarating to the spirit. He had looked into a mirror and he had not felt cheapened by what he saw. This struck me as the soundest of all art criticism.

Mrs. Heiser moved to set my fears to rest. The statue that would go to Washington, she said, was one of three bronze castings made of Victor Kahill's original plaster sculpture that was exhibited at the 1939 New York World's Fair. But it is neither the one at Bailey Island, nor the one standing in Canal Plaza in Portland. The Department of the Interior, she said, had selected a site for the statue between Maine Avenue and the Potomac River, necessary authorizations had been secured from the U.S. Congress, and everything seemed to point to a dedication of the statue in the spring of 1982. A little more money was needed, Mrs. Heiser added cautiously, since the fiscal climate prevailing in Washington at this time dampened any hopes of getting public funds to transport the lobsterman to the capital and getting him properly set up on the banks of the Potomac.

The Maine Lobsterman will not change the course of history in Washington, but it may serve as a reminder of our belief in the individual, because if there ever was an occupation that thrived on the free principle of life, it is lobstering. It may be inaccurate to say that lobstermen love freedom — in its fullest sense — more than farmers or merchants or industrial workers, but it is my own conviction that they do. They are alone on the surface of the sea, in foul weather and fair, and they seem to consider this the ultimate in prizes. The occupation itself speaks of the free spirit of man.

Nothing is perfect, though, and I must point out that already the statue of *The Maine Lobsterman* is a little out of date. The statue shows the lobsterman pegging the claw of the lobster, a job that in recent years has given way to banding. This is not a profoundly disturbing flaw, if indeed it is a flaw at all. It is, rather, the empty oratory of the other statues in Washington that is embarrassing because the spoken words don't seem to change much over the years or even the centuries. I'm glad that *The Maine Lobsterman* will have a spot beside the river and away from the halls of Congress. When the warm breeze of springtime blows along the Potomac, I believe a lot of pilgrims will come upon the Maine statue with surprise and delight, a renewed testimonial to the old truth that accomplishment is always more satisfying than promise.

Growth Industry

An item that I imagine was of minor interest to the reading public caught my eye in the newspaper the other day, and while other readers may have passed lightly over it, there was something there that struck me as a little foreboding. The item said that the number of lawyers in Maine was growing by at least a hundred each year, and it implied that this was perhaps the state's leading growth industry. Knowing lawyers, I have a hunch that the growth industry will not be lawyers but litigation; an idle lawyer yearns for the courtroom like a landlocked sailor yearns for the sea.

There was a time, not too long ago, when neighbors settled their differences over a backyard fence, but it's now nip-and-tuck for a law-abiding man to keep out of court. Litigation, the dispassionate element in our society, sweeps us into the vortex of legal proceedings whether we wish to be involved or not. According to the news report, the new lawyers now descending upon the state are drawn not by the sweet odor of prospective litigation but by the lifestyle offered by

Maine: its coast, its woods, its clean air. Maybe so, but in the lawyer's world it's litigation that makes the wheels spin, and to enjoy Maine's coast and clean air these lawyers are going to have to find some disagreements that need settling. An ominous modification is foreseen here for the application of Parkinson's Law, which holds that the work load automatically expands to accommodate the work force.

Still, it's not all bad. Sharper competition and a wider selection of legal services should eventually work to the advantage of those going to court by lowering prices on routine work. I don't know if this has happened yet because I look upon courts with the same uneasiness that an alligator would display in a handbag factory, and I keep as far away from the courthouse as possible. I think few people ever win anything in court; it is more a question of who loses least. Anyway, it stands to reason that with a lot of lawyers around, especially young ones who are feeling the first pangs of hunger, fees should drop. That should be a touch of good news for any of my neighbors who may discover themselves entangled in the web of the law.

A few days ago in Portland I walked past some lawyers' offices and was reassured by the appearance of normality and peace which seemed to prevail. The weather was fine and unseasonably moderate, the traffic slight, and the pedestrians moved indolently as though they were glad to be outside in the sunlight. A squirrel started across the street, then thought better of it and went back to the park, where it rocked on its haunches and gazed at me appraisingly; I may or may not have some peanuts hidden away in my pockets. From one of the buildings an elderly man who was unmistakably an attorney appeared. He was a Dickensian type, complete with watch chain and dandruff, and I was sure that there hung about him the odor of old lawbooks. For a second our eyes met and my anxiety returned; was he thinking of me in terms of *State of Maine v. Stinnett*? But he buttoned his overcoat and moved on down the street, and I shook off my apprehension. It occurred to me suddenly that another element in my data mix or genetic blueprint, as the high-tech people like to put it, is a fear of bankers, who I feel are constantly watching me for signs of profligacy. Only a few days ago I hurried from my Brunswick bank when one of the male tellers glanced at me disapprovingly, his forehead wrinkled. Was he asking himself, "What is Popular Account 5462-4036 doing with that new sports jacket when his balance is so slight?" A sensitive man feels these things.

California, of course, is the state where one retains a lawyer even before a family doctor is selected or a school is picked out for the children. Suits and counter-suits are filed there as casually as one subscribes to a magazine. Only a few days ago I received a letter from a friend who is visiting in Beverly Hills and who had just had the opportunity of tasting the full flavor of California life. I quote from the letter: "Yesterday I stopped for a red light behind another car. I was driving an automatic transmission, and I'm used to a straight stick so I keep forgetting these cars have a tendency to inch forward if you don't keep your foot on the brake. My car inched into the car ahead. A man and his wife poured out of the car, and the woman said, 'You broke my fingernail and dislocated my neck.' I laughed at the joke, saw there were no scratches on the bumper, and started to get back into my car. The man was taking down my license number and demanding my papers. 'Whiplash,' he said. 'Are you kidding?' I asked. 'Nothing's happened.' I pulled over to the curb to let the traffic pass, and when I got back the man was asking his wife to go to the drugstore on the corner and call an ambulance. I said, 'I think you're both insane,' and got in my car and drove away."

Well, California is a long way from Maine both in distance and in attitudes, and I don't think that the lawyers now streaming into Maine are going to cause the winch of litigation to be given another turn. After all, lawyers aren't the first occupational group that has been attracted to Maine; doctors, teachers, architects, and — God forgive me — writers have come here because it is an uncrowded and unspoiled state. I know about the latter group because twelve years ago I was one of them. And the more I think about writers coming to Maine, the less menacing the lawyers become.

Harmony

A few days ago, I encountered an elderly lady standing beside a car on the Maine Turnpike, and since it was raining hard and the lady's car was obviously disabled, I pulled over and asked if she needed help. She explained that she had a flat tire but that a mechanic was already on the way, and her problem was solved. "I think I should tell you," she added, "that you are the fourth person to stop and offer help. I'm from Long Island, and I don't think this would happen there. Not four people."

Not one, if I know New York. The crash of colliding steel and the shattering of glass will bring witnesses to the windows in every neighborhood in New York, but cries for help routinely fall on deaf ears. If it takes a catastrophe or a disaster to arouse New Yorkers from their isolation, it may be because they feel that at the moment of the accident there is someone out there who is having a somewhat rougher time of it than they are. And they want to make sure of it.

I was walking along Park Avenue one bright autumn day recently when, in the block ahead, I saw an enormous crowd of people spilling into the street. In the center of the throng was an ambulance. As I passed, I saw a white-coated attendant pull a spectator away from the door so he could close it. The spectator wore a look of hurt betrayal, as though, holding the best seat in the house, he had suddenly been evicted for no just cause. One night in New York, I heard a nightclub comic conclude his act by paying a quaint tribute to his audience. "You've been such a good audience," he said, "that we're going to throw open the doors and let you see a street accident." It was a joke — but was it? The more I brood about this, the less certain I am that it is funny.

My own romance with New York, never a very tender thing even in that first wondrous moment of discovery, long ago foundered, and some time ago we decided to go our separate ways. New York stayed where it was, and I came to Maine, and neither of us — so far as I can tell — has regretted the separation.

I often wish I could see New York the way her admirers do, and the way the poets do, and the way strangers do who come there from other cities and other countries, but I cannot. Right now a very fashionable term among New Yorkers is the "happening," which describes almost any event that cannot be precisely or instantly categorized. I have a terrible suspicion that if executions were made public again, they would be the damndest happenings to hit New York. Broadway and the theater district would have to close up.

I must now take you across the country to Seattle, where, as in Portland, Maine, the city is currently locked in discord over what has come to be known as adult entertainment. Scientists were brought in to study the Seattle situation after temperance forces there contended that topless waitresses and dancers increased the sale of drinks in the bars where they worked. This theory was promptly shot down in flames by the scientists, who — after perhaps tasting the full extravagance of the situation — found that when topless girls were dancing, drink consumption fell off markedly. I could have told them that without leaving my island.

My experience with this type of entertainment occurred last winter when in Boston I visited a Combat Zone spot that had achieved considerable local notoriety as a result of a police raid. The dancers — there were two of them — rather than looking complaisant were both visibly nervous. One, in fact, couldn't have been more uneasy

133

if she had been a stakeout for a bank robbery. I left midway through my first drink (a fact that may be of interest to the Seattle scientific task force) and when I arose from my table I was given a look of dark reproach by the waiter, who more than anything resembled a seal that had dropped its fish. I feel there is a message in this for the embattled people of both Portland and Seattle, and like all great truths it is fairly simple. The whole matter of adult entertainment will be decided not on the basis of morality, but on the element of boredom.

There's one more subject that must be considered while I have hold of your lapel, and that is the deplorable state of modern architecture. If an author writes a poor book, it ends up on the remainder table of a bookstore, and the sensibilities of the public are not offended. And a disastrous painting inevitably finds its destiny in an attic somewhere. But a forty-nine-story office building, or a motel, or a high-rise apartment has a permanence that cannot be ignored. It sits there as a public outrage year after year, a massive cinder in the eye of the beholder. Maine has its share of these monstrous buildings, and the most positive thing I can say about them is that the construction is often of such quality that they won't last long. Even that thought holds little consolation.

But this morning on Route 24, between Brunswick and Harpswell Neck, I came over the brow of a hill and saw a small farmhouse that was so beautiful that I stopped the car to stare. Like a snowflake or one of those gentle waves that lap the timbers of a wharf, it was perfect. It fit the landscape, which was composed of rolling meadows with a quick glimpse of the sea from a hilltop, and it possessed that mysterious thing which the Greeks called harmony. It was made to be lived in and not to win some design award, and its livability shone through. I started the car and drove away, my faith renewed. If we can still build something as beautiful as that simple farmhouse, the future isn't frightening.

A Good, Reliable Villain

It is a fine day today, with perhaps just a little bit too much breeze coming up the cove, but so far as I am concerned any breeze at all is too much. I am not doing justice to wind, as one of nature's priceless elements, because frankly I hate the very guts of wind, but I know there are those who glory in what a sailboat crew would call a spanking breeze. Any man who rows around very much in a fairly clumsy skiff knows that a breeze is his enemy, and one that becomes totally

Clausewitzian the moment he arrives at a landing float or a dock. It is then that the breeze does its greatest mischief, forcing the rowboat into all kinds of entanglements with other boats, banging the oarlocks against the dock, rolling and pitching the skiff until it is almost impossible to stand or to secure a line, and causing it to take in water over the side so that, as a parting gesture of pure spite, one goes ashore with both feet soaked to the ankles. No, a little wind goes a hell of a long way with me, although I am well aware of the fact that this statement places me on a collision course with the sailboat set. As long as I've gone this far, I'll go a little further. I don't even like that clanking of halyards against the mast that most sailors consider a rhapsody. To me it's as annoying as a persistent water drip, and maybe worse. It's louder.

I have noticed with dismay a growing tendency in this country to avoid criticism of anything, even wind, because of the likelihood of offending this group or that one, and I think this is an unhealthy attitude. Progress has always depended upon criticism. What this country needs right now to clear the air is a good, reliable villain. By this I mean a scoundrel who accepts his villainy as part of his character and whom we can count on not to turn soft in the final reels. The trouble now is that he couldn't belong to any identifiable minority group lest a scream of outrage go up that the entire group had been described in something other than the noblest of terms. Even Darth Vader, remember, is dead and is carrying on villainous work only by means of a life support system.

I recall, quite a number of years ago, when Hollywood issued a remake of *The Three Musketeers* in which the villain, the Duc de Richelieu, was shown in civilian clothes because the Catholics objected to his being depicted as a Cardinal — a fact that was pretty generally known throughout the sixth grade. The Jews then blocked, at least temporarily, the showing in this country of *Oliver Twist*, a British film, because the villainous Fagin was identified as a Jew. The blacks, Mexicans, and Chinese quickly sought and achieved protection from misrepresentation, and as the field narrowed, the quality of villainy declined. The next loss was almost incalculable: the redskins went on the warpath. "Distortion of Indian life and character in films and other media has fed the barriers of misunderstanding and distrust," the Indians formally notified the film industry, which was an Indian way of saying they were fed up with the-only-good-Indian-is-a-dead-Indian routine, and they had fired on their last wagon train.

And so it goes with the farmers, OPEC, the pedestrians, the Protestants, the vegetarians, and the people who own goldfish. They are all sensitive. Shortly before he died, Al Capp, the comic strip artist, said, "I've got to the point where I refuse in my strips to make a vicious character a solvent man." Presumably the solvent minority would holler "foul." Well, at a time like this, the movie industry, the television studios, the novelists, and the comic strip artists can be grateful for a man like me. I am available for villainous engagements and attitudes, and I draw the line nowhere. I would scalp the Wells Fargo stagecoach driver as cheerfully as I would stampede the herd on the outskirts of Abilene or remove the strategic pin from the engine of the training cruise submarine. Usually I would try to throw in something extra: when I shoot the sheriff, I would steal his badge.

The thing that disturbs me about the sweeping pretense that all minorities are noble and flawless is the dishonesty and hypocrisy inherent in the contention. No group is untouched by villainy; in our hearts we realize and accept that truth. It is only in our public posture that we must pretend.

The most attractive thing about my offer to be a villain is my lack of minority affiliation. I belong only to the human race, a rather loose organization which, considering the state of affairs which it has brought about throughout the world, can hardly afford to claim libelous misrepresentation.

Moreover, as I said before, I hate a stiff breeze. That's for openers.

8

The Great Predator

A Friend Indeed

I've always held to the belief that nature's gifts are never frivolously bestowed, and since a sperm whale's brain is six times larger than that of the human being and since only a small part of it is used for survival, the rest is undoubtedly engaged in thought-forms which exceed anything mankind has yet dreamed of. The brain of the moose, on the other hand, is not a lavish endowment, but even so I suspect the moose is smart enough to see the absurdity in the contention of Maine's Department of Inland Fisheries and Wildlife that the best way to help the animal survive in Maine is to shoot it.

I recall from my youth a cartoon strip character called "Fearless Fosdick," a cretinous detective. In one episode, Fosdick was attempting to run down a shipment of poisoned beans. Looking through a first-floor window, Fosdick saw a citizen raising a forkful of beans to his lips, whereupon he whipped out his service revolver and shot the man dead. "Thank God," Fosdick breathed, "I got him in the nick of time." There's something about this wooly thinking that characterizes the Department of Inland Fisheries and Wildlife's attitude toward moose hunting. They seem to be telling us that there's nothing quite so healthy as a dead moose.

In 1982 over 60,000 "sportsmen" applied for the 1,000 moose-hunting permits which the Department of Inland Fisheries and Wildlife decided to issue. I have placed quotation marks around the word *sportsmen* to denote questionability of the term, if not outright derision. The shooting of an animal as big as a horse with the powerful and highly refined weapons now produced by sophisticated arms manufacturers may qualify as sport, but I doubt it. Hunting moose with a hand-launched rocket grenade would be hardly more ridiculous. But these 60,000 prospective hunters, I assume, agree with the department's

The Great Predator

philosophy that the best way to make the State of Maine secure for moose is to slaughter them, and since even the most optimistic estimate of the state's moose population is 20,000, these hunters could have done wonders for the cause of moose in Maine. This has always been the attitude of those who consider animal life worthless. The scientists in whose laboratories dogs are starved for sixty-five days and living rats' brains are sucked out through tubes claim that their research is for the common good, and the Japanese and Norwegian whalers have very well-rehearsed reasons why whaling is beneficial to all concerned, including the whales. In the context of the sperm whale's remarkable brain and its incredible capability, the blubber boilers, oil separators, bone saws, and assorted equipment of the whaling ship seem obscene.

There was a time when nature imposed a predator-prey ratio on wildlife, and it worked, as nature always does, until interfered with by the most awesome predator of all time — man. It was this predator, eager to get into the woods and start shooting, who conceived of the "over-density" theory that promptly repealed prevailing natural laws. The vast wilderness areas of Maine, the hunters argue, cannot support 20,000 moose and the kind thing to do is to blow the brains out of as many as possible with high-powered rifles. Moreover, 60,000 friends of the moose volunteered last year to put aside their Saturday television habits and go out into the country to perform this humane public service.

The Department of Inland Fisheries and Wildlife's pronouncements on the matter of moose hunting seem to suggest that the department is drifting more and more into the world of Fearless Fosdick. The moose killed by the hunters, the department says, are subjected to tests which help determine the health and general condition of the animals. I would say, even from a distance, that the health and general condition of these moose are very bad — couldn't be worse, in fact. Moreover, the department has been quoted as saying that hunting will enable it to "detect any threats" to moose, although it seems to have overlooked the most real and ominous threat of all — the hunter.

Over two-thirds of the moose killed in the two hunts that have been authorized by the department to date have been adult bulls, the department has said, which "suggests" that the breeding population feels little impact from the hunting season. This baffling statement also seems to suggest that an adult bull is of minor if any importance in the moose-breeding setup, a presumption which I believe is not supported by the facts. The erotomania of a bull moose in rut is rumored to be a spectacular thing indeed, and to say that it plays no important part in moose family planning is like saying the sun plays no part in plant growth. Moose mating is no bucolic and romantic poem.

In New York State the moose is believed threatened with extinction and has been placed on the state's endangered species list, although the federally financed Endangered Species Unit is itself on the endangered list as a result of Reagan Administration frugality. The resurgence of moose in Maine, after they were nearly all killed off by hunters, seems to be such an exhilarating thing that it is provoking a response bordering on the hallucinative. The Natural Resources Council of Maine, whose grip on reality is fairly steady, admits there are issues involved here "which transcend data" and has asked its members to disregard symbolism and emotionalism and give it guidance. Well, it won't get guidance less emotional than this. Right, NRC?

Maine Too?

Man has built an extraordinarily queer world that gives an observer not the slightest notion of what he, the builder, is like. On one hand, he labors in an operating room for tedious hours substituting a good heart for a failing one, while on the other hand he engages in acts of meanness and cruelty from which a predatory animal would turn away in disgust. When an individual or a group of individuals engages in calculated acts of cruelty, we can seek some protection for our consciences by distancing ourselves as far as possible from the offense, but what detachment is possible when one's state government is committing the act? Like all ethical problems, it leads back ultimately, of course, to man himself.

I have just read a newspaper report of Maine's selection of fourteen trappers to employ leg-hold traps in catching coyotes suspected of killing sheep. "When the coyote goes to take the bait," the article says, "it will step on a buried trap, setting off a spring that releases steel jaws that snap around a coyote's leg." What happens then? Well, the newspapers don't care to deal with matters too unpleasant, so the reporter backs away at that point, leaving living flesh in the grip of steel. The coyote, however, cannot back away, much as it tries; it remains there, in agony, throughout the day and night until the trapper eventually comes to put a bullet through its head and end its pain.

A book published recently quoted the wife of the owner of Alexander's Department Stores, with a rather extraordinary answer for those questioning the morality of slaughtering animals to provide pelts for fur coats. "We aren't killing," she is quoted as saying, "any animals that aren't *supposed* to be killed." I imagine Maine holds pretty much to the same viewpoint where coyotes are concerned, so I will limit my comment to the method which the state's Department of Inland Fisheries and Wildlife employs in bringing about the — excuse the expression — "final solution" of the coyote problem.

Some states — Massachusetts, Florida, and Hawaii are among them — have banned leg-hold traps by law, since the best that a trapped animal can hope for is to chew off an imprisoned leg, an option often taken. Lacking the ability or the courage to do this, an animal can remain in a trap for days or until it dies of exhaustion, starvation, cold, or the attacks of other animals. It is true that laws exist requiring trappers to "visit" their traps each twenty-four-hour period, but only sixteen states have such laws, and Nevada requires a trapper to visit his lines only once a week. The other states have no laws at all requiring regular visits to traps, and, indeed, any law regulating the protection of wildlife is beset with enforcement problems. Since animals lack the means to report violations, the compliance record left to the honor system is quite often pitiful.

I am uneasy that Maine feels it cannot tolerate a few coyotes that have wandered in from the west, but I am even more embarrassed by the means it is taking to rid the state of the visitors. I think any state is making a distressing error of judgment when it relies upon a barbaric and inhuman means of accomplishing its purpose, regardless of the need or the nobility of the objective. Thomas Baily Aldrich once wrote that "civilization is the lamb's skin in which barbarism masquerades," and I can't help but feel there is some local application in this comment. The coyote has wandered across the face of the United States for years without finding a welcome, and it may well be that its society is distressing and that unusually severe steps have to be taken to get the idea across that Maine is not the ideal spot in which to settle. But a leg-hold trap is not the answer. In the first place, aside from the cruelty of the device, a leg-hold trap is not selective — it catches anything that is hapless enough to step on it, including dogs, cats, and other mammals. For several days I have been trying to erase from my mind a photograph, which I saw recently in a newspaper, of a small raccoon that had lost both of its front paws in a leg-hold trap. It had been brought to an animal shelter and was trying to eat something from a saucer, its two stumps barely supporting its forward weight. Trappers refer to unwanted animals caught in traps as "trash," and they estimate that seven of every ten animals trapped fall into that category.

Clearly, Maine wants no coyotes, but what is occupying the

thoughts of some of its citizens is the suspicion that the state is going about the task in a way that may make it no better than the coyote. In my opinion, which is not a humble one, the state should aim a little higher than that. I possess no desire to prevent either the State of Maine or the coyote from fulfilling their separate destinies, but I plead — and the coyotes and assorted "trash" agree with me — that it be done without the assistance of the leg-hold trap.

9

Invited and Uninvited Guests

The Chipmunk and I

I never really knew if he was a chipmunk or a very small squirrel, but for some reason he fixed himself in my mind as a chipmunk and I always thought of him as that. He was quite small, extremely officious and pompous, and assumed, quite early in our relationship, that my Maine house was his and that I, not he, was the intruder. But for a couple of summers a mutual forbearance prevailed. As long as I kept a supply of Oreo cookies on the kitchen counter he managed to tolerate me, and as long as he didn't do too much damage to the place I convinced myself that he was an appealing little chap and rather companionable to have around. Ultimately it was the Oreos and doughnuts — he also had a fondness for doughnuts — that proved his undoing; he got fat, clumsy, and mischievous.

His mind revolved constantly around sweet pastries, and where chocolate was concerned his self-control vanished entirely. He knocked glasses off the shelves in the middle of the night, he gnawed into anything that wasn't lead-lined, he went into the oven of the stove — don't ask me how — after a piece of apple cobbler, and he became so obese that he could no longer jump from the wing chair to the stone fireplace chimney. The last time he tried, he missed by at least a foot and fell on the fireplace screen, as sorry a chipmunk spectacle as I've ever witnessed. Holding on to the screen, he glared at me malevolently; obviously I had moved the chair back and deliberately caused him to miscalculate the trajectory. It was what he deserved for trusting a human in the first place.

But, as I said, in the early days of our relationship, things went smoothly enough. When I walked around the island he followed me, chattering constantly or fussing and fuming over things that were not to his liking and for which he obviously blamed me. He could not abide rain — it drove him instantly into the house — and I think he held me responsible for this too. In fact, his list of grievances against me was impressively long, and I think he would have banished me from the island had it not been for the fact that I was, after all, his Oreo connection.

Once, when I had been away for a week, I returned with a bagful of groceries, which I placed on the doorstep while I went to the water tank to see if rain had raised the level during my absence. When I returned to the door I heard a rattling in the bag, and two mischievous eyes glared out at me. Satisfied that there were Oreos in the bag, he jumped out, and when I opened the door he preceded me into the house. For a fleeting second, I entertained doubts as to who was master of the house, and I half expected him to bark an order to me as he led the way into the kitchen.

It was only when he started gnawing holes in the walls and floors that I finally came to the conclusion that deportation to an uninhabited island was the only solution. Even when I knew what had to be done I was slow in coming to a decision; I had grown used to the chipmunk and in my heart I knew I would miss him. Without knowing it, he became very helpful in finally forcing the issue. One day I awoke and there were two large holes, side by side, in the wall of my bedroom. He had gnawed one to gain entrance and the other to leave by, an extravagance clearly beyond my limit of tolerance. The next night he ate a hole the size of a small apple in the floor of the kitchen. He had thrown caution to the wind; now I could hear him gnawing away during the night, sometimes letting himself into the kitchen cabinet, sometimes going through a wall to get from one room to another. When I would interrupt him at his work, he would scamper away, hurling all manner of threats and curses at me, only to be back on the job within minutes after I turned my back.

I started work on the trap early one Sunday morning. I made a long, narrow box, with a stick through the top that was delicately balance on a notch, and connected to the top of a hanging door by string. The slightest nudging of the stick from inside would cause the door to drop. I tested it three times before baiting it with a doughnut and placing it under a tree behind the house. I read a book for half an hour and then wandered back to see what had happened. The chipmunk had somehow retrieved the doughnut, and was sitting on top of the trap holding the last of it in his two front paws. I carried the box into the kitchen where I set it on the counter and baited it with an Oreo. I had hardly reached the front porch when I heard a dull thud, and I hurried back to the kitchen. He was trapped, and in his rage he was making a fearsome noise. I grabbed the trap and raced to the dock.

It took ten minutes to get to Cloud Island, and all the way the chipmunk reviled me from inside the trap. I cut the motor, pulled the boat up on the rocks, and opened the trap. The chipmunk leaped out, glared at me a moment, and disappeared into the underbrush. Back at my own island, I worked a bit, napped, and tried to read. But it was quiet, unnaturally quiet. There was no rustling in the leaves, no gnawing, no glasses falling from the shelves. I slept fitfully that night and awoke early. I went out on the sundeck and gazed in the early morning light toward Cloud Island. I don't know what I expected to see, but it appeared the same. Later that morning I went over to the mainland and drove to the shopping center, where I bought three pounds of Oreos. I took them to Cloud Island and spread them out on the rocks near where I had released the chipmunk. The least I could do, I reasoned, was to ease the transition to a new way of life. I never saw him again, but when I went over the next day with a dozen doughnuts, the Oreos were gone.

Entertaining

Late last month, on a bright October day, I closed my island home for the season. I hauled the float, stored the boats, and shuttered the house for winter. It was late afternoon by the time I left the island, and I decided to break the homeward journey at a motel, where I ventured to ease my reentry to mainland life by catching the news on television. I flicked the switch, but instead of Walter Cronkite, I found a lady giving advice on how to be a good host or hostess. My summer and autumn had been busy with guests, and I sat back to see if there was something to be learned about the care and feeding of visitors. It didn't take me long to decide that I wouldn't much care to visit this TV lady. She didn't seem to entertain the kind of guests that I have in Maine.

This lady was from somewhere in Long Island, and she said she expected her guests to bring their own Porthault sheets with them, as well as some kind of board that goes under the mattress if they wish a firm foundation. To my knowledge, there has never been a Porthault sheet on my island, and I have a much simpler solution to the back problem. There are five bedrooms, with beds of varying ages and resiliency; let them bounce around on a few of them until one strikes their fancy. It's no more complicated than that.

But what really made me lay my book aside and pay attention

to the television screen was when the lady explained the necessity of planning in advance some party games — she especially mentioned a costume party — and "some gay trips to the village for fun and diversion." This mention of a costume party struck a responsive note in me, since my daughter had only recently been entertaining some of her friends from San Francisco on the island, and, California being what it is, the clothes they normally wore at cocktail time were *all* costumes, in my opinion. One chap was partial to floor-length caftans, while another wore some plaid trousers so vivid that I wouldn't have touched them with tongs. If I had taken this crowd into the village for fun and diversion, I would never have gotten them back to the island. Cundy's Harbor isn't ready for this sort of thing.

The people who come to coastal Maine to visit usually aren't looking for discotheques and Porthault sheets, I'm pleased to report, but are seeking something totally different. I've found they like to sit on the rocks and stare at the sea, or row around the cove examining the driftwood left by the high tide, or gaze at the lobster boats through binoculars. This latter attraction seems to possess endless fascination; the guest invariably grunts with dismay when a short is thrown back into the water. One night last summer, a gentleman in his late eighties, the author of one of America's greatest folk dramas, was visiting me, and late in the evening he picked up his brandy glass and said he was going to step out on the sundeck for a breath of fresh air before retiring. When he had been gone for thirty minutes or so, I went outside to satisfy myself that he was all right, and I found him standing at the railing gazing silently at the stars. I inched back into the house, not wishing to disturb his reverie. A host or hostess doesn't have to provide funny hats when a show like that is being performed in the sky.

I've discovered a strange characteristic common to all people who visit in Maine. Without exception, they are captivated by scallop shells. I don't believe I've ever had a guest that didn't return to the house from a foraging session at the shoreline without a handful of scallop shells. The shells are usually washed in the kitchen sink and laid out carefully to dry in the sun. They are invariably left there, and after the guest departs I frisbee them back into the water. Just the other morning I recognized an old friend; it was the third time this year that I had tossed it back.

It's my opinion that, contrary to what the lady on television said, the best thing one can do with a guest is to leave him or her alone. Leave a stack of new books in sight, put out the ice bucket and a few bottles, see that a few chairs are on the shady side of the sundeck, and tell the guest you'll see him later. I think you'll find this a more contented guest than one taken to the village for fun and diversion. The scope of a host's talents are measured by the extent to which he provides the very things that a guest had hopefully in mind when the invitation was presented. I have run a few private tests of my own, and I have yet to find a guest who gives a damn about Porthault sheets and costume parties.

I don't mind a guest possessing peculiarities, provided they don't get out of hand. A recent guest, a former nightclub singer, walked around all weekend holding a glass of water in her hand, from which she occasionally sipped. It was odd, but not upsetting. I reasoned it was a throwback to her nightclub days when everybody had a glass in hand. And being a bachelor, I am plagued by lady guests who want to rearrange the furniture in my living room; the assumption being that any man living alone doesn't know the first thing about home decoration. I've gotten used to this, too. On Sunday afternoons, as soon as I get back from delivering them to the Portland airport, I move everything back to its former location. I regard it as nothing more than a minor part of the pageantry of entertaining guests.

"Dear Mrs. Irving..."

A gull's life — a Maine gull's anyway — is an endless cycle of rain, fog, wind, snow, and calm, with a great deal more of the first four than the last. Coastal people don't think highly of gulls, I have noticed, and I have often wondered why the gull has never managed to build itself any political power in the lobstering and fishing communities of Maine. They wheel overhead in the most magnificent flight patterns of any airborne creature alive (nowhere else does there exist such profound knowledge of the aerodynamics of flight), or they float watchfully in calm waters offshore, or they can sun themselves on rock ledges, but coastal people ignore them as though they don't exist. They will fight raucously among themselves when a fisherman is tossing scraps overboard, but generally speaking a gull is a dignified bird that accepts the day's offerings with reasonably good cheer, and eats enough mosquitoes in the course of a summer to give it what it feels should be a better standing in human society than it now possesses.

My interest in gulls is due, in large part, to the arrival in waters adjacent to my island several years ago of a gull of such high moral character, such steadfastness, and such dependability that through her I have come to know the real meaning of rectitude and nobility. She arrived on a nasty, raw day in spring and took up residence on a sparsely thicketed headland, together with her mate, a shiftless, womanizing gull of such unscrupulous character as to make her saintliness all the more outstanding. Even when there was a chop in the sea, I saw her out there bobbing on top of the waves, keeping an eye out for whatever might be floating on the surface that she could bring in for an evening meal. Her mate, more often than not, was at the Harpswell dump in the company of younger female gulls, and never to my knowledge did he bring anything home but discord. That he came home at all was remarkable, and toward the end of the summer he indeed stopped.

I have never taken any solid pleasure in reading about animals with human names, always feeling myself in the presence of a cuteness that tended to restrict my breathing, but I am compelled to record that the pair of gulls, over a period of time, became known as Mr. and Mrs. Irving. I am not certain how the names came about, nor is it particularly important; what I recall is that the pair, and most notably the female, worked their way into the island household and almost reached the point where they were consulted about the daily menus and shopping lists. Actually, this wasn't as far from the truth as it may appear because after dinner I often rowed over to the headland and left stale bread and table scraps on the rocks where — forgive me — Mrs. Irving could find them. The next morning I would find the rocks neat and clean, no lettuce draped over the juniper plants, no orange peels floating in the water. Mrs. Irving was an exacting housekeeper.

Most gulls' efforts to integrate into the social life of the neighborhood meet with constant and ruthless rebuffs. Young boys are forever shooting at them with rifles, boat owners place wind-driven devices on the decks of their crafts to frighten them off, and dogs chase them if they alight ashore. I don't know how the male gull of my pair handled this oppression, but the female felt no need for any sort of affirmative action program and, indeed, gave no hint that she was discouraged or grieved at this ancient hostility, holding firmly to her belief in the ultimate triumph of the gull over discrimination.

One day last summer a postcard arrived from a recent guest addressed to Mrs. Irving, and while this was a little too fey for my tastes and I was ready to drop it into the wastebasket, my young grandson had a dissenting opinion. This, in his view, was a clear case of interference with the mails; the card had been left in our mailbox and we had the inescapable obligation of seeing that it was properly delivered to the addressee. Since an ethical question had been raised, I abandoned my position and agreed to row the boy and the card over to the headland. The trip took perhaps ten minutes, during which time I was trying to figure out how the boy would handle the matter of delivery, since the gull certainly would not let either of us get close to her. In my mind's eye, I saw him trying to stuff it under her wing, like a process server forcing a summons on an unwilling litigant. But the boy possessed no uncertainty. He placed the card, address side up, on a large rock, and secured it with a smaller one. "That'll hold it," he said, "at least until she reads it."

I wish I could say that was the end of the matter, but it wasn't. The next day, shortly after breakfast, the boy asked me if I had time to row him over to the headland. He didn't say what was on his mind, but he didn't have to; I knew he wanted to check on the postcard. He jumped out of the boat when the bow grated into the sand, and he came back a few minutes later, a strange look on his face. "The card's gone," he said. "The rock's there that weighted it down, but the card's gone." He didn't seem at all mystified by the card's disappearance. He pushed the boat off with one foot, and settled down in the stern seat facing me. "It's the first postcard she ever got," he said, "and I guess she's showing it around."

You don't suppose — of course not. I must be losing my mind.

The Mouse in the Typewriter

If you have read this far, you may as well hang on and learn how to get a mouse out of a typewriter, because that is the subject of today's sermon. Writers need a typewriter just as an astronomer needs a telescope or a farmer needs a tractor, and since so many things will give a writer an excuse for not writing, it is unfortunate indeed when a typewriter gives up, because this furnishes the writer with a legitimate reason for calling it a day. Early this morning I knew something was malfunctioning on the keyboard when the *m* key grew sluggish, only to be joined during the next paragraph by the comma. Writers all have their peculiarities, and mine is an overwhelming affection for commas; I write like commas grow on trees. I can live quite a while with a sluggish *m*, but I want my commas to come promptly when I tap the key. The advantages of the new electric typewriters, I am told, are many, but they are not for me. I am tapping at this moment on an ancient Remington-Rand, which requires stamina as well as nimbleness, but it possesses a stubborn righteousness and strikes me as an honest machine in every sense of the word. When my commas began backing up on me, I knew something was wrong, and I lifted the plate beneath the space bar to have a casual glimpse of the innards of the machine, much as one would lift the hood of a Model T to see if the fan belt were broken or the spark plugs were blackened. I had never before seen what I saw now.

A good-sized mouse had built a comfortable nest under the typewriter, and the noise of my typing had driven him up into the machine. His tail had somehow come to rest in that tiny groove where the *m* and comma keys drop, and I could tell by a glance at his face that he was badly frightened and wanted very much to return the typewriter to me and look elsewhere for shelter. I lifted the typewriter, cushion and all, and carried it out to the small porch of my study, where I set it down very slowly and carefully on the porch. I tilted the machine over on its side and walked down to a big rock beside the sea, where I sat for a while to give the mouse time to get himself and his possessions moved out.

Ten minutes later he was still there. But it was clear now that he was stuck and unable to move. He had wedged himself tightly against the back plate, and some protuberance from the machinery was pressing into his side. Terror had now replaced simple fear in his eyes, and his breath was coming rapidly. Mice, I had often heard, could flatten themselves almost to a ribbon when they needed to slip through a small space, so I left the scene again to ease his panic and to give him another chance to free himself. But when I returned he was still in the typewriter and the conclusion was clear: if he was going to get out, he would have to be freed by someone. He couldn't do it himself.

Being without a typewriter is a serious matter for a writer, as I have said, and while it languished I found myself languishing. I faced a magazine deadline, which was serious, but the mouse faced an even more serious deadline; he couldn't live too much longer with that piece of machinery pushing cruelly into his stomach. I possess no skill at all with tools, but I fetched the tool kit and prepared to disassemble the typewriter. I would do as little as possible, I decided, since I had no confidence whatever in the likelihood that I could ever reassemble it. I tilted the machine up on its back, and began.

There is a bell at the end of my wharf, which I ask visitors to ring when they come to the island, and at this moment the bell sounded. I put down the tools, took a look at the mouse — he seemed to be weakening — and went to the wharf to meet my visitor. It was the son of a neighbor on the mainland, a youth in his early teens, and he had come over on a minor errand. "Have you a minute?" I inquired, and he said that he did. He was a handsome, extremely likable chap, who talked very little. I led him to my study, where the typewriter was lying on its back on the porch. "Look inside the typewriter," I said. The boy hesitated. "A snake?" he asked. I shook my head. "Look," I said. He dropped on his hands and knees and peered into the machine. "Stuck?" he asked. I nodded. His eyes swept the inside of the machine expertly. Without looking up he said, "Hand me the screwdriver." I took the screwdriver from the tool kit and put it in his hand. "Steady the typewriter," he instructed me. He worked swiftly; after loosening a nut at one end of the plate, he moved to the other end, and handed me two nuts to hold. He put down the screwdriver and lifted off the back plate. The mouse shook himself, jumped out of the typewriter, and darted under the porch of the study. The drama drained from the situation like a flash.

The boy asked me for the nuts, screwed the back plate into place, and got up from his knees. "Bet he won't come back there anymore," the boy said, as we walked back to the wharf. When I got back to the study, I placed the typewriter back on the cushion, and lifted them both to the stand. I could have done it, I told myself, but the words swirled around my head without conviction. The boy had saved both the mouse and the typewriter, while I would surely have sacrificed one or the other. But I was pleased with the way the drama had ended. So pleased, in fact, that I ran a sheet of paper into the machine and produced an entire row of commas.

Blue Jay Bigotry

Four years ago I was mugged in New York City's Central Park by a blue jay, so when one appeared on my island recently, I gave it a chilly reception. I realize that this is not the same bird, having winged its way from Manhattan to Maine, but I am capable of conveying guilt by association, and a blue jay, to my way of thinking, is a bird to keep your eye on. The Central Park episode came about early one morning when I was walking my dog in a particularly overgrown area not far from the Seventy-second Street entrance on the West Side. I was bareheaded at the time and I received the full force of the assault on the top of my head. I was stunned and bleeding, but not so stunned that I didn't hear the flutter of wings and catch a glimpse of my assailant circling around the top of the shrubbery, preparing for a second dive. That this jay clung to the Clausewitzian theory of total annihilation was obvious, and I could see at a glance that it had no intention of permitting me time to arm defensively. Tugging at the dog's leash, I retreated quickly; in my personal principles of warfare, I have striven to elevate the character of retreat and to remove it from a position of disfavor.

I was as surprised as the next man to learn of the belligerent nature of a jay, but since the attack I have picked up a little more information on jay behavior. One chap to whom I told the story took the position that I must have wandered into an area adjacent to a nestful of young jays, but, since this came from a man who feels the bird world is overflowing with love and good intentions, I was inclined to dismiss his comment. A full-fledged bird man is like a cat man (or woman) in that he will tolerate nothing that reflects discredit on the object of his admiration and will insist that the creature must be described in only the noblest of terms. I say the hell with that. Blue jays, like anybody else, have to recognize standards of good conduct and simple justice. Whether I had wandered into a poorly defined area of home defense or not, I was still the victim of an attack that for sneakiness and stealth made Pearl Harbor look honorable.

Another fellow with whom I discussed the attack showed no surprise at all. Nodding his head affirmatively as I told the story, he said that a jay had made life miserable for his cat and, in fact, had frequently tried to kill it. The moment the cat appeared outdoors, the jay would divebomb it repeatedly, eventually sending the animal into a severe depression which slid downhill into a full nervous breakdown. The cat got so that, even in the house, it would emerge from under the furniture casting its eyes wildly overhead and scurrying in panic back to cover if anything cast a moving shadow on the floor.

I had been raking leaves on the island when the blue jay appeared, and my hand went instinctively to my head to make certain that my hat was on. The jay's manner was uneasy, and I deduced that it was on a scouting expedition rather than an invasion: a visit to feel me out, more than anything else, with a view to pitching stakes permanently if things looked stable. I am familiar with most of the birds that pause at the island during migration or that come over to settle, since I feel that their reasons for fleeing the mainland are probably the same as mine. Mostly I get robins or grackles, and upon their arrival I always set out some grain or stale bread just to let them know they are not considered intruders. I made no move to get anything for the jay, which struck even me as bigotry, since I was making a sort of racial judgment about the bird rather than seeing it as an individual. What I am facing here is a problem of supremacy; I am suspicious of the jay, and in my distrust of it I want it to leave the island. What I almost said was that I wanted it to go back where it came from, but

I caught myself in time. Intellectually and morally, I'm in an impossible situation.

Clearly, something has to be done, and before people start thinking I'm burning crosses over here to scare off blue jays, let me recount an experience with a hummingbird that showed up unexpectedly one day last summer. I was reading on the sundeck at the time, when I looked up and saw the hummingbird working its way casually through some petunias and geraniums. After hovering a moment in midair, obviously not too pleased with the prevailing sugar level, it sped off toward the southern end of the island. The next day I stopped off in a nursery and bought a five-pound can of hummingbird syrup and a dispenser to hang on the branch of a low shrub. Although I checked the syrup level almost daily, the hummingbird nourished its own resentment and never came back. I'm going into a new summer now with a four-pound inventory of hummingbird syrup which I would like to move, and I am wondering — a little slyly — if it is too implausible to assume that blue jays may have a sweet tooth. I don't know what blue jays have and don't have, but I would venture a guess that after consuming four pounds of syrup, nausea would be one thing they would have, to say nothing of cavities. I know what *I* would have; I would have the island to myself again.

Balanced Alliance

The world looks different from under a boat when one is lying on one's back, scraping the hull. It is a dirty job under any circumstances, and smelly as well, but while most boat owners go to any lengths to avoid it, I get a certain amount of satisfaction from it. There is nothing dynamic about the job, as there is about sawing wood, for instance, and I think few men of scholarly instinct would consider it an acceptable vocation. Yet it bestows strange prizes. For one thing, it shores up a sagging self-regard by reasserting one's mastery over the excesses of the sea, and for another it is the kind of job that doesn't end up in mixed success. You scrape the surface, and the hull is clean; it's difficult to see how one could do a sorry and discreditable job.

The thing that appeals to me about scraping the boat that I have been working on today is the tantalizing thought that perhaps one's psyche could be as easily cleaned — that delusion, deception, prejudice, anxiety, selfishness, and fear can be scraped away, leaving an individual in an orderly and secure state. The thought stayed with me as I labored. This was a splendid delusion, of course, but it was one delusion that

I didn't care to scrape away. There was something like this in a science fiction novel I read some years ago, I now recall. Science fiction is not a normal indulgence of mine, but I read this book because the author was a friend of mine and I knew that sooner or later he would ask me a probing question — writers are tricky — that could be answered only by revealing whether or not I had read his book. In the novel, criminals were psychologically demolished and made over, much as I have scraped away the barnacles and marine growth from the bottom of my boat. All of this came back to me this morning when I was wondering why the gift of serenity and well-being could not be had by a thorough scraping of the badly entangled ganglia that create and transmit human emotions. As I dragged the putty knife along the fouled hull, I imagined that I was scraping away those free-floating fears that have attached themselves to me over the years — this tangle of shells now being dislodged is absurd notions of right and wrong implanted in a youthful mind by parents moved by ignorance and good intentions; this clump of matted seaweed is superstitions born of coincidence and carefully nurtured through boyhood; this evil-smelling growth is a collection of outgrown and unworkable ethics that long ago should have been replaced by reality; this clinging barnacle is a groundless but persistent guilt that never should have existed in the first place. It's amazing how reasonably good conduct can come from any of us with circuits so overloaded.

I crawled out from under the boat and walked to the house for lunch, only to find a porcupine nestled in a tree by the kitchen door. A porcupine on an island where there is a dog in residence is about the worst of all possible situations. It is an accident on the way to happening. The porcupine had walked across from the mainland on an exposed ledge and mussel shoal at very low tide, and taken refuge in the tree. It gazed at me blandly. The tide had turned, but there was still an escape route for the porcupine if it could be persuaded to move promptly. I tried throwing sticks, but it only moved sluggishly out further on the limb. I tried firecrackers. I tried shaking the tree. Then I brought out the rifle as a last resort. I don't kill animals.

The quickest solution, of course, would be firing a .22 rifle bullet through its head, and that is precisely what most Maine country people would have done. I think I would like to be able to do it; in a sense I envy people who can dispose of things so neatly. But from somewhere — probably from one of those overloaded circuits — a voice questioned my right to dispose of things, neatly or otherwise, if in doing so I also dispose of a life. I must assume that the porcupine values its life as I value mine; it is the most important thing in the world to him and certainly outweighs a transient convenience on my part. I took the rifle back in the house and brought out a large trap, the property of a neighbor. I baited the trap handsomely and set it at the foot of the tree. If the porcupine goes in the trap tonight, I'll take it over to the mainland tomorrow and turn it loose. Meanwhile, the dog will be kept in the house.

Back under the boat, I had a new riddle to ponder, or, if not a new one, then an old one with new seeds of mischief. In scraping the moss and clutter off the psyche, why couldn't I simplify my life by eliminating the porcupine? No great displacement would have occurred, and I would have enjoyed a new kind of freedom, one that would affirm the notion that human beings are more important than animals and that the earth is big enough to absorb the loss of one porcupine which was foolish enough to trespass on an island where it did not belong. I followed this dismal line of thought as far as I could, but I knew there was no conviction anywhere in it. Human beings must have an intimate, spiritual connection with other living things, and Nature does not give man any particular hierarchy, regardless of whether he possesses a .22 rifle or not. So the lesson for today was that scraping barnacles off the bottom of the boat is a fine thing, but the bottom must be left intact. A balanced alliance between human beings and animals, I suspect, is all the stronger when the rights of one or the other of them are impaired, and the rifle is still left in the house.

Gulls

It was on a warm, sunny morning in late winter, one of those days when the ground is soft underfoot and one smells the earth for the first time in months, that I managed to take a load of out-of-date food down to the mussel bed for the gulls. I'm pretty much alone among my neighbors, and indeed among most Mainers, in my fondness for gulls; they complain harshly and they are rogues by nature, but their knowledge of aerodynamics fascinates me, and I can endlessly watch them soaring in the tricky sea breezes and gliding in for a landing, tilting the entire fuselage upward at the last moment to enlist gravity as a brake, then touching down in the water with the lightness of a feather. They have forgotten more about flight than Boeing will ever know, and if some stale bread, a leftover cake from Christmas, and a box of rice whose invasion by mice is irrefutable, will help to pay for some of the performances I have watched, then the price is reasonable.

A friend of mine from Boston told me the other day that gulls are so smart that the transitive verb *gull* means to outwit someone, and it was the most noteworthy piece of original thinking I had stumbled across in some time. A person who is gullible, it follows, can be easily led down the pathway of deceit by a gull, and if there is one among us who has not at some time been given the shaft by a gull, let him hold up his hand. My most recent betrayal occurred last summer when I arranged an alfresco lobster luncheon on the rocks for some guests from San Francisco. On matters of this kind the gull must always be kept in the forefront of one's thinking, and the fact that I permitted myself to be diverted from this awareness was the cause of my undoing. My mind had strayed for a few moments to tangential matters, to the selection of a wine and the dishevelment of the salad, and when I made my second trip of preparation to the site of the luncheon, I could see that very little remained from the fruits of my first trip. The rolls were gone, the salad had been finely picked over and only scattered leaves of lettuce remained, and one gull, possessing a wry if undisciplined sense of humor, had left a coarse acknowledgment of the repast on the table cloth. On a rock ledge fifty yards away, two gulls still argued noisily over a soggy roll.

Every man has his prejudices, his notions of error, the articles of his own faith, and if my neighbors have the distaste for gulls that they pretend to have then I must assume that there is something in the society of gulls which I have not yet encountered. Certainly the wharves and harbors of Maine would be the worse without gulls, who rid the premises of lobstering and fishing detritus more promptly and more efficiently than a municipal clean-up crew could do. What preserves the flavor of my neighbors' discontent, I suspect, is the gull's casual attitude toward guano, especially on boats and dock railings. I won't attempt to gloss over this stumbling block to better relations, but in fairness to the gull I think I should point out that the bird does considerable good work and seldom, if ever, gets any credit. Only a few weeks ago, a Portland newspaper carried a news story about a lobsterman lost two days in a heavy fog, and when asked how he had managed to keep off the shoals, he replied: "I listened for the gulls." An unusual amoung of squawking, he explained, meant rock ledges were close by. Here was a man, without realizing it, thanking his enemy for his salvation.

Several years ago I wrote of a female gull that made her home on a ledge a short distance from my island. She was spotlessly clean, industrious, and not easily ruffled, not even by her mate, who was as slothful and lecherous as she was prim and high-minded. I watched them through the glasses quite often late in the afternoon, and my jaw would tighten when I saw him come flying in from the Harpswell dump, where he had spent the afternoon in the company of younger and more complaisant females, full of excuses, his feathers soiled, his manner reeking of guilt. At that time I made inquiries around the neighborhood to see if gulls mated for life, but no one seemed to know or, for that matter, care. My neighbor was painting lobster buoys in his shed when I asked him, and he laid the brush carefully across the top of the can and looked at me searchingly. "You gone completely crazy?" he asked.

Early last summer the lady gull disappeared and hasn't been seen since, and I have speculated that she finally reached a point of desperation and moved to another locality, where she would not be haunted by unpleasant associations. Quite often in the hours before twilight I used to sweep the glasses across the rock ledge, but she never reappeared and, for that matter, neither did he. The gap between them — their lifestyles, their moral outlooks — was so great that I can't imagine it could be bridged successfully, yet there is always the possibility that she took him away with her, betrayed once more by his lies and promises of reform.

On days like today the gulls gaze at me curiously when I toss the food into the water; I have to move back a few feet from the shore before they swoop in close to claim it. Shadows pass quickly over the sand and pebbles at my feet, there are hoarse cries in the air and the sound of wings stroking the wind, and when the food is devoured, calm and peace return to the deserted shore. On late winter days, the wind blows free and loose over the marshes and through the tangle of juniper and bayberries on the high ground. Without a community of gulls silently facing into the sea breeze, the landscape would be one of bleakness and solitude. They add the single note of spiritual serenity.

The Ideal Guest Is an Accident of Nature

The summer of 1979 will be remembered by most people in Maine for the persistently unappealing quality of its weather, but it will remain green in my memory for an altogether different reason. It was the summer that I had an endless succession of guests on the island, coming and going in an aimless pattern that gave my neighbors on the mainland the suspicion that I was perhaps operating some new sort of shunpike motel. Of all of the things that the owner of an island can do, none is more ticklish and demanding than having guests. Guests breed tension, especially guests from New York, and I have discovered that tension on an island tends to become vortical, sooner or later sucking everyone into the maelstrom. Often the only thing that will clear the air is a good fight or a good drunk, and while both are extreme and both are effective, I prefer the latter of the two solutions. Only once have I had to deport a guest, a chap who came to the island more like an invader than someone who had come over for a visit, but that was an odd adventure and I had rather not dwell upon it.

The other evening by the fire, winter having again laid the hand of stillness and isolation upon the land, I fell to musing about the summer's guests and was startled to realize that people from the same locality all possess pretty much the same attitudes and peculiarities. Fresh water is a precious commodity on this island, since it has to be gathered from the rooftops during rains, a circumstance I seek to impress upon guests before they get a chance to fill tubs or let the spigots run too long. There is a well, but its water is brown and distasteful, and even that disappears with the first dry spells in July. Californians, I have noticed, get the idea immediately, and indeed become so niggardly in regard to use of water that I sometimes wonder how I can daintily get across the idea that a bath is not completely out of the question. On the other hand, New Yorkers disregard the instructions entirely, and when a guest from New York is in residence, I hear spigots running and toilets flushing far into the night. The psyche of the New Yorker is conditioned to ignoring instructions; pay attention to one authority, they reason, and soon your independence will be hacked to pieces by all of the others. Every day I give New York guests an emotional sermon on the need for thrift where water is concerned, but I can always tell by the look in their eyes that I have failed. No contact has been established.

The most adventurous guests are from the South — from Mississippi and Alabama and Georgia. They can't wait to explore the cove and the ledges, to race boats, to gather and clean mussels, to take saunas, to go swimming at midnight, to take picnic lunches to deserted islands. I don't know how to account for this, but I do know why New Yorkers are the least adventurous of all. New York City is a lively and dynamic place which provides, in one form or another, every type of entertainment of which the mind of man can conceive.

Conditioned by such a plenitude of choice, New Yorkers are helpless when facing the necessity of creating their own diversion. I often see them on the sundeck looking at me expectantly, waiting patiently for me to suggest something for them to do.

There is no telephone on this island, a fact that is scarcely noted by guests from small towns or rural areas but which is regarded as a serious deprivation by those from big cities. Every time a boat goes to the mainland, city guests clamber aboard to make, as they put it, "a couple of important phone calls." Since I often go from two to three weeks without putting a receiver to my ear, I wonder about the urgency of those calls. More than anything, I suspect, the guests are reassured by the ringing and by the answering voice. They are in touch; never mind with whom. One fellow, an advertising man, clutched his address book under his arm, in the manner of an evangelist clutching the Bible, and when he dropped his coins in the telephone I could see the lines of anxiety disappear from his face for the first time since his arrival. He was again connected to his life-support system.

An ideal guest — for an island, anyway — is an accident of nature. You don't find one by culling your address book, because past performances are worthless when used as a measure of probable island behavior. A good guest just comes along, adapts comfortably to an indolent and uneventful way of life, respects the fragility of the island ecology, and is quite content to take a book and a cup of coffee and slink off to some sunny rock for a few hours' reading. A man doesn't forget that kind of guest.

10

Writing

A Flimsy Business

I wish I could say that Maine is a fine place for a writer to work, but I'm not really sure. It offers too many distractions, it suggests too many things that need to be done *before* the writing starts for it to be ideally suited to the writer's needs. Anyone engaged in the flimsy business of writing is always uncertain and a bit aimless; there is no coffee wagon coming by to fix the passage of time, no camaraderie or clever remarks from the girl in the next office to relieve tension and drag the writer from the reverie into which he may have drifted. The writer works alone, producing only clusters of words, surely the most whimsical contribution of all to the gross national product. He works without structure, without direction, without supervision, and nothing worthwhile will come of it as long as his mind is hampered and cramped by boundaries, real or imagined. It is my experience that the most devastating and destructive boundary of all is that which separates writing from some physical occupation that needs to be done and, more urgently, needs to be done now. The float of the dock needs to be painted before the new plywood deck warps, and since the radio promised rain tomorrow it should be done today. The big skiff, which is to be given a fiberglass coating, must have the copper paint scraped off first, and since the tide is low I should get at it now when I can flip it over easily. If it is really going to rain tomorrow, I should clean the pine needles out of the gutters today. Why am I sitting here writing when these important things go undone?

    The most baffling thing in the writer's day is when to start writing. When I brought my breakfast out to the sundeck this morning, the warmth embraced me and I thought the sea had never looked lovelier. A lobster boat was working its way through the ledges at the entrance to the cove, and before hauling in a trap the lobsterman glanced at me and waved. I waved back, but I saw that his attention had shifted to the job at hand. There was a slight breeze from the sea, but it barely ruffled the oak leaves that partially shaded the deck. My dog was barking furiously, and by standing up I could see that she had been marooned on a mussel shoal by the incoming tide. There was enough time for me to finish breakfast before getting the rowboat to haul her off. Meanwhile, her attention was diverted by a large starfish, which she had pulled out of the water and was examining curiously. I touched the newly painted deck railing and saw that it was dry; time for the second coat. A day like this was made for painting and certainly it was not made for writing. I finished breakfast, had a second cup of coffee, and went down to the rowboat to get the dog. Already there was forming in my mind a list of important things that I should do on such a fine day, and writing was very close to the bottom of the list.

Some years ago I was living in southern France writing a novel, and the day I began working on the book I set up a schedule that turned out to be both practical and productive. I arose at five o'clock, ate a roll and drank a cup of coffee, and was at the typewriter by five-thirty, where I remained until one o'clock. At that point I quit for the day. But coastal Maine is not the Cote d'Azur, and here I own my home, have roots deeply planted, and am concerned about the weather, the general conditon of my property, the health of my plants, the affairs of my neighbors, and the coming and going of the mailman. Since these things all claim high priorities in my thoughts, it is natural that they share handsomely in the division of my time. When I awake to find the wind blowing from the northeast and the sky overcast, I think of writing. I know it isn't the way it should be; it's just the way it is.

I wonder if other people who lead unstructured professional lives have these same difficulties, and whether they find the distractions of Maine to be as overwhelming as I. Perhaps not artists, for many of the things that cause me to dawdle — the fog lifting from the rock ledges, the suddenly discovered clump of wild sweet peas nestled in the crevice of a rock, the blue heron searching the tide line for an evening meal — are the very things that send the painter off searching for his sketch pad. Why shouldn't it work that way for writers?

My neighbor unknowingly did me an act of unkindness a few days ago, but he is a generous man and never dreamed that the ways of a writer are as errant and capricious as they happen to be. He called to me from the end of my dock and said that he had caught too many mackerel, and would I bring a pan down as he would like to share them with me. And now the knowledge that more mackerel are out there in the cove — and perhaps some striped bass, as well — is in possession of my mind. I may address the typewriter halfheartedly, but in my heart I know there are lustier pursuits to which I could devote my time, and it's just a matter of a few hours — maybe even minutes — before I'm out beyond the boathouse digging a few sea worms for bait.

People Say You're a Writer

Some people say that a writer, if he has a burning desire to write, can work as well one place as another, but I think this is not only inaccurate but a perversion of the facts. Writing is an odd way for a man or a woman to make a living; words are the property of us all, and it seems illogical that some of us take the common wealth and twist it to serve our own ends, much as though I would charge a sailing ship for the right to sail past my island. Somerset Maugham had an interesting concept of writing, holding to the belief that an "idea acquires substance by taking on a visible nature," the visible nature, of course, being the written word. I don't know how many writers feel they are shoring up an idea when they work, but I firmly believe that most people harbor in the deep recesses of their minds the notion that given the opportunity they could write great books, just as they are certain that under the proper circumstances they could be great actors. The fact is that writing is grimly tedious, difficult beyond my ability to describe it (there's one writer's admission of failure, right there), harrowing, and fiercely competitive. A writer, groping in the dark for a graceful way of expressing what is in his mind, needs all the help a generous Providence can supply, and that some can work better in one place than in another is not only correct but not even news as far as I am concerned. I have discovered several places that accommodate my own tastes, and the best of them all is the rustic workroom on this Maine island where I am at this moment. Today is probably the most glorious day of the year, and I have moved my typewriter out on the flimsy porch where I can see the sailboats passing on their way to the open sea and where I can smell the pine needles and bayberry when the autumn sun strikes them. The boxer is inside, snoozing on the couch (writers need a couch as much as boxers do, which is a bone of contention between us since she feels my reasons for incumbency are both weak and inadmissible), and the only thing that can divert me from my work is beauty, which, of course, is the most diversionary thing in the world.

I have been told that Ireland is an extraordinarily hospitable location for writers to reside and work, but I think that Maine also serves the serious writer well. There is a great deal of tolerance in the atmosphere of Maine, and a writer in an intolerant climate is usually a writer in misery. My neighbors, almost all of whom take their living from the sea, have never expressed any curiosity about the peculiar way that I support myself, although I'm sure it must cross their minds when they see the irregularity of my coming and going from the island. On second thought, that's not entirely true; one of my neighbors, a lobsterman, mentioned it one day when the two of us were sitting at the end of my dock drinking beer and discoursing brilliantly on a variety of subjects. "People say you're a writer," he said. It was a flat assertion, but I knew my neighbor well enough to recognize it as a question. I acknowledged that I was, but I added that if I had my life to live over I would probably choose to be something useful. My neighbor thrives on self-deprecation, and I could see by the look on his face that he approved of the way I had stated the matter. "What in hell do you write?" he asked, a little profanity sneaking into his conversation under any circumstances. "Books? Magazines?" I nodded affirmatively in both cases. "Does it pay good?" he wanted to know. "Only fair," I said, "but it lets me live anywhere I want and, like you, I don't have a boss. I don't like bosses." We sat there in silence for a few moments. "I never had a boss in my life," he said, "except when I was in the army." He took a long drink from the bottle. "Of course," he said, wiping his mouth on the back of his hand, "that isn't counting the old lady." He stepped into his boat and pushed away from the dock. "Take it easy," he said. The business of writing was no longer a mystery to him; it had suddenly acquired a visible shape.

More than anything, in my opinion, a writer needs to be let alone, not only by his neighbors but also by his government and his friends, and I suppose that is why Maine strikes me as an ideal place for someone to engage in this questionable business. It is the nature of Maine and its people to confer the prize of privacy upon those who want it, with no questions asked and no resentment felt. An island, of course, affords a degree of privacy found nowhere else, but writers as a rule are gregarious people, and I'm not sure that too many of them could stand the solitude that island life imposes. Moreover, an island breeds lassitude in some people, and that is the virus that writers fear most.

Still, what nourishes one man, serves another poorly. A well-known writer from Mississippi, standing on the porch of this study early in the summer, looked across the cove and said, "I not only couldn't write here, I couldn't even carve my initials on the porch railing." Here was a man who recognized the enemy when he saw it, even if the enemy was beauty.

The Last Priority

Today is a fine day, almost perfect in fact. The sky is blue, the water is green, and there is a light breeze from the northeast stirring up a small chop in the cove. It is the kind of day that I would like to row around the rock ledges and the forested shore of the cove, maybe even going ashore to kick around the plastic bottles and see what treasures the tide may have deposited there since my last visit. This is a highly satisfactory way of killing a late summer day, especially if afternoon torpor has set in and one has sense enough to wander around and find a sheltered spot for a short nap. I yield to no man in my admiration for an afternoon snooze, and I think it best when taken on sudden impulse and in partial, if not direct, sunlight. The sun heightens indolence, causing ambition to disappear just as it bleaches color from fabric. There is something in my soul that craves a summer afternoon, lives for summer afternoons; I am designed and built for hot weather. Some people are forever seeking what they refer to as "activities" — something diversionary that will occupy their time — but I recoil from the word. What I am looking for are those little inactivities, those exquisitely untroubled moments when there is no pressure to do anything at all, and for some reason they seem far more plentiful on summer afternoons than any other time of the year. If I seem to speak with authority on this subject, it is because I am very sure of the path I am treading; I know an inactivity when I see one. To be blunt, show me a lazy summer afternoon and I'll show you how to turn off the adrenalin like closing a spigot.

I have just been reading an article on writing by Kingsley Amis, the British novelist, and I came across a passage that was like stumbling over a wastebasket in the dark. "They [writers] guard their free time as jealously as their working time," he wrote, "and if free time is to be invaded by work of any sort there must be no sense of obligation about it." A great many people outside the literary world or on its fringes hold to the belief that writers are invaded by a fury that compels them to write, that they are helpless when this virus finds its way into the bloodstream. Nothing could be further from the truth. I know a few compulsive writers, but generally speaking writers get their work done only by severe discipline, shame, or mounting debt. In my own case, it often takes all three to get me into a room with a typewriter. Why Amis thinks that writers jealously guard their working time causes me to doubt the man's sanity, and I can only say that I could show him a thing or two about how writing time is not jealously guarded here in the U.S.A. that would open his eyes. There is the boat to be beached and painted, the loose board in the wharf to be replaced, the wood to be sawed, the sauna stove to be cleaned, the plants to be watered — hell, I could give Amis an almost endless list of things that need to be done, and all of them have priority over writing. He is, of course, on much firmer ground when he speaks of the writer guarding his free time, but the problem here is that only the writer knows when free time begins and ends, and he is not to be trusted. It isn't as if one has an office where common decency, if not the boss, requires one to arrive at a certain time and socialize only at the water cooler until the day's work is completed. Most writers work at home without supervision of any kind, and their skill at devising delays becomes sharpened over the years until it reaches a point where it is a wonder that they connect with a typewriter at all.

I must confess, too, that there are occasions when time starts off as working time and before you know it, it has slipped across that vague and shadowy line into free time. Late last autumn, while writing an essay, I rowed over to a small island with a notebook in which I intended to list all of my impressions so that when I returned I could write what I hoped would be a savory little essay, a sort of eclogue, on the lasting glory of a bright autumn day. I found the right spot, and dutifully began making entries in the notebook. However, I was lying in the sand, leaning on one elbow, and when I add that I was in direct sunlight I am sure that the discerning reader will know what happened next. Water from the rising tide, lapping at my foot, awoke me in time to retrieve the notebook, which was floating gently just offshore.

The leaf on which I had written my notes was dry when I got home, and after changing my shoes I went to my study and wrote the article. It was my hope then, as it is now, that my readers appreciated the spirit of enterprise that went into that work. Less energetic writers, those who fail to do the necessary field research, would have let their readers down by producing something less authoritative. For my part, I discovered not only the rewards of virtue, but also the pleasure of observing work time merging congenially with free time.

And if a short snooze is the main attraction of a dreamy summer afternoon, it isn't bad either, on a lazy afternoon in autumn.

A Letter

I had a letter today from a chap in Kentucky who said that he had read some pieces I had written and that they had moved him to send me some of the essays he had written for a Louisville newspaper. He suggested modestly enough that this may be an unfair swap, but I don't think so. I read a chapter from a book he enclosed, and it struck me as such a splendid chronicle of the human spirit that I had difficulty putting it aside and getting back to work.

Living on an island creates not only physical isolation but in some ways an emotional one as well, and I am cheered when I learn that an unknown writer in Kentucky (unknown to *me*, that is) is stumbling around in the dark just as I am, trying to get his thoughts down on paper, trying to have his say. The business of writing is an unsubstantial and wispy enterprise, and few people are inclined to take it seriously, as they do driving a truck, say, or running a hardware store, or teaching school. I guess actors, dancers, and artists all face the same sort of skepticism about their life's work, since they don't have regular working hours, don't meet at the water cooler, and don't go to an office picnic each summer in the country. For many years I inhabited a magazine office in New York, and while I felt like a paroled prisoner when I walked out, I find the work I am now doing infinitely more exacting despite the intoxicating air of freedom in which it is carried out. I have commented before on the lowly place which writing occupies on the list of important things vying for an island owner's attention, and I don't mind pointing out again that completing this essay may occupy my mind but not my heart. The skiff needs scraping and painting, a shutter came loose in the March wind and needs some attention around the hinge, and the chimney on the sauna is tilting at a drunken angle. In my opinion, all of these jobs would edge out writing in any consideration of basic values alone.

The writer goes his way, seldom satisfied, only rarely fulfilled, acutely sensitive to criticism, yet for some reason not flinching from the sustained endeavor that is demanded of this strange craft. The writer regards the laborer with an enviously accusing eye, secretly yearning to possess his ability to come home from a day's work and sit on the porch steps in his undershirt, drinking a bottle of beer, and looking forward with eager anticipation to the seven o'clock sports roundup on the living room TV. He knows this isn't for him and never will be, this capacity to turn his mind to idle speed, to detach himself completely from the work at hand, to pause in what he is doing with no spillover into whatever is going to occupy him next. Somewhere — offstage, perhaps — his mind still wrestles with words, and they in turn wrestle with thoughts, seeking always to turn one into the other. One hopes for the soaring leap of imagination, but too often the dream is reduced to a patient analysis of the shards of half-forgotten conversations, of things read, of recollected excitement. All of us, unless totally insensitive, must eat some despair, the writer I believe more than most.

So I am heartened when a letter from Kentucky finds its way to my island in Casco Bay and informs me that something I have written at some time in the past has brought to a reader some meaning, or entertainment, or a tiny illumination to the puzzle of why man continues to seek answers to marvelously unanswerable questions. A few evenings ago I came across a photograph in a magazine of a chimpanzee's hand wrapped protectingly around the hand of Jane Goodall, the anthropologist who has come closer than any human being to understanding the chimpanzee and breaking down the barriers between them and us. The photograph warmed me with a strange inner radiance, the same sort of spiritual glow I felt when I received the letter and the book from the stranger in Kentucky. It was as though, after a long winter, I had just heard the spring peepers.

What I read of the book I liked immensely, but I noticed that the author lied like a dog in writing the preface. "I hope you get as much pleasure from reading this book," he wrote, "as I have in writing it." This is all standard nonsense which writers feel is required of them, much as lawyers are fond of "whereas" and "nolo contendere" and the Latin phrases which justify their employment in a society that could easily do without them if English were consistently used. I think that if the author of that book revised the preface with an honest eye, he would drop off that sentence. It gives off a hollow ring. His words are too well chosen to be casual, his thoughts are too gracefully expressed. If you ask me, he worked like a cottonfield laborer on that book and he was happy as hell when it was finished.

11

Love Letters to Maine

The True Prize

In reading the recently published essays of E.B. White, I was struck by a sentence that, although it expressed my own feelings precisely, I would never have thought to express. Headed north, White asserted, he always felt better after he crossed the Piscataqua River. During all of the years that I drove to Maine from New York either to open my summer place or to visit friends in winter, I experienced this same feeling when I crossed the bridge and moved from New Hampshire into Maine. For some reason — it seems absurd when I write it down — I always sounded the horn of the automobile as a sort of celebration of my arrival, a premature ritual, it turned out, because I lived a long way from Kittery. Nonetheless, the act of crossing the bridge placed me within the State of Maine, and this was enough to provoke a homecoming blast even if — as often happened — it drew rearward glances from other motorists. Suddenly, I told myself, the sky was more improbably blue, the air was more bracing, the water glistened and sparkled in a way that was unknown to the south, and altogether I was fortunate indeed to have returned to the last place on the eastern littoral of the United States that was still unspoiled. A friend of mine confided to me that he invariably kissed his wife when he crossed the bridge after having been away for some time, which only makes me think that White was responding to a fairly common impulse, although he was the first to put it into words. It occurs to me now that E.B. White, my friend, and I are not native-born Mainers but rather are adopted sons and perhaps possess the extraordinary zeal that often seems to accompany conversion. In my heart, though, I have the suspicion that natives feel the same way, even if their natural restraint may lessen the likelihood of their blowing horns or kissing their wives to mark their return.

This is the sort of subject that doesn't tolerate much probing or poking around because it is a matter of appreciation, and one either has it or one doesn't, but it appears to me that Maine binds its children to it with a cord that has the strength of anchor chain. I am a Virginian by birth and quite possibly by nature, and while there is much about my native state that I admire, it doesn't touch me the way that Maine does. It is said that the people of Oregon have a fierce and possessive fondness for their state, and I accept this although it is hearsay only because I know very little about Oregon. What I have seen of Oregon resembles Maine in many respects, and there may well be some strange component in those wild and unspoiled coastlines, separated by three thousand miles, that acts upon the heart and mind in much the same way.

During the past summer, a neighbor dropped in unexpectedly one afternoon, and over a drink our conversation veered around to some difficulties he had been encountering. As is often the case, idle chatter dissolved quickly into confidentiality. "I'm thinking about pulling up here," he said, "and moving on." I was surprised. He was a native of Maine, and I wondered how he would adjust to California or New York or Boston, or wherever he intended to resettle. Unable to contain my curiosity, I asked where he intended to go. "Oh, a little further down east," he replied. "No place particularly. Down east." Of course. Where else would one go?

Pondering one's affection for a place is a little like pondering one's affection for a woman; the answers that turn up are never satisfactory and seldom tell the whole story. I would say that it was the coast of Maine that captured my heart — the coves, the headlands jutting into the ocean and taking the full fury of winter storms, the unpredictable weather, the quiet people who make their living from the sea — but I know there is something else that is too elusive for me to define. I feel at home in Maine in a way that satisfies me very much, and I suppose there is nothing more complicated about it than that. When I go away, I'm always glad to get back, and there's no other place I feel that way about.

One afternoon during this past fall I was taking a leisurely walk with my dog when rain, which had been threatening for several hours, started to fall. A glance at the sky showed it meant business, and I called off the walk and started for the house. It was coming down steadily when I went inside, and after starting a fire I stood at the window and watched the drops spatter against the glass. The wind sprang up, making whitecaps in the cove and bending the small birch trees, and in a few minutes the window was blurred and I could no longer see the sea. I sat there through twilight, drinking a cup of tea and arising only once to light a lamp, and my spirits soared as the storm increased. I was warm and dry and secure, and there was no need for me to do anything more than I was doing. Man has sought the comfort of this feeling from the time he first built a home in a cave, this feeling that is haunting and mysterious except to the understanding and the sympathetic. I feel it often in Maine, and that is the true prize.

Second Choice

I have recently completed a long trip across the United States, saying warm and friendly things on radio and television about a book I had written, and I returned with the deep conviction that outside of New England the State of Maine is a mysterious and little-known territory and that a recitation of its shining virtues brings looks of bewilderment. Maine figured more prominently in that long journey than it should have, due to a peculiarity which demands some explanation. The book was an account of travels and adventures in odd corners of the world, and inevitably the interviewer would maneuver me into facing what he or she considered the craftiest question of all. I learned to detect that sly smile, as they closed in for the kill. "Of all the places in the world that you have visited," the interviewer would ask, "what place is your favorite?" When I said, "Maine," I invariably confronted an expression that could only be described as incredulity. Often, thinking they had not heard me correctly, the interviewer would ask, "Did you say *Maine*?" I learned to nod affirmatively and await the next question, which never failed to come. "Why Maine?" the interviewer wanted to know. The perplexity was always genuine.

There would have been no show of surprise had I declared that the most wonderful spot in the world, in my opinion, was Capri or Bali or Rio or Hong Kong, but Maine seemed too implausible to be taken seriously; somehow it could not mingle in democratic equality with the more famous glamour spots of the globe. And its implausibility touched even me; how could I explain, in the three minutes remaining on the studio clock, the way I feel about the grandeur of Pemaquid Light, the sheer cliffs rising from the Atlantic on Monhegan Island, the majesty of Mt. Katahdin's summit breaking through a ground fog, or the blue brilliance of a Maine lake on a hot summer day? The fickle yield of pleasures for a traveler are not easy to put into words under any circumstances; one likes a certain place because there is something in the air which is lacking someplace else. The world is laid out haphazardly, and the traveler must trust to luck, perhaps more than most people.

A man appearing on several talk shows a day has a great deal on his mind, but I was startled to make a discovery one day while talking on a Chicago television program. The usual question had been asked and the usual answer given. The host of the show, instead of asking me why I preferred Maine to any place in the world, went on to inquire what was my second choice. In the flimsy business of conversational broadcasting, one soon develops a fixed line of repartee, like an old-time vaudeville comedian who knows where the surefire laughs exist when the going gets tough. Thus jolted out of my usual routine, I paused uncertainly for a moment and then replied that Finland was my second choice. I had no ready explanation for my fondness for Finland, I explained, but felt it was probably an emotional thing that would require a good deal of probing before any solid answers could be found. I was wrong about that; back in my hotel room that night as I was pondering the day's happenings, my reason for liking Finland came to the surface very quickly. Finland is a great deal like Maine.

I spent a couple of weeks once in the lake country of eastern Finland, hard by the Russian border, and I was constantly struck by the similarity between that country and the State of Maine. There were the deep forests of spruce and fir, the cool, clear lakes, the odor of wood smoke hanging in the winter air, the small towns, the unhurried life. And the spruce forests growing along the Gulf of Finland in the south, and the Gulf of Bothnia in the west, come down to the sea exactly as they do in Penobscot Bay and Casco Bay and Machias Bay. There are differences, of course, because part of Finland lies beyond the Arctic Circle and most of it is on the same latitude as Hudson's Bay, and while Maine winters can hardly be categorized as mild, they lack the deep, locked-in frigidity of the countries lying far to the north. Maine's North Woods are inhabited by moose while Finland's are inhabited by reindeer; that says something, too.

Certainly one of Finland's most notable contributions to the world has been the sauna, a delight that I have demonstrated to my satisfaction can be transported to Maine without the slightest loss of appeal. A few years ago a small Finnish sauna was erected on the Maine island where I make my home, and I have been surprised at how solidly the sauna ritual has become established in my life. Standing on a rocky promontory, a few feet from the edge of the sea, the sauna offers exactly that same combination of cleanliness, relaxation, and feeling of contentment that has made it a part of Finnish culture for a thousand years or more. It travels well, but I realize now that it really didn't have to travel far.

Homesickness

A writer's business is everywhere, the direction of his travels often as eccentric as the progress of an epidemic, and it was on the wings of just such a whimsical journey that I found myself recently in Ireland. The season was late spring, a time that I seldom venture from Maine because it is the period of the year that requires a responsible man's presence at home, and the guilt at witnessing a Frenchman or an Englishman or an Irishman repairing his fences or painting his house is usually pervasive enough to spoil the trip. But Ireland, I was surprised to find, provoked a vastly diminished guilt, and I think it was because the Irish country looked so much like Maine that I often had the feeling that I had never left home.

To be honest, I must report that I am a coastal Mainer, but most of the time I was in Ireland I was reminded not of the coast but of interior Maine — of the gently sloping hills, of the fences made of fieldstone, of the small streams running clear and cold through the meadows, of the massive rock outcroppings on the crests of the hills. And there's the weather. Day after day (this was late spring, remember) I awoke to what the Irish in their poetic way referred to as "a soft day," but what a less fanciful Down Easter would regard as mist, overcast, and drizzle. As nearly as I could tell, the vocabulary of the Irish does not embrace the word *rain*.

Most of the time I was on a small boat going up and down the Shannon River, and, except for the frequent locks, it could as easily have been the Androscoggin or the Kennebec or the Penobscot. Cattails grew in the swampy areas that drained into the river; the fields were green and moist; the hedgerows made strange patterns on the hillsides, dividing fields and pastures for purposes long ago forgotten. When we approached a lock, it was our custom to tie up at the riverbank, and more often than not I would take a bicycle we carried on the foredeck of the boat and pedal along a path to the lockkeeper's house to notify him of our arrival. Since there were not many boats plying the Shannon at that time of the year, the lockkeeper was often involved in duties far less frivolous than seeing that pleasure boats passed through his lock, and there were times when he had to be fetched from a distance. It was these expeditions that I enjoyed the most. The countryside was coming alive with an almost explosive quality, jonquils bloomed in profusion beside the path, and, as I had found in Maine, Nature's way of absorbing human conflict was at work. I discovered the same quiet and solitude on the paths that I had long ago found on the rocks of coastal Maine.

When I glanced at a map to measure the progress of the boat, even the names gave me the strange sensation of being at home. There was Bangor, in County Mayo, and of course, Belfast, and even Waterville, just south of Dingle Bay. Irish talk is lively and picturesque, as is the speech of the Down Easter, and it is filled with images and pictures. Nothing is too trivial to be described in detail. Like the man of Maine, the Irishman's conversation is marked by cadence, a kind of interior rhythm, that gives it distinction, and I found that I seldom tired of listening to even commonplace remarks. One morning I walked a mile or so with an ancient lockkeeper, pushing the bike beside me as we talked, and when he learned that I was a writer he invited me to return during the summer and make my home in his cottage. When I explained that I never left Maine in the summer, he nodded with understanding. "I've never been to America," he said, "but I've often been told that Maine is much like this country. There's no sense in moving from one part of Heaven to another, is there now?" I agreed there wasn't.

Near the small river town of Boyle, I left the boat and bicycled into the village to spend a night at the local hotel. I awoke early the next morning, and after a hot bath, started down a country road to the boat landing several miles away. The sky was blue, the air clean and cool, and a gentle grade descended toward the river. Cows grazed in the fields on either side of the road, and I passed small stone farmhouses that were just coming alive with the first activity of day. A farmer, carrying a bucket into a field, stopped in his tracks and stared at me curiously. I waved, and he waved in return. The roadside was a tangle of vines and small trees, and the ditch on my right contained a small stream struggling to get to the river below. When I rumbled across the wooden bridge spanning the river, the planks were wet with dew and the tires of the bicycle left a straight line behind me. There was no sound except for some cows in the trees of a hedgerow, and from far away in the direction of Boyle came the muted sound of a truck. It was so much like rural Maine that I felt a twinge of homesickness. There are differences, of course, but I won't try to catalogue them. Maine is much bigger than Ireland, but I don't think that means much, one way or the other.

Substance

I have just returned from some islands in the Pacific to an island in Casco Bay, and while the sight of palm trees ringing a blue lagoon is an undeniably romantic sight, I must confess that I stepped ashore here last night with a feeling of intense delight. The Pacific islands may call to a certain kind of wanderer, but I am not among them; I prefer this rocky islet, with its tangle of bayberry and juniper, and the forest floor carpeted with pine needles, and the crisp autumn air that promises to get crisper, and with gulls wheeling in the blue sky. There is a substance to this island that I don't think those Pacific islands possess; they seem temporary, like a motion picture set that will be demolished when the film is completed.

It was late in the afternoon when I arrived here, and after dropping my suitcase in the kitchen and putting my necktie on the back of a chair, I went down to the rocks at the south end of the island, a spot that has always struck me as an ideal location for reentry into island life. The tide was coming in quickly, pushing rockweed ahead of it, and a warm, moist breeze was blowing from the east. It was warmer than it should have been this time of year, and there was no doubt but that rain was in the offing.

A blue heron was standing in some eelgrass a short distance from me, fishing for small crabs and minnows, and my presence obviously displeased it. Herons know that a human being has to be kept under constant surveillance since there is no telling what foolishness he may undertake, yet having to watch me lessened its fishing efficiency. Its dilemma was plain. It struck at a shiner that had appeared as a silvery flash in the eelgrass, but missed. It straightened quickly and turned its head in my direction to see if I had witnessed the failure. Squawking loudly, it lifted off from the eelgrass, its great wings flailing the air. Sailing low over the water, it landed gently on an exposed mussel shoal. This seemed more to its taste; at least it could disregard me and give full attention to its work.

I have always had a low opinion of that time of day when the tide is dead low and all of the mud flats are exposed, but in truth it is at low tide that most of the secrets of the sea world are revealed. The tide now was flowing, but it had only just turned, and was creeping across the low stones and invading the crevices in the rocks. A few mussel shells were floating, but they would soon fill and sink;

the slightest ripple in the surface would cause them to disappear. A small, dark grotto under a rock began to fill, and it gave off a strange clapping sound as though applause was coming for some unseen performance. The sound was echoed a moment later by a cormorant a short distance away, which began beating its wings furiously as it took off from the water to fly to a nearby rock ledge.

I became suddenly aware that the sun had disappeared and that it was beginning to get dark, but it was pleasant sitting on the rocks and although it was very still, there were few mosquitoes. A boat came into the cove, very fast, judging from the sound that drifted across the water, but it passed on the other side of the island and I didn't see it. Another blue heron soared in close, saw me, retracted its landing gear, and flew on. No one has ever asked my opinion of the blue heron but I'll offer it anyway: a blue heron is a very unsociable bird.

A still twilight on the Maine coast is a thing of beauty, and the tropical island I had just left seemed pale to me now. The wind sprang up again, shifted quickly, and for a moment I was treated to the rich odor of lobster bait coming from my neighbor's boat which was moored a short distance away. Not much can be said for the odor of rotten fish heads, but when diluted properly with moist, salt air coming in on the evening tide, it is comforting and reassuring, somewhat like the odor of kerosene given off by an oil lamp.

A boat came slowly around the northwest tip of the island, and in the gathering gloom I recognized a man who, so far as I could tell, was the only native coastal person I knew who did no work whatever. His manner suggested that he did not wholly condemn work but that it placed a barrier between him and his working neighbors. He saw me on the rocks and waved.

It was then that the moon came up over the rim of the sea in the east, and laid down a path of gold between me and Yarmouth Island. It was a breathtaking sight, made all the more overwhelming by the silence that had seized the stage. There was only the sound of the incoming tide slapping gently on the rocks as that immense copper ball turned slowly to burnished gold as it rose in the sky. In the shallows a clump of rockweed rose and fell gently, and from somewhere came a heron's complaint, hoarse and solemn and sad. Moonlight on a South Pacific island could be resplendent, I am sure, but I feel it would be curiously insubstantial. Here on the Maine coast, standing on these rocks, was something marvelously infectious, something sensual and profound. It made my long journey home a fulfillment.

Going Back

What is monotonous to one man is exciting to another, and I tell myself that each spring when I soar afloat on the celestial feeling that precedes the opening of my island home for the summer. I am a sensible man and I have made this spring journey exactly fourteen times, so there is no way to rationalize my elation as I tie up boxes, sort out books, and pack clothes for a trip that is still weeks away. Being a traveler both by nature and by occupation, I find that no more than a half-hour is needed for me to get ready for a trip to Nepal or Malaysia or the Amazon jungle, but when I contemplate crossing that narrow bit of Casco Bay to my island, hardly more than a moat when I'm being realistic about it, I freeze up, I tremble, my eyes glaze over, and I display all of the foolish symptoms of a feverish lover planning a honeymoon. Nepal is beautiful, Malaysia is exotic, the Amazon jungle is adventurous, but this is the *real* journey. When I pull away from my dock on the mainland and head for that clump of spruce and pine rising out of the sea, I am following my heart. Ahead of me is a rendezvous, an exciting drama in which I play a walk-on part: the whippoorwill whose mournful song lures me to the windward end of the island at twilight, the murmur of the spring wind moving through the boughs of spruce and causing the great oaks to sway gently against a darkening sky, the blue heron squawking in disdain and resentment at my return, the gulls wheeling low over the house, a field mouse startling my dog by suddenly scurrying under a pile of leaves. I feel like an intruder, but I know that feeling will pass. "It's our island, too," I say aloud to the dog, but that is to reassure me and not her.

There is something mystical about the sea that seizes certain people, just as others are possessed and bewitched by the moon, and it may be that I am one of them. I remember as though it were yesterday my father taking me on an overnight steamer trip down the Chesapeake Bay, and although I could have been no more than ten at the time, every sensation and insignificant detail of that brief voyage can be retrieved by me in an instant. The morning of the sailing was one of the most unbearable anticipation, and when the steamer began to tremble and vibrate as the engines started, I felt a tightening of the throat such as I had never experienced. The next few minutes were a blur of sensations: voices shouted out orders, bells rang, hawsers were hauled up on deck, and then the whistle shattered the air with such a dull roar as to cause me to reach for my father's hand. I stood at the railing and watched the wharf and the workmen begin to recede, to slip away backward, and then only the boat was real and dependable, and I let go of my father's hand and ran to the other side of the steamer to see what things were happening there. Later, there was the clang of a bell in the water, and my father, who had moved across the deck to be with me, said that was a buoy, a channel marker to guide the pilot, and in a few minutes we were moving rapidly out to sea. My father left the railing and sank into a deck chair, but I remember standing there. There was a flash of sunlight on a tall building behind us, and that was the last thing I remember about the land we had left. The air now was wet and smelled of salt, and the ship began to roll slowly. It was a pleasant motion and a puzzling one. I tried to adjust to the roll but I found it wasn't easy; I let go of the railing and tried to walk naturally, and I felt very foolish when I stumbled. But it was wonderful, and I wanted to watch the rush of white water away from the bow long after my father had called to me and said it was time to go to our stateroom.

When I am on the island I do not forget for a second that I am surrounded by the sea; it does not intrude upon my thoughts, rather it is a knowledge that rests in my mind and never goes away. The sea seeks a man out; it occupies his mind even though his guard is up. Moreover, I know now without looking at the sea whether the tide is coming in or going out; this is something that happens subtly and imperceptibly, as one knows without looking up when the sky has become overcast.

The discerning reader, the one who looks between the lines for hidden and unconscious meanings, will suspect by now what I am trying to say is that I am seeking to reverse the long process of evolution and crawl back into the same sea from which my ancestors so laboriously pulled themselves many millions of years ago. I would refute this theory vigorously, yet I know that an island is not a sound pulpit from which to proclaim one's independence of the sea. I am dependent upon the sea for many things and the most important of them is emotional equilibrium and peace, which I find on that island to an extent I have found nowhere else. If that's a confession, let the psychologists make the most of it. Meanwhile, I'm packing my possessions in order to get back there as fast as I can; if my ancestors made the big mistake eons ago, let me be among the first to start the process of correcting it. If anyone else feels this way, I'd like a show of hands.

Coming Home

A few years ago when I lived in New York City and commuted to Maine each weekend, the transition was about as extreme as it could be, since I moved from an overcrowded rock island with eight million neighbors to another rock island with no neighbors at all unless one counts some gulls, a few blue herons, some field mice, a squirrel or two, and an itinerant porcupine. Demographically speaking, this transition could wreck the emotional equilibrium of most New Yorkers who grow morose and anxious when not pushed around by crowds, but to me the solitude of the Maine island was healing, refreshing, and even exhilarating. No depressurization was necessary for me on Friday nights when I arrived at my dock in darkness, and I felt even more at ease a short time later when I reached the island, tied up the boat, and made my way up the path, carrying a small suitcase and a bag of groceries. The contrast of the Maine island with what I was used to all week was actually exciting in an odd way; I felt a breathless sort of reverence for its silence, its cleanliness, its simplicity, its timelessness. It was as if the island had been left behind by time but not by me; I had been there only the week before, and I knew what magazines were on the coffee table and what had been left in the refrigerator and where my oilskin coat was hung.

I went back to the island recently, after an interval of several months' traveling, and I stepped ashore with more than the usual anticipation. For more than fifteen years this small island has loomed large in my life, and at some time — some *unidentifiable* time, because I don't remember when it began — I grew to consider it home. Now the self that I had left there merged with the new arrival, which is coming home in the finest sense. Everything I saw as I walked up the pathway to the house confirmed memory: a glance showed there was enough wood in the woodpile to carry me to warm weather, there was a comforting stack of propane tanks against the wall of the boathouse, only a few trees had fallen to the winter gales, and the small sauna on the windward tip of the island stood forlorn but intact. I was struck again, as I always am when I have been away long, by the silence in the deep forest and the quickness with which the world that I have come from recedes.

Noise has become so much a part of our lives that we often aren't aware of it, unless we pause to listen to it or come suddenly upon a place where there is almost a total absence of it. Then little sounds intrigue us — the sudden whirring of the refrigerator or a clock ticking or a woodpecker drilling into a rotting tree trunk or the wind sighing in a spruce tree. These sounds are soothing because they are familiar, and to me they speak with eloquence. They tell me I am home again. I crumple some yellowed newspapers in the fireplace, throw on some kindling, and in a moment flames are leaping up the chimney. The fire is more than a ritual. A house closed during winter months accumulates cold and holds it stubbornly; it takes a steady fire almost twenty-four hours to dispel the chill. Woodstoves do it more quickly, but I have come to be content with the leisurely way that the living room fireplace moves the comfort line slowly backward through the house, as spring is said to move inexorably northward eighteen miles a day. In a few hours it will be warm in my bedroom, where now I see my breath.

    I make all of the small gestures of arrival. The flags go out on the sundeck, a signal to my friends in the lobsterboats that I am again in residence. I bring the binoculars from the shelf in the living room, and make a sweeping search across the water to see what changes have occurred since I left, what new things have been deposited on the sand of the other shore or in the eelgrass. I unlock the door to my tiny workroom — a handyman's cottage when the island was the property of a more affluent owner who, unlike me, did not prize privacy so greatly — and toss a briefcase on the couch. The chimney of the sauna has come to lean with the wind, and I push it straight with a long stick. I open the door and lift out the table which came from Finland with the sauna and for which I had never discovered any useful purpose. A mouse scurries along the baseboard inside the sauna, his bright eyes clearly regarding me as an intrusion. The first fire in the sauna stove will induce him to resettle elsewhere, most likely in the pile of wood and leaves now banked against the side of the building. One year a nest was built in the sauna chimney, a situation I discovered only after lighting the season's first fire and being baffled by the sight of smoke pouring from the sauna door. When I took the chimney down and shook it, an entire family of mice exited, along with the shredded remnants of what had been a highly prized wool rug that I had brought back from Mexico.

    Within a day or two, Maine seeps into me; I pick up where I left off. My neighbors on the mainland, whom I seek out for a word here, a handshake there, tell me, each in his or her own way, what has happened since I was last here. There is no time for indolence because there is too much to be done; plants must be brought from town and set out, the sundeck must be painted, debris from the trees must be picked up and burned on the rocks at low tide, leaves must be raked up from around the house, the telephone must be reconnected in the shack on the mainland — the list is endless. But the first night we are here, the dog and I sit by the fire in contentment; everything else seems a theater of unreal life. The only reality is here.

Postscript

This is about a quiet day in late autumn that was not really memorable except for the golden shafts of sunlight that slanted through the forest where the leaves had been, and a strange melancholy that invades the heart with the shortening of the days. There seemed to be more than the usual lichen on the rocks and tree trunks, and the smell of dying ferns, now brown and dry, found its way into that blend of forest odors dominated by spruce and pine needles, by crushed bayberry, and by the musty scent of rotting leaves. It was a day when there was no time for hurrying, no place for any great accomplishment.

It was the day I was to close the house where I live for five months of each year. I do not think of it as a summer house, because it lacks the makeshift character of most summer houses. It is home to me — the place where I feel more comfortable and at peace than anywhere else. I once raced halfway around the world to get there to recover from an illness, and when I finally sank into my own bed and saw the curtains fluttering in an early afternoon breeze and heard the hollow sound of a blue heron at the sea's edge, I knew that everything was as it should be and that I would soon be well again. Closing the house, a few weeks ahead of the first snowfall, is not a lighthearted undertaking; it is too much like saying goodbye to an old friend. I am never sure what changes will have occurred to either of us when next we meet.

Most of the real work had been done. Linens had been put away, matches collected, rice and cereal hidden in metal containers to thwart the squirrels, who have a dozen imaginative ways of getting into the house. Little remained except the custom of walking one last time through the forest and sitting on the rocks and staring at the sea — the futile things a man will do in the hope that he can store up something substantial to tide him over the winter. This is all part of the ritual of disengagement, when clutching at the familiar and comforting is the most important need of the human heart.

The swift blur of modern life has robbed us of too many prizes that we once took for granted: the blended scent of a hundred tiny blossoms in a meadow on a hot day in July; walking a hedgerow during the first snow of autumn, when you secretly hope it will snow all night but you know it is just a flurry; waking in the night to hear the soft drumming of a summer rain on the roof.

But on a quiet day such as this, one can take life up again without its anxieties, its complications. This is not farm country; few coastal areas are. My neighbors make their living by fishing for lobster, or by clamming, or by gathering Irish moss from the rock ledges. I see small shingled shacks, lobster traps stacked in neat piles, brightly painted lobster buoys drying in the sun, or dinghies tied to sagging docks, their floorboards always under several inches of water — which presumably is the way lobstermen prefer them to be. I've never in my life seen a lobsterman with a dry dinghy.

The last walk around the place serves a purpose not just sentimental but unexpectedly practical as well. I find my saw lying in the leaves where I abandoned it after sawing up a piece of driftwood a few days ago. It would have gone unnoticed but for a glint of sunlight reflecting off the steel handle. I take it to the boathouse, grease the blade with outboard oil, and hang it on a nail. In New England, abuse of a tool is almost as unforgivable as abuse of a member of the family.

At the shoreline, I climb to the summit of a rock where I come every morning to breathe the fresh sea air and force the sleep from my brain. It is low tide, and I think of Rachel Carson's beautiful description of the smell of low tide: "that marvelous evocation combined of many separate odors, of the world of seaweeds and fishes and creatures of bizarre shape and habit, of tides rising and falling on their appointed schedule, of exposed mud flats and salt rime drying on the rocks." A tiny pool made by a cleft in the rock is a prison for some small species of sea life which threshes wildly about, rippling the surface of the pool. At the foot of the rock, buried in the tangle of rockweed, the violet shell of a mussel glitters and a small crab skitters, barely beneath the surface. One wonders what ethics and logic prevail in nature's checks and balances beneath the sea.

At this season, the insistent clarity of the light is the most dramatic thing in the whole pageant of seasonal change. In winter and spring, mists and fog often obliterate the view, and in summer, a light haze settles over the landscape, softening detail and blurring objects at a distance. But as autumn slips into winter, the air becomes clear as crystal. From the top of the rock I see sharply the docks and dwellings on Yarmouth Island, even a flag snapping in the sea breeze, all now suddenly revealed.

A few days ago, driving along the Maine Turnpike, I passed a groundhog. It was early in the morning, and I got the impression that he had just awakened. He was sitting erect and seemed to be stifling a yawn, and as I watched, he scratched the back of one ear absent-mindedly with a front paw. He gazed at me curiously, and then, as he receded in my rearview mirror, I saw him duck back into his hole. Possibly the sight of human beings speeding down the highway on such a nice day dismayed him, or maybe he felt that he had made a mistake by rising too early.

Sitting on the rock, I think of the groundhog and wonder at the neatness and order of his life. He has one home and he sees no need for any other; whatever that burrow contains is a perfect arrangement according to his whim, fortune, and need. On the other hand, my possessions lie in boxes and suitcases, waiting to be loaded in the station wagon. This is a vulnerable state for a man to be caught in, living neither here nor there, and my anxiety is deepened by the suspicion that perhaps something vital is being left behind.

I come down off the rock and enter the forest again. There is an ancient pine tree that I am always surprised to find still standing each spring; it has been dead for many years, and its trunk has been perforated by woodpeckers. Now it is home to innumerable beetles and bugs, and squirrels. I push it as hard as I can and it doesn't move. I will see it another spring.

The wind is out of the northeast, cool and crisp, and the water in the cove is ruffled. In a few more days the first snow will come, and although it will probably just dust the ground, the one after that, or the next, will mean business. The house is already uncomfortably cool, despite the fire which is kept going in the living room. Last night, when I got out of bed to arrange a new pyramid of logs in the fireplace, I noticed that my breath was forming steam — a warning not to tarry much longer. It's time to go, but it seems extraordinarily bad planning to depart such an absorbingly lustrous season of the year. It's like leaving a play midway through the last act.

Miss Carson was not troubled, as I am, by the passage of autumn and, unlike me, she found nothing melancholy in the shuttering of a house for winter. Instead, she discovered something infinitely healing in the repeated refrains of nature: "the assurance that dawn comes after night, and spring after the winter." I will try to think about that on the long drive back to the city.